A REAL COWBOY LOVES FOREVER

STEPHANIE ROWE

A REAL COWBOY LOVES FOREVER

(A *Wyoming Rebels* novel)
Copyright © 2017 by Stephanie Rowe
Cover design © 2017 by Kelli Ann Morgan,
www.inspirecreativeservices.com

ISBN 13: 978-1-940968-56-8
ISBN 10: 1-940968-56-9

For further information, please contact:
Stephanie@stephanierowe.com

Dedication

For Joe

Acknowledgements

Special thanks to my beta readers and the Rockstars. You guys are the best! There are so many to thank by name, more than I could count, but here are those who I want to called out specially for all they did to help this book come to life: Malinda Davis Diehl, Leslie Barnes, Kayla Bartley, Alencia Bates Salters, Alyssa Bird, Donna Bossert, Jean Bowden, Shell Bryce, Kelley Daley Curry, Ashley Cuesta, Denise Fluhr, Valerie Glass, Heidi Hoffman, Jeanne Stone, Dottie Jones, Janet Juengling-Snell, Deb Julienne, Bridget Koan, Felicia Low, Phyllis Marshall, Suzanne Mayer, Jodi Moore, Ashlee Murphy, Elizabeth Neal, Judi Pflughoeft, Carol Pretorius, Kasey Richardson, Caryn Santee, Amber Ellison Shriver, Summer Steelman, Regina Thomas, and Linda Watson. Special thanks to my family, who I love with every fiber of my heart and soul. And to AER, who is my world. Love you so much, baby girl!

A REAL COWBOY
LOVES
FOREVER

Chapter 1

THERE WERE DAYS when Maddox Stockton felt there wasn't enough water in the world to wash off the filth caked on his soul.

Today was one of them.

He stood on the front steps of the Rogue Valley sheriff's office, staring grimly out at the blowing snow. It was cold, even for a guy like him who didn't bother to feel much of anything these days.

The door closed behind him, but he didn't turn as the local sheriff, Dane Wilson, walked out and stood beside him. "You sure you don't want to crash at my place, Maddox? It's going to be a hell of a drive."

"No. I need to get back." But Maddox didn't move. He just stood there, letting the bitter Wyoming wind knife through him, welcoming the way it bit through his jeans like a she-devil out to savage him. Cold was better than feeling nothing, which was how he went through most of his days. The days when he did feel? Hate, guilt, and a whole shitload of other emotions that served no one.

Dane shoved his hands in his pockets, standing beside Maddox as they watched the wind whip the snow around. The only two trucks left on the street were theirs, just like when they were teenagers. Just like back then, tonight they were the only two in town who had nowhere to go. Just him and Dane. All that was left of the kids who had once thought their darkness wasn't forever.

They'd been wrong. The darkness *was* forever, and it was their own souls that kept it alive.

"Always another bad guy to track down, eh?" Dane mused.

Maddox shrugged. "Who can give up on a childhood dream come true?"

Dane laughed. "Yeah, because every little boy's dream is to become a bounty hunter who spends his days with scumbags who would be happy to shoot you between the eyes if it kept them from going back to jail."

Maddox cocked an eyebrow at his longtime friend, the only person in the entire world besides his brothers, who he considered worth trusting. "As said by the man whose desk is next to a jail cell."

Dane shrugged. "This is Rogue Valley. Not much bad shit happens here anymore since—"

He cut himself off, but Maddox knew what he was going to say. "Since my bastard dad died, right? It's been like a damned oasis since he spared the world his presence."

"I was going to say, since the Stockton brothers grew up and became somewhat respectable."

Maddox laughed at that one. "You know damn well that only Travis, Zane, Chase, and Steen have become respectable, and that's only because they were lucky enough to find women who were so loyal and amazing that my brothers couldn't walk away."

Dane cocked an eyebrow at him. "You sound jealous."

Maddox took a deep breath and flexed his hands. "No jealousy. I'm happy for them. I didn't think there was any chance that anyone with the last name of Stockton could ever be happy, but I'm glad I was wrong. I'm glad that they're getting a chance to live the life they deserve."

Dane turned to look at him. "You don't want it, too? I'm not gonna lie, sometimes I'm jealous as hell at what they have."

Maddox met his gaze. "Don't waste your energy, bro. Neither of us can ever get that close to someone like their women. The poison inside of us will eat away at anything good that tries to come near us, until there's nothing left of the light that used to exist. We'll kill the light, Dane. You know it."

"What are you, a poet?" But Dane didn't argue.

Because Maddox was right.

The two men stood there for a few more minutes, letting the frigid wind slice into them, before Dane finally sighed. "I'm going to head out." He glanced at Maddox. "Always good to see you when you're in town, bro. Make sure you stop by next time."

There was an edge to Dane's voice that drew Maddox's attention. He narrowed his eyes, studying his friend. "What's wrong?"

Dane hesitated, and Maddox suddenly tensed, realizing that something was going on with his friend. "What's up?"

But Dane simply shook his head. "Nothing."

"Lie."

"Yep." Dane didn't bother to deny the accusation, because they knew each other too well to be able to lie to one another. But he also didn't expand on it. "Drive safe, my friend. There are too many bad guys left in this world for you to kick the bucket just yet."

Maddox grinned. "You got it. Catch you later." He followed Dane down the snow-covered front steps, turning right to head to his truck, which was parked down by the corner. He pulled his cowboy hat low over his head, his boots kicking through the snow as he walked. He knew it was going to be a hellish drive, and he should've left earlier. But it had felt good to chill with Dane, and take an hour to forget who he was and the legacy he carried with him. Besides, he was heading south, away from the storm. As long as he got out of the area before it hit hard, he'd be fine.

He reached the corner, and his truck chirped as he unlocked it. But just as he was reaching for the driver's door, the warm glow of lights from way down at the end of the street caught his attention. He frowned, counting the storefronts, then scowled when he realized it was the café belonging to Lissa, the fiancée of his brother, Travis.

Why was she still at work? He knew Travis was out of town to play a benefit concert back East, which meant he wasn't around either to drive Lissa back to their place, or to make her go home before the weather got impassable.

Maddox thought grimly of the long ride in front of him, but even as he ground his jaw at the thought of driving in heavy snow by delaying his departure any longer, he didn't hesitate as he slammed his door shut.

There was no chance he was going to drive away until he knew Lissa was safe.

Scowling, he shoved his hands in the pockets of his heavy coat, slogging through the snow as he strode down the sidewalk. The town center was empty, completely abandoned, because even the hardy Wyoming residents were hunkering down before the storm hit.

But as he walked, an SUV towing a rental trailer pulled up in front of the café, making him groan. If someone walked into the café needing a meal, it would be almost impossible for him to pry Lissa out of the kitchen. He swore under his breath, but he didn't slow down. If he had to be a complete ass and kick the customer out the door with an empty stomach so that he could make sure Lissa shut down and got out the door safely, then he was fine with that.

People thinking he was a classless bastard was nothing new to him, and he had long since stopped giving a shit what anyone thought.

Besides, what was the point in fighting it?

They were right.

Chapter 2

THE CAFÉ WAS *open*.

Tears filled Hannah Crowley's eyes as she quickly pulled her SUV up to the curb. The moment she had the car in park, she put her head down against the steering wheel and closed her eyes, trying to keep her emotions in check. Relief rushed through her, deep, penetrating relief. There was someone who she could ask for help.

She wanted to cry with relief, frustration, and grief, but as she had so many times over the last six months, she simply scrunched her eyes shut, and fought back the emotions. She was so exhausted that it took a moment longer than usual, long enough that she knew she was at the very end of her ability to cope.

But being at the very end meant she still had a thread to hang onto, so after a moment, she took a deep breath, plastered a smile on her face and lifted her head. She looked over her shoulder, expecting to see a peacefully sleeping child, but instead she was met with the solemn stare of the little girl who had become her daughter six months ago, in a grief-filled transition from niece to daughter. Those blue eyes were exactly the same as Hannah's sister, Katie, had had. Every time Hannah looked at little Ava, she saw Katie staring out of those eyes. Dear, precious Katie, who would never see her daughter grow up.

Hannah managed to smile, not a half smile, but a broad, genuine smile, the only kind that ever seemed to bring a smile to the face of the little girl who had once been so happy. "Good news, pumpkin. The café is open. We'll grab a bite to eat while I get directions, and then we'll be at our new place before the storm hits. Ready for our first venture into our new town?"

Ava nodded, but she said nothing, remaining silent, just as she had every day since Katie had died. Her blue eyes were wide, fixed on Hannah, as if she were afraid that if she looked away, Hannah would disappear.

Hannah's heart tightened, because she knew what it felt like to be afraid that the one adult in her life would disappear, and it made her want to cry to think of Ava being burdened by the same fear that she and Katie had grown up with, fear that had become a grim reality when they were teenagers. "I promise you, baby, it's all going to be okay now. It's you and me, and we're warriors. Got it?"

A tiny smile curved the corner of Ava's mouth, and she nodded again. She held up three fingers in a "W," and Hannah did the same.

Hannah reached back and unhooked the car seat that Ava had almost grown out of, and the little girl quickly climbed into the front seat and settled on Hannah's lap, wrapping her arms around Hannah's neck. Hannah squeezed her tightly, pulled a pink stocking cap down over Ava's head, and then climbed out.

The wind was vicious, ripping the breath out of her lungs. Hannah coughed, trying to catch her breath as Ava buried her face in Hannah's shoulder. Holding the little girl close, Hannah hurried through the driving snow toward the storefront.

Hannah caught a glimpse of tables and chairs set up in a cozy warm environment as she approached, but there was no one inside. For a split-second, dread raced through her. What if someone had simply left the light on and gone home? What if there was no one there?

Fear gripped her. What would she do? She'd been driving around for over an hour, and aside from the café with its lights on, she hadn't seen anyone else around, nobody who could tell her how to get to her destination. There didn't appear to be any hotels, at least that she had found, and her cell phone had no reception. If she were alone, it would be bad enough, but there was no way she could weather the oncoming blizzard in a car with a four-year-old. Whispering a little prayer under her breath, she leaned her shoulder into the glass door and pushed.

The door opened easily, and she almost cried with relief as she stumbled into the warm interior. Tiny bells suspended from the hinge jingled, announcing her presence. Almost immediately a woman called out from the kitchen. "Hello?"

Someone was there! "Hi!" Hannah walked forward, careful not to slip on the weather-beaten wood floor. "Are you open?"

"For a woman in need? Always." The swinging door to the kitchen opened, and out walked a woman with brown hair in a ponytail, jeans, and a Wildflower Café sweatshirt. She gave Hannah and Ava a smile so warm and inviting that fresh tears surged in her eyes. Hannah quickly blinked them back, embarrassed by the show of emotion. Since when did she need a friendly face? She didn't. She had long ago learned to be self-reliant.

It was just that she was so exhausted, and in a tight spot. Yes, that was it. She didn't *need* a friendly face. She just needed a little bit of guidance. "I'm new in town, and I'm having trouble finding the house I rented. My GPS doesn't work because I can't get cell service, and I was hoping maybe you could give me directions." As she spoke Ava nestled her head more tightly against Hannah's shoulder, not even looking at the woman. Ava had once been the most gregarious and effervescent little girl, and it broke Hannah's heart to see how she hid her face.

"Yes, there's only one service provider that gets cell service around here. It's a hassle to out-of-towners passing through." The woman patted the deli counter. "Come sit. I'll whip you up something to eat. My name is Lissa McIntyre." She smiled at Ava. "What's your name? Are you hungry? Maybe a grilled cheese or some mac and cheese?"

Ava didn't lift her head from Hannah's shoulder as she sank down on the stool. "My name is Hannah Crowley and this is Ava. She would love some macaroni and cheese, and I'll take anything you have in the fridge. A sandwich, or salad, or anything you have left over. There's no need for you to go to any trouble."

"It's no trouble at all." Lissa grabbed two glasses and began to fill them with water. "What's the address of the place you're looking for?"

Hannah recited the address from memory, and didn't miss the flicker of alarm on Lissa's face. "What? What's wrong?"

"You're planning to go there tonight?"

Hannah nodded. "I have a one-year lease. You know where it is?"

"Yes." Lissa set the glasses in front of them. "It's

been empty for almost three years. Are you sure that the heat and electricity are on? Have you seen it? I don't even know if all the windows still have glass in them. Plus, the driveway's almost a mile long. You'll be stranded there for at least a week if the storm is as bad as they're saying it's going to be."

Exhaustion surged back over Hannah again, but she lifted her chin. "I have plenty of food. Flashlights. Batteries. Blankets. We'll be fine. The real estate agent I rented it from promised me that it was all set to move into. He said he would turn the heat on, and that there's a generator even. I think we'll be fine, if we can just get there before the storm hits."

Lissa folded her arms over her chest. "I don't think you should go there."

Hannah sighed. "I don't have anywhere else to go."

Lissa frowned. "I have an apartment upstairs, but it's currently being renovated, or I'd invite you to crash there."

Hannah was touched by the offer, but she shook her head. "It's no problem. I really want to get settled anyway. If you can just give me directions—"

"I know!" Lissa's face lit up. "Come home with me. We have plenty of space in our house. You can crash there until the storm is over, and then I'll take you to your place."

"You'd let us stay with you?" Hannah gaped at her, stunned by the offer. She could tell from Lissa's expression that she was completely serious. "You don't even know me. Why would you invite me to stay at your house?"

Lissa looked surprised. "Because you have a little girl, and you guys need to be taken care of. Why on earth would I even consider letting you go to the old Anderson place on a night like this? Of course I would make sure you were safe."

Hannah stared at her, still not understanding.

Lissa sighed and softened her voice. "When I first moved to town, I never would've made it if the woman who owned this café hadn't looked out for me. And now, I'm the owner of this café, and there's a woman with a little girl, who has just moved to town, who needs help. Ten years ago, I was you, sitting on that stool, only I was seventeen, broke, alone, and pregnant. I know what you're feeling right now, because I've been there. The very last thing I would ever do is abandon you. We're not strangers, Hannah. We're sisters."

Tears filled Hannah's eyes, and she had to look away as memories of her sister came flooding back. Katie would've taken care of strangers just like Lissa was. Their childhood had made Katie into someone kind, with a huge heart, who needed to take care of the world, the way no one had taken care of them. That same childhood had made Hannah unable to reach out to anybody except her mother and her sister, the only two people in the world she trusted, and they were both gone now. She managed a small smile. "My sister would've loved you." The words slipped out before she knew what she was saying, and she merely bit her lip, knowing she would never be able to keep it together if Lissa asked any questions about Katie.

But she didn't. Understanding filled Lissa's eyes, and she sighed. "My sister died when I was in high school."

Hannah's throat clogged, and she nodded, barely able to handle the empathy and sadness in Lissa's eyes.

Lissa smiled. "See? You sitting on that stool really is me ten years ago. How on earth could I possibly not make sure you're okay? It's settled then, don't you think? You guys can eat while I wait for the last pies to finish baking, and then we'll all head out to my place." She nodded, clearly satisfied with the decision as she set the placemats and utensils in front of Hannah and Ava. "You want some coffee?"

Lissa's kindness and generosity reminded her so much of Katie's, that it made Hannah concerned for Lissa, just as she'd worried about Katie all those years. She had spent her life trying to protect Katie from the softness of her heart and her trust of people, and she had failed in the end to keep her sister safe. She couldn't let Lissa follow the same path. "You can't possibly let me into your house. I could be dangerous."

Lissa laughed then, a gentle, warm chuckle that seemed to wrap around Hannah. "Oh, come on, Hannah. I've seen plenty of people in my life who are truly dangerous, people not worth trusting. You aren't one of them." She winked. "Besides, my house is on the Stockton ranch, and there are four huge Stockton brothers all living within shouting distance of me. They'd rescue me in a heartbeat if there was even a hint of danger, so it's fine. They'd be thrilled to have someone else to take care of." She winked. "It's in their genes to take care of people who need help, even if they would deny it all the way to their graves."

Something deep inside Hannah tugged at her, a yearning to accept Lissa's offer to crash at her house for the night. The thought of being surrounded by people who would protect her, whose natural instinct was to offer help, was almost too much to even imagine. But as strong as the yearning was to accept it, Hannah knew she never would.

She had learned too long ago that the only person she could count on was herself. Well, also Katie, but her beloved sister was no longer around, and their mother had long ago passed away.

It was up to Hannah to take care of herself and her

daughter, and she wouldn't know how to put their well-being in the hands of others, even if she had to. So she managed a smile and shook her head. "Thank you so much for the offer, Lissa, but we'll be fine. If you could just write down directions to my new rental place, I'll be all set."

Lissa folded her arms across her chest, her forehead furrowing into a frown. "I really don't think you should go up there tonight, with the approaching blizzard. You don't even know if the electricity will be turned on! Plus, I don't know how to give directions. It's a bunch of back roads with no street signs. You'll never find it."

Hannah's resolution flickered. "You can't tell me how to get there?"

Lissa shook her head. "I'd have to drive you there. It's impossible to describe."

Hannah thought of the storm outside, and knew she would never ask Lissa to drive in it just for her. What was she going to do? She couldn't go home with this stranger who'd so kindly opened her house to her and Ava, but there was no way she was going to risk getting lost in an approaching blizzard with a four-year-old in the back seat. Desperation rushed through Hannah as she frantically tried to think of another solution, something other than imposing upon Lissa. "What if—"

Lissa's gaze suddenly flicked behind Hannah, and a smile lit up her face. It was a smile of such joy that Hannah knew Lissa had just seen someone she loved, someone who mattered to her. For a split second, envy flooded Hannah, a deep, almost unbearable sense of longing to have someone look at her like that, or to feel that way about anyone...but as soon as she thought it, she sat up taller on the stool.

No. There was no room in her life to make her self-worth dependent on someone else's approval. She would provide all the love that she and Ava needed. Her heart had already been broken by the passing of her mom and Katie, and she had no more heart left to risk by turning it over to anyone else.

Lissa beamed at Hannah. "Perfect timing, it seems to me, don't you think?"

"Perfect timing?" At Lissa's delighted nod, Hannah swiveled on her stool to see who was coming in. She turned just as a shadow passed by the front window, and the door opened. There was a jingle of the bells, and then a man in a cowboy hat stepped inside.

No. She was wrong. He wasn't simply a man. He was a rough and rugged cowboy, a dark, brooding loner with insanely broad shoulders, dark blond hair curling under his snow-covered cowboy hat, and blue jeans that hung low and loose over his hips. His jaw was angular, accented by a day's whiskers, and he was at least six feet tall. He was pure male and testosterone, dangerous and devastatingly handsome, in a stay-away, tormented-male kind of way. He was scowling, looking so irritated with the world that her heart turned over, because she knew the world that he was seeing. That was what she saw as well, when she looked around: darkness, danger, and isolation.

"Maddox!" Lissa called out his name, the happiness evident in her voice.

Maddox flashed her a smile, the kind of smile that made Hannah's heart tighten, because it was the kind of smile she also gave most of the world. A smile that was in name only, hiding all the weight inside her soul. It was a smile that said his heart had long ago forgotten how to smile. "Hey, Lissa," he said. "How's my favorite future sister-in-law?"

Hannah didn't even hear Lissa's response. She was too consumed by Maddox and the sheer power that

15

seemed to be emanating from him. His voice was deep and rough, rolling through Hannah like a warm caress designed to smooth all the rough edges of her heart, and lighten the deepest shadows of her soul. Even Ava shifted in Hannah's arms, lifting her head to look at him.

As if sensing their perusal, Maddox slowly turned his head to look at them. The moment his emerald green eyes settled on her, Hannah's stomach shivered, not with fear, but with something else. Awareness? A spark of life? A sudden desire to take a deep breath and step out into the sunshine?

She didn't want this. She didn't want to notice him, or any other man. She just wanted to get to her new home and start her life over, a life where there was no more pain.

But, as Maddox stared at her, something inside her shifted. Unbidden, almost against her will, she smiled at him. She didn't mean to. She didn't want to. But there was something about the heavy burdens in his green eyes that made her want to reach out to him, to offer him the kind of light that Katie used to give everyone she met.

For a long moment, he simply stared at her. Not smiling back. Not giving any kind of indication that he'd even noticed her overture.

As he stared at her, Hannah's smile began to fade. Who was she kidding? It was Katie who had always known how to help people, not her. And why would she think *she* could offer relief to this tall, broad-shouldered man who could clearly take care of himself?

But just as she began to lower her eyes and turn away, he nodded at her. A single nod, so slight it was barely discernable, but she saw it. Instinctively, she knew that that little nod had been far more significant than any smile he could have given her.

A smile would have been fake.

The nod?

It had been real.

She smiled then, a real smile, her first real smile in months.

Chapter 3

HER SMILE WAS like oxygen and sunshine had merged together to give life to the darkest, most barren of existences.

That was all Maddox could think of as he stared at the woman sitting on Lissa's barstool. Her eyes were a deep, expressive brown, framed by long, black eyelashes that seemed to protect the shadows etched in her eyes. There were circles under her eyes, and her face was pale. She looked exhausted, the kind of exhausted from a life-time of hardship, not from a day or two of inadequate sleep. When he'd first seen her, his initial thought had been that she was like a lost puppy, who needed a hug, a warm bed, and someone to watch over her so she could sleep without fear.

But when she'd smiled at him, all those thoughts had fled. Her smile seemed to plunge right through all the barriers he'd erected over the last thirty years, unleashing a raw, visceral surge of emotion that he hadn't felt since the day he walked in and found his mother dead on the couch. He had shut down after that, a gradual destruction of his humanity, with the final blow being that night when he was seventeen.

He was hard. He made sure he was hard. It was the only way to survive, and it was, quite frankly, all he deserved. But with this woman staring at him with... kindness? Empathy? Concern? It felt as if she saw in him the same humanity that he'd crushed so long ago, and it made him want to suddenly breathe again, as if he'd stopped breathing years ago.

Then, the little girl clinging to her so tightly lifted her head to look at him, too. Her white blonde hair was tangled, her eyes were wide, and she was staring at him as if she'd never seen a human being before. Her face was solemn, much too solemn for a small child. Instinctively, he smiled at her, trying to coax a smile in return.

She stared at him for another moment, her face staying completely serious.

Maddox's smile widened, and he wrinkled his nose at her, just as he did with his brother's baby. He made the same face that made his tiny nephew crack up, and this little girl didn't disappoint. A little dimple appeared in her right cheek, before she ducked her head back against her mom's shoulder.

Satisfaction thrummed through Maddox, and his smile was real as he glanced again at the woman's face. She looked shocked, staring at Maddox as if he were from another planet. His amusement faded, and hardness settled around his heart again. Yeah, that's what he was used to. People looking at him like he was a fucking psychopath, which wasn't far off from the truth.

His jaw hard, he dragged his gaze off her, and settled it on Lissa's face. She was watching him with a small smile lifting the corners of her mouth. Her amusement made him frown even more deeply. "Shouldn't you be home?" he growled at his soon-to-be sister-in-law. "The driving is going to get bad really soon."

"I will, as soon as my pies finish baking. Just another ten minutes or so."

"Pies?" He couldn't keep the disbelief out of his voice. "You're staying around in this weather for *pies*?"

"Yes, because that way, I can freeze them, and they will be all set for whenever I can open again." Her smile widened. "Have I ever told you how much I appreciate the fact that all you guys watch out for me?"

He nodded. "All the time." He stayed by the door, not wanting to get involved. He just wanted Lissa to get out of there and to get home safely. With Travis out of town, it was his responsibility to make sure his brother's fiancée was safe. "It's time to leave, Lissa. The wind is picking up, and visibility is starting to go down. When it really starts to snow, driving is going to be impossible." As he spoke, his gaze flicked to Lissa's guests again. He'd seen them drive up in the SUV with the U-Haul trailer attached. Where the hell were they planning to go? They weren't going to be able to get too far in the storm. Not that they were his problem. They really weren't. "Where you headed?" he asked them, before his plan not to worry about them had even finished forming in his head.

"The old Anderson place," Lissa answered. "Maddox, this is Hannah Crowley and her daughter, Ava. Hannah, this is Maddox. He's one of my eight future brothers-in-law, although he doesn't live on the Stockton ranch. Yet."

Maddox sighed with irritation. "You know I'm never going to move onto that ranch. You guys need to lay off. It gets annoying."

"Of course it gets annoying. Eventually, you're going to get so tired of us pressuring you to live there, that it's going to be easier for you just to move onto the ranch and build a house there, than it is to deal with our incessant, annoying harassment." Lissa grinned as she said it, looking completely unrepentant.

Maddox couldn't help but grin. He didn't like women. He didn't trust women. But his brothers who had settled down had chosen well. He particularly liked Lissa, because she somehow made him smile when no one else in the world could. Not often, but once in a while. "No chance."

"There's always a chance," Lissa announced cheerfully.

He sighed and glanced back at Hannah. He was getting restless, and had to get this settled so he could get on the road. "The Anderson place? On Ridge Street?"

"You know it?" Hannah's face lit up. "Would you be able to give me directions? I haven't been able to find it, and my GPS doesn't work without cell service. Lissa says it's too complicated and she would have to drive me, but of course I would never let her drive me in the snow. I just need to get there. Maybe you can give me directions?"

Her eyes were incredible. They'd been beautiful when she'd been staring at him warily, exhaustion weighing heavily, but now, they were literally sparkling with energy. Son of a bitch. He suddenly wanted to walk across that café, sit down on the stool next to her, and try to think of everything he could say that would bring that kind of life into her eyes. It felt like she was pouring hope right into the darkest recesses of his damaged, blackened soul. "Your eyes are riveting."

Her eyes widened, and he heard Lissa cough. Swearing, he realized what he'd said. He stepped back, his back brushing against the front door. "You'll never find the Anderson place in this weather," he said gruffly. "You need to crash in town."

"I'm not staying in town," Hannah said. "Ava and I need to get to the house, and get settled in. I can't believe it's that hard to tell me how to get there." She looked back and forth between them. "I just need directions. Please."

There was a desperation in her voice that pricked at him. He fisted his hands. "Don't be stubborn. That place has been abandoned for years. It's probably not even habitable. You can't go there."

Lissa clapped her hands. "That's what I told her. I invited her to come back to my place to stay, but she won't. Tell her that she needs to come home with me. It's the only solution that makes sense, but like you said, she's being stubborn—"

"I'm always stubborn. It's part of my charm," Hannah said.

He almost grinned. "Stubbornness isn't charming." But even as he said it, he knew he was lying. She was charming as hell, and he appreciated a woman with enough strength to fight for what she wanted. Weak or vulnerable women terrified him, because they reminded him of his mother.

"Of course stubbornness is adorable," she countered. "I'm completely captivating. So, please, succumb to my manipulative charms and tell me how to get there."

He folded his arms over his chest. "There's no chance in hell that I'm going to send you off to try to find that place in this weather."

Hannah sighed and looked at Lissa. "Is this what you meant when you said they're protective?"

Lissa grinned. "Yep. See? So, you need to come home with me."

Hannah's face fell, and Maddox felt a stab of guilt at the anguish on her face.

"I really don't want to impose upon anybody," she

said with a weary sigh. "It's been a long trip, and I just really need to get settled in our place. We need to get started."

Maddox saw the raw vulnerability on her face, and suddenly he understood. She wasn't being stubborn. She was simply trying to create a foundation to hold herself up. He had been that desperate once. He also understood her need not to go home with Lissa. It was the same reason he refused to move onto the ranch with his brothers. He needed his own space, and he needed to be careful to never get too close to anyone again, so that when he snapped and fulfilled the legacy he was destined for, there would be no one close enough for him to destroy.

He met her gaze, and felt himself falling into those brown eyes. So much pain. So much grief. But at the same time there was an indomitable fierceness, the one trait that his mother had never had, which was why she had died. The exhaustion on Hannah's face made it clear that, despite her fierceness, she had so little reserves left. She needed to be home, he knew it. He could see it on every line of her face, and the way she held her daughter so tightly.

Swearing, he glanced outside at the blowing snow. He needed to get the hell on the road, or he would be stranded in Rogue Valley, too. But when he looked back in the café, he saw the two women watching him, both looking at him like he held the key to everything. He clenched his jaw, and then Ava lifted her head off her mom's shoulder and looked at him. Those silent blue eyes stared at him, wrapping around his heart, and he swore, realizing that there was no chance in hell he was going to drive out of town until these three females were safe. He'd come to the café to make sure Lissa was safe, and now Hannah and Ava were also on his list.

He sighed, swearing under his breath as he realized

he might as well just accept the truth, that he was sunk. Glaring at them all, he jerked off his coat, tossed it on a chair, and strode into the café. "I'll finish the pies, Lissa. You get the hell back home. Once they're in the freezer, I'll escort Hannah and Ava to the Anderson place. Got it?" But as he spoke to Lissa, he couldn't keep his gaze from sliding over toward Hannah as he approached the counter.

There was no way for him to miss the sheen of tears as they filled Hannah's eyes at his words, and suddenly he knew he'd done the right thing. His life was dirty and gritty, and there wasn't anything pretty about it, but he knew in that moment, that he'd done something that mattered.

"Really?" she whispered. "You will?"

"Yeah," he said gruffly. "It's not a big deal. I was headed that direction anyway." Which was passably true.

She smiled, a smile so genuine that he smiled back. Yeah, that felt good.

Lissa, not surprisingly, frowned at him, however. "What if the heat isn't on? What if the house isn't actually habitable?" She folded her arms over her chest. "There's no way —"

"I'll check it out. If it's not okay, then we'll head to the ranch. Okay?"

Lissa narrowed her eyes at him, then finally nodded. "Okay, but I'll stay and finish the pies, so you can get going with them. It's a much longer drive out to the Anderson place than it is for me to get back to the ranch."

Maddox ducked behind the counter, grabbed her coat from the hook by the kitchen door, and held it out to her. "I've been in your kitchen before. I know what to do. Get out, or I'm going to call Travis and tell him that the woman he loves is taking unnecessary risks with her safety. You want him to worry about you when he's in

25

New York, unable to get back here to help you?"

Mentioning Travis's worry for her did it. Concern flicked in Lissa's eyes, and she inclined her head. "Okay. I'll go. But I want you to text me and let me know whether you're bringing Hannah and Ava to my place or not. And the pies will be ready in ten minutes." She hesitated. "I don't want you to overcook them—"

"I know how to tell if pies are done." He helped her get her coat on, moving her toward the kitchen. "Text me when you get back to the ranch. Get out."

Lissa turned, and gave him a quick hug. Then she winked at Hannah. "Welcome to Rogue Valley, Hannah. The café is open almost every day, so even if you end up staying at the Anderson place tonight, you come see me when the storm is over. You need a friend, and I'm here for you."

Maddox didn't miss the flash of longing on Hannah's face, and he sure as hell noticed the way she stiffened, as if trying to talk herself out of her need to respond to Lissa's overture. Clearly, Hannah was a loner, like him. He felt a flash of regret. Being a loner might be the only way to survive, but sometimes it completely sucked.

He held the door for Lissa, watching until she went out the back door, and the door swung shut behind her, leaving him alone in the café with an oven full of pies, and two females who were going to be in serious trouble if he didn't deliver for them.

He wasn't good for women. He knew he wasn't. He'd learned that lesson a long time ago. Swearing, he closed his eyes. How the hell had he just gotten himself into this situation?

Not that it mattered. He was in it, and now he had to see it through.

Gritting his teeth, he turned around to face the two females counting on him.

Chapter 4

T HE MOMENT THAT the back door shut behind Lissa, Hannah suddenly realized that she'd made a huge mistake. She was alone with a strong, dangerous man, and she had a little girl to protect. Dear God. Suddenly, the images of her sister's battered body and her mother's bruised face flashed through her mind, and her heart started hammering with panic.

What had she been thinking? She had been so desperate to be a part of the affection between Lissa and Maddox that she'd agreed to something insanely foolish, and potentially dangerous.

She knew about men. She knew how dangerous they could be. And yet, she'd walked right into this.

She immediately stood up, holding Ava tight. "You know," she said, trying to keep the strain out of her voice as she tried not to look at Maddox. "Why don't you just write down the directions? The snow is getting worse, and I really should head out now. I don't think it would be wise for me to wait until the pies are ready. I'm sure I'll be able to follow your directions well enough, when I add them to the ones I already received from the realtor."

Maddox studied her, his arms folded across his chest as he leaned his shoulder against the door jamb and cocked one leg to the side, in a casual, jaunty pose that made him look even more imposing than he already did. "I have never hurt a woman in my life, and now isn't the moment when I'm going to start."

She blinked, replaying his words in her head as she stared at him, startled by how he'd zeroed in on the exact reason why she was suddenly nervous. For a split second, she wanted to just drop her shields and admit that she was terrified of everything, but instead, she pulled her shoulders back and summoned strength she could barely access. "You mean, you *are* going to start hurting women at some point in the future? It just isn't going to be this particular moment in time? Because that really doesn't make me feel safer."

His jaw tightened, and his eyes narrowed. She expected him to defend himself, but he said nothing. He just stared at her, his expression hard and cold. There was something in his eyes that made her hesitate. She realized suddenly that she'd hurt him. Deeply.

She thought of how much Lissa had clearly adored him. Of how he'd gotten Ava to smile. Of the weight in his eyes. Suddenly she knew that she'd been wrong to judge him so quickly. He was a protector, not someone who would hurt the innocent. Heat flooded Hannah's cheeks. "I'm sorry," she said, meaning it. "I didn't mean to offend you."

He shrugged, lifting one shoulder, but she didn't believe his casual response. There was too much tension in his body, too much darkness in his eyes. She sighed, recognizing her own limitations. Based on all the evidence,

she was pretty certain that he was completely trustwor-
thy. The problem was with her own inability to trust any
man, not just him. He didn't deserve to be insulted because of her own lack of capacity to be normal. She
sighed, wanting to take away the insult she'd just tossed
at the man who had been so kind to her and Ava, as well
as Lissa. "I just meant, that I feel like I should go. I didn't
mean anything personal by it. I just—" She hesitated, not
sure that announcing that she basically saw all men as
potential threats was the right way to go.

"The question is," Maddox said, his voice low and
rough as he watched her, "are you safer trying to find the
Anderson place alone in the storm, or here with me?
That's the million-dollar question, isn't it?"

There was something in the way he asked it that
made her pause. Even Ava lifted her head to look at him.
There was an edge to his voice, a raw bitterness laced
with self-hate that made her heart turn over. She looked
at him more closely, and this time, she noticed the small
scar on his temple, and the scars on his fingers. There
were small round scars on his left forearm that looked
like burn marks. Small, round burns about half a centi-
meter in diameter, marks that looked like they'd been
caused by a...cigarette?

No.

She had to be imagining things. Her gaze snapped to
his, and the sudden raw pain she saw in his eyes told her
she'd been right. Someone had burned cigarettes into his
arm at some point in his life.

Silently, he unfolded his arms, and turned and went
back into the kitchen, leaving her and Ava alone out
front.

Hannah closed her eyes, her throat tightening. What
had happened to him? How old had he been when he'd
gotten those scars? She wanted to run after him, to hug

him, to offer him the comfort that she'd never gotten all those nights she'd been so scared as a child.

But she didn't move. Katie had been the hugger. Katie had been the one to offer comfort. Hannah didn't know how to do that. All she knew was how to erect shields around her, barriers that would keep people out. Besides, Katie's love had gotten her killed, and there was no way that Hannah was going to make the same mistake.

She would never trust anyone, especially not a man, especially when she had Ava to protect.

She should leave. Right then. Get in her car and drive until she found a place to stay. Men scared her, and Maddox clearly had the kind of violence in his past that terrified her. She should run, take Ava, and...

Ava touched her arm, and Hannah opened her eyes. Ava touched her lips with her fingers, and then rubbed her belly, indicating that she was hungry. Hannah grimaced. "I'm sorry, baby, but I think we should go—"

Just then, the kitchen door swung open. Hannah jumped as Maddox walked out, carrying two trays. One of them had a sandwich and a salad on it, and he set that in front of Hannah. The other one he held up to Ava. "This is my secret recipe," he said, his voice gruff. "Only special kids get to eat this. So far, only my niece and nephews have gotten to eat it, but I can tell that you're particularly awesome, so you get to be in the inner circle."

Ava watched him, her eyes wide.

Maddox set the tray down in front of her, and both Hannah and Ava leaned forward to see what was on it. It was macaroni and cheese, but somehow Maddox had managed to arrange it into the shape of a dog. He had used chocolate chips for the eyes, a strawberry for the nose, and French fries for the whiskers. "His name is Alfred," Maddox said, his voice softening the longer he spoke. "He's a magic dog. Once he's in your belly, he stays with you forever as your guardian angel. He's always there to hug you if you need it, and to chase away the bad dreams. All you have to do is say his name, and he'll be there for you." Maddox set a glass of chocolate milk down. "And drink your milk. It's good for you. Got it?"

Ava nodded vigorously, watching him with rapt attention.

"Good." He glanced at Hannah. "You need to eat, too," he said, his voice still gruff. "You look like you're going to pass out."

She blinked, startled by the way his deep voice seemed to wrap around her, enveloping her in a sense of warmth and safety. She stared at him, unable to look away from his gaze. There was so much emotion in there, pain, hardness, regret. And something else. A yearning. A longing. For what? She cleared her throat. "Thank you," she whispered. "I—" She stopped, not sure what to say.

Silence fell, and for a long moment, they stared at each other. After a moment, he nodded, and stood up. He didn't wait for an answer. Without another word, without another look, he turned and walked back into the kitchen, letting the door shut behind him.

Hannah stared after him, her mouth open in shock. "Alfred?" she whispered to herself. Alfred the magic dog. How on earth had Maddox realized what Ava needed? How did a man so tough and hard know what a traumatized four-year-old needed?

Ava scrambled off Hannah's lap onto the adjacent stool, and pulled the tray over. She leaned forward, so she was eye level with Alfred. Her lips moved, and Hannah knew she was whispering something to the dog.

Tears suddenly clogged her throat. Dear God. Ava was whispering to the macaroni dog. Talking, for the first time in six months.

Ava finished her conversation, then she leaned over and kissed Alfred on his strawberry nose. Hannah's throat tightened as Ava picked up a fork, grinned at Hannah, and started eating, a small smile curving her mouth.

Hannah smiled back, ruffling Ava's hair as the little girl started shoveling the food into her mouth, eating with more vigor than she had in six months.

For a long moment, Hannah sat there, stroking Ava's hair, watching her daughter eat, aware of the sounds of pots clanking in the kitchen as Maddox moved around. Something clanged, and he swore under his breath, just loud enough for them to hear.

Ava looked at Hannah, and then giggled, her eyes dancing with mirth, clearly highly amused that they'd caught Maddox swearing.

Giggles.

Whispers.

Shoveling food in her mouth as if she could never get enough to eat.

Three things that Hannah hadn't been able to make happen for Ava...until now.

She knew why it had happened now.

She could see it in the way Ava was swinging her feet, and the relaxed set to her shoulders. Ava felt safe. Maddox, with his broad shoulders, gruff voice, and macaroni dog, had made Ava feel safe.

Maddox had given them their first moment of feeling safe in years, maybe ever, and yet, Hannah had basically accused him of hurting women. He was the same man Hannah was afraid to be alone with. The same man who had made Lissa light up. The same man who had made Hannah feel safe when he'd said he'd escort them to her new place. He'd made her feel safe, until her mind and her own baggage had interfered, dragging her into the horrors of her past.

She looked at her sandwich, at the salad he'd put together for her, on his own, without even asking if she was hungry. She closed her eyes. On an instinctive level, she was terrified of the man in that kitchen, of his immense strength, of the darkness he undoubtedly carried inside him, but at the same time, she knew in her gut, that she was seeing him through her own filtered lens of hardship.

The man had made Ava a macaroni dog, for heaven's sake. He might have flaws, but there was something inside him that was worthwhile. She knew it, even if she was too afraid of him, or any man, to admit it. She didn't have to trust him. She didn't have to let him into her life, or see him for even one moment after tonight, but she did have to do one thing.

She owed him an apology.

Chapter 5

MADDOX KNEW THE moment that Hannah stepped into the kitchen. He didn't know how, because he hadn't heard her, but suddenly he knew she was standing in the same room as he was. He closed his eyes and braced his hands on the counter, not turning around.

Ten pies were lined up on the stovetop, and the pot-holder was still in his hand. He didn't want to look at her. He didn't want to see that expression on her face again, when she realized how dangerous he was, how blackened his soul was.

He was used to people looking at him like that. He had truly thought he didn't care anymore. He had honestly believed that on that night when he was seventeen, he had shut down enough that it would never bother him again, when someone looked at him like the monster he was.

And it never had bothered him. Not until the moment

that he'd seen that expression on Hannah's face, when she'd been holding her daughter so tightly, her eyes wide with fear as she had announced her need to get on the road.

He had had no words to respond.

And now she was standing behind him, as if he were expected to turn around and talk to her, as if he was a normal human being. As if all the crap of his past wasn't firmly entrenched in every fiber of his being.

"Maddox?"

He grimaced at the sound of her voice, at the way it spread through him like kindness and warmth. Her voice was beautiful, like the sounds of birds on an early morning ride just as the sun was rising and nature was waking up. Shit. He hadn't thought of those rides on his favorite horse in a long time. What the hell? Why was he thinking about Big Red again? He'd left horses and his memories behind long ago.

He cleared his throat. "I'll be ready to go in about five minutes." He didn't turn around, and didn't give her the chance to say she wanted to drive in the storm by herself. Fuck that. He might be scum, but there was no chance he was letting Hannah and Ava out into the storm alone. "I'm going to put the pies in the walk-in freezer, so they should be okay, even going in hot." He kept his voice hard and steady, focused. "You can follow me in your car."

She sighed, a deep sigh he could feel in his gut even from the other side of the kitchen. He ground his jaw, his muscles becoming even more tense. What the hell did she want from him? This was all he had. All he fucking had to offer.

He heard the creak of the floor, and knew she was heading back to the front of the café. It was exactly what he wanted to accomplish, but he couldn't suppress the stab of regret that he managed to alienate the first woman that had made him feel anything in years. Hell. He didn't want to be dealing with this—

Suddenly, he felt the whisper soft touch of her hand on the back of his shoulder. He froze, going absolutely still, his breath freezing in his chest. Her touch was so gentle, so soft, softer than anything he'd ever felt in his life. Every one of his senses honed in on the sensation of her fingers against the back of his shoulder, trying to imprint the sensation in his soul so he would never forget how it felt to be touched like that.

"I'm sorry, Maddox." Her voice was as soft and kind as her touch, gently nestling its way past the armor he'd worked so hard to reinforce over the years.

He cleared his throat, still not turning around, afraid that if he moved at all, her fingers would slide off him, and he would never feel this again. "No apologies necessary." His voice was gruff, hard, almost harsh. He grimaced when he heard what he sounded like, but he didn't know what else to say. He felt like he didn't have another voice anymore, but for the first time in a long time, he wished he did. He wished he had another way to talk to her, to this woman who was touching him as if he was some treasure to be honored and nurtured.

"Sometimes an apology is necessary." Her voice was still soft, but he heard the crack of emotion. "I owe you one."

It was that hint of vulnerability that made him turn around. He simply couldn't turn his back on her, even if it meant losing the whisper-light physical connection between them. The moment he turned to face her, and she raised those brown eyes to his, his breath stuttered again. "God," he whispered. "You're like a single ray of sunshine, drifting through the darkness. I could breathe it in forever. Never apologize for who you are."

Her eyes widened, and belatedly, he realized what he'd said. Shit. He wasn't the guy who talked about sunshine and hope, not anymore.

Her hand slid down his arm, and fell to her side. His entire soul seemed to call out at the loss of her touch, and he was viscerally aware of the fact that she hadn't simply pulled her hand back, but had prolonged the contact, as if she too had come to life from that mere touch.

She lifted her chin, as if she were summoning resolution. "I do owe you an apology," she said firmly. "I insulted your kindness and your offer of help. I want you to know that my reaction to you had nothing to do with you. I..." She hesitated, but before he could interrupt, she caught herself and seemed to find the energy to finish what she was saying. "I have trust issues when it comes to men," she said succinctly, her gaze steady on his face. "That's *my* baggage, not yours. I appreciate your help, and I would love for you to escort us to our new place so we can get there safely."

There was so much vulnerability in her eyes that Maddox couldn't hold onto the detached coldness he lived by. But he knew he should. This woman was vulnerable. She could not let her guard down around him. She simply couldn't. Which meant he had to keep the walls up for them. "Ironically," he said. "Your hesitation was the appropriate response when dealing with me. I'm not a good guy. I come from bad stock, and it's just a matter of time until it wins. You saw in me an evil that is truly there." Crap. He hated saying that out loud. He absolutely hated acknowledging what he really was, especially to her.

She stared at him, searching his face as if trying to see into his very soul.

He let her. She needed to know what he was.

"You would never hurt me," she said softly, breathing

out a deep sigh of relief, as if she was so pleased to have finally figured out the truth about him.

Except she was wrong. "I'm not a good guy," he said again, ignoring the way his chest tightened at her words. "Don't look at me like I am."

But she did. She kept studying his face, and then her gaze dropped to his forearm. He knew what she was looking at. He knew that she could see the scars from the cigarettes his dad had put out on his arm so long ago.

"Who did that?" she asked, her voice gentle.

He stiffened. "My dad." He hadn't meant to answer her. He sure as hell hadn't meant to pour out the baggage from his past, and when the flicker of sadness rushed over her face, he wished he hadn't. But at the same time, he had to get that empathy out of her. He had to make her understand that tainted blood ran in his veins. "My dad was a piece of shit, and he taught me all I know." He meant the last as a warning to her, to make sure she understood that the monster who sired him still lived within him.

To his shock, Hannah reached out, her fingers drifting over his scarred forearm. He went still, staring in shock as he watched her hand brush over the old scars, as if she could wipe away all the pain that had accompanied them. "I'm sorry," she whispered. "There are some men in this world who are so bad. I'm so sorry your dad was one of them."

He wanted to tell her that he was one of them too. He really did. But the words stuck in his throat. He simply couldn't do it. He couldn't say the words that would make her run away.

She raised her gaze to his. "Have you ever hurt anyone physically? Ever?"

He swallowed. "I got in fights as a kid. I...do what I have to do. I'm a bounty hunter. My job is...ugly sometimes."

She didn't look away. "Someone like me, I meant," she whispered. "Have you ever physically harmed someone innocent? Someone who you could break if you hurt them. Have you ever hurt anyone like that? Hit them? Struck them?"

The mere idea of it made a cold chill grip his spine. He couldn't imagine anything more abhorrent. "Fuck, no. Never."

She raised her eyebrows, searching his face. "Not once?"

"No way." He swore. "I'd cut off my own arm before I'd strike an innocent, but the monster that would is inside me. I'm my father's son. The violence is a part of me. The destruction of all things beautiful. Not just physically, but spiritually." He brushed his finger over her jaw, quickly, lightly, just needing to touch. "Like you. I would crush that light that shines so beautifully through you. I'm that kind of bastard." Hell. Had he just said that aloud?

Hannah studied him for a long minute, and he saw wisdom in her eyes that belied her age. "If it were in you, you would have hurt someone by now," she said softly. "Men like that...they can't stop themselves. It starts small, but it's always there. If it's not there yet, Maddox, it won't ever be there for you." She touched his arm again. "Even with these."

"Don't believe in me, Hannah. Just don't."

She smiled sadly. "I don't believe in anyone, Maddox, but you make me want to change that."

He saw the truth in her eyes, and suddenly, he wanted to be the one to make her believe again. He wanted to be that good guy who would teach her that some men were decent human beings, that there were people she could count on, that the world could be safe. But he wasn't that guy. He knew those men existed, because his brothers were those kinds of men. He saw the way Chase, Steen, Zane, and Travis treated their women and kids, and he *knew* that his brothers had somehow risen above the hell that haunted them all.

But he wasn't like them. He was worse, so much worse. There was no happy ending for him. Silently, he reached up and brushed his finger over Hannah's cheek. One touch. Just to see if her skin was as soft as he'd thought.

It was.

She didn't pull away, and for a long moment, they stood there in silence, with his hand against her cheek, and her fingers gripped around his scarred wrist. In less than an hour, he would be on the road, back to his job, back to his life, but this moment...this moment was one he would hold onto for a long time, because it was the first time he'd felt like a real person since his mother had died.

Because Hannah was looking at him with trust, even if he didn't deserve it. That was all it had taken to make him feel human again: just the expression on her face when she looked at him. It was breathtaking.

The kitchen door suddenly opened, and they both dropped their hands as Ava poked her head in. She looked back and forth between them, and then smiled and held up her empty glass.

Hannah let out a nervous laugh. "You want some more milk, pumpkin?"

Ava nodded, holding the glass silently toward Maddox. There was absolutely no fear in her face, just a contented certainty that he would provide.

Fierce protectiveness surged through him, a raw need to draw both females into his space so he could shield them from whatever had caused the shadows in their eyes. He wasn't a protector. He was the guy who people guarded against, but in that moment, he knew his role had changed. He would do whatever it took to keep them safe, even if it meant keeping them away from him.

But right now, they needed him. And he needed them, more than he'd ever needed anything. He needed their sunshine.

So, he took a deep breath, and let go of the walls he'd worked so hard to build up. Not forever. Just for the next hour, until he had them safely set up in their new place. When he was back on the road, he'd be back to himself. But right now, right now he needed to be the guy that they both saw when they looked at him. "One chocolate milk, coming up."

The smile he got from both of them was a gift he knew he'd never forget.

Ever.

Chapter 6

A S MADDOX DROVE further and further down the long winding driveway that led to the old Anderson place, he became increasingly convinced that it was a bad idea for Hannah and Ava to move in right before the storm. His truck was bouncing over the ruts in the dirt road, and snow was piled up high on either side. It had clearly been plowed since the last storm, but there were sticks and branches littering the ground. The driveway was over a mile long, and it was pitch black, and completely isolated.

The blowing snow was whipping across his headlights, and he couldn't tell if fresh snow had started to come down yet, or if it was still ground snow blowing. But his dashboard said it was below zero, and that was without the wind chill. It was cold as hell, and this place was much more isolated than he had remembered.

Behind him, the headlights from Hannah's SUV flashed as she followed him. She had stayed close, as was necessary with the increasingly poor visibility. Every time he glanced in his rearview mirror and saw those headlights, he thought of Hannah and her little girl in that dark interior, trusting him to get them to safety. There was no way in hell they would've ever found this place, because the road signs were nonexistent, and the midwinter snowdrifts were already high.

He turned the corner and his lights flashed on a small, snowy cabin. The steps had barely been shoveled, and there were shutters closed over the windows, as if no one had been there in years. There were no lights on, and there were tall trees all around. His headlights flashed over the old barn beside the house, and he grimaced when he saw how ramshackle it looked. Was the house in equally poor condition?

He didn't know what real estate agent Hannah had used, but he had a bad feeling that the house had been misrepresented. This rural homestead was no place for a single mom and a little girl in the middle of a Wyoming winter.

No wonder Lissa had been so insistent that Hannah and Ava go back to her place. He'd been here plenty of times growing up, helping out with the horses, but he had never noticed how isolated and alone it was. Hell, he generally liked things that didn't involve a lot of other people. He still wouldn't have noticed how isolated it was, except for the fact that Hannah and Ava were behind him, and his mind wouldn't stop picturing the two of them in that house.

He parked the car, and by the time Hannah pulled up next to him, he had made his decision. There was no chance that he could allow Hannah and Ava to stay there with the storm rolling in. It simply wasn't safe. She had no cell service, he doubted there was a working phone line, and he didn't even know if there was electricity.

They would be stranded alone once the storm hit, for a few days, without any knowledge of how to survive if the shit went south.

No chance.

He was out of his truck before Hannah had even put her car in park. He jogged around her hood and knocked on her window. She rolled it down and grinned at him. "How cute is this cabin? It's like from a storybook!"

He blinked, startled by her comment. "It's completely isolated out here."

"I wanted privacy. It's perfect." She twisted around in her seat. "What do you think, pumpkin? Did you see the barn? We could get a horse in the spring. Would you like that?"

Ava unhooked herself from the car seat and climbed into the front, nodding fiercely. She held up two fingers, and Hannah laughed. "Yes, of course. We can get two ponies, so we can ride together, and they can have a friend. Does that sound good?"

Ava bobbed her head enthusiastically and threw her arms around Hannah's neck.

Maddox frowned. "You can't stay here. It's so isolated. No one will be able to get to you if you need anything, and you don't even have cell service."

"It's an adventure!" There was no mistaking the excitement in Hannah's eyes, and on Ava's face.

He scowled more deeply. How could they not see what a bad situation this was for them?

"Are you ready to go inside, pumpkin? There are three bedrooms, but I get the big one, because I'm the mom."

Ava wrinkled her nose at Hannah, and then Maddox had to step back as Hannah shoved her car door open.

Maddox frowned as they got out. "I really feel like you should go to Lissa's, and start your move-in after the storm." The wind was whipping fiercely, biting through his clothes. He didn't like Hannah and Ava being out in it. "It's really cold."

"Of course it is. It's Wyoming." Hannah wrapped her arms around Ava, and climbed out. A house key dangled from her fingers as she stepped around Maddox and headed for the front door.

Maddox swore under his breath and caught up to them, his hand out to catch them if either of them slipped on the treacherous ground. They made it to the front step without incident however, and Hannah easily slid the key in the lock, using the light from their headlights to see what she was doing.

Maddox looked over his shoulder, scowling as he noticed that the snow was thicker now, indicating that fresh snow was starting to come down, as opposed to just being stirred up from the ground. The storm was moving in, and it was coming fast. Before too long they wouldn't have any options at all, other than to hunker down exactly where they were.

He didn't like being out of options.

"Oh, it's adorable."

Hannah's awed exclamation caught his attention, and he looked back at the house. She had turned on the lights, illuminating what appeared to be a living room/family room. There were two old couches, with wooden arms and backs, decorated with faded cushions. The coffee table had picture books on it, and there was a wood stove in the corner. To the left was a wide doorway that gave him a view of an old, worn out kitchen with a battered wooden table, old chairs, and tired curtains. There was a weathered rag rug under the kitchen table, and the stove looked like it had been there for forty years.

Hell, the whole place was probably a fire hazard waiting to go up in smoke.

Hannah, however, walked inside, her face illuminated with happiness. "It's perfect," she whispered. "Don't you think, Ava?"

To his surprise, the little girl nodded and squirmed to get out of Hannah's arms. When Hannah set her down, Ava ran across the room, jumped on the couch, stuck her hand between the cushions, and then held up an old, faded stuffed dog. It was light brown, with floppy ears and a droopy tail. The thing looked like it had been stuck there for decades. He had no idea how Ava had noticed it.

She looked up at Maddox then, and held up the dog, beaming at him.

He frowned. "You want me to take it?"

She shook her head and patted her belly, then put the dog on her stomach.

Hannah sucked in her breath. "It's Alfred," she whispered. "She found Alfred. Didn't you, Ava?"

Ava bobbed her head, grinning at Maddox so happily that something inside him turned over. He'd made up that dog thing for his youngest brother, Travis, when he'd have nightmares about going to sleep in that hellhole that they'd grown up in. He hadn't thought about Alfred for years, but something about Ava had made him remember.

He crouched in front of her. "It looks like Alfred decided to come out and see you for real. He almost never does that, you know. Only very special girls get to meet him for real. You take good care of him, and he'll take good care of you. Got it?"

Ava hugged Alfred to her chest, and nodded fiercely. Then she pointed down the hall, and at Hannah's nod, she took off running, clearly checking out the rest of the small house.

Hannah sighed as she watched Ava run, then turned back toward Maddox. "Thank you."

Maddox shrugged. "It's just a story."

"It's not just a story, and you know it. It's a life pre-server for her, and you meant it that way." Hannah cocked her head, studying him, and Maddox shifted, uncomfortable with the way she was looking at him, as if he were a saint.

"We need to get going to Lissa's," he said gruffly. "The storm's coming in fast."

Her eyes widened. "To Lissa's? Why would we go there?"

"Because this place—"

"Is perfect." She touched his arm, a light touch that made everything in his gut tighten. "We'll be okay, Maddox. You can go. I know you need to get on the road."

He swore under his breath. "You're staying?" He didn't need to ask. He could see the determination on her face, the way her jaw was set and her eyes were steady and determined.

"Of course." She turned away. "I just need to find the heat. It's freezing in here."

Maddox watched her as she made her way to the wall, walking along as she looked for the thermostat. The wind was howling as it battered the walls, and the shutters were banging. It was going to be a hell of a storm, one that was likely to take out power, and shut down the roads.

He glanced at the wood stove. Only three pieces of wood. He thought back to when he'd been here as a teenager, and remembered a woodpile out near the barn, at least seventy-five yards from the house.

"Found it!" Hannah called out from the kitchen. "It should warm up soon."

Soon? With the old heating system, it would take a few hours to get it to a livable temperature, and that was assuming the power didn't go out.

Hannah walked out of the kitchen. "The fridge and stove work, and there's water, so we're good!" She smiled at him. "Thanks so much for getting us here. I can't thank you enough." She glanced back at the hallway, where Ava was still running around. "It was so important to get her settled. She needs that. Thank you." Weariness flashed across her face, and Maddox suddenly saw that same vulnerability that he'd seen when he'd first walked into the Wildflower Café.

She no longer looked like the fierce, indomitable spirit who was willing to move into a worn-out cabin in the Wyoming tundra in the middle of the night. She looked like a woman who had been ruthlessly dragged through hell, a hell that was still trying to drag her down. She was swaying slightly, as if staying on her feet was taking the last bit of strength she possessed. He noticed again the circles under her eyes, and how pale she looked.

Instinctively, without thinking about it, he rested his hand against the side of her face. He frowned. "Your skin is cold. Too cold."

She raised her brows. But he felt her lean into his touch ever so slightly. "It's zero degrees in here. Of course my face is cold." But even as she said it, he felt her body shiver despite her heavy parka.

"Are you sick?" He narrowed his eyes, protectiveness surging through him. He took note of how narrow her shoulders were, of the way she hugged her arms to her chest, of the way she bit her lower lip. All of them were signs that she was struggling in a way she was refusing to admit.

She shrugged. "Who has time to be sick?" But even as she said it she sighed, and he felt the weight of what she carried in her breath, her voice, and her eyes.

He knew what that weight was. He carried his own

share of it. He thought back to what she had said about her wariness around men, and a dark protectiveness and anger settled around him.

Whatever the reason she had to park herself and her daughter out in this hellhole, he had to respect it, because she was a survivor. But as he stood there, his hand still on her cheek, feeling the trembling of her body, he knew he wasn't going to get on the road and drive away until he was sure that they were all set.

He had driven in blizzards plenty of times in his life. What was one more? Fuck it. He had to stay until everything was in place to his satisfaction. It wouldn't take long, and then he could go. His fingers tightened against her cheek, and her gaze went to his. For a moment neither of them said anything. It was just the two of them, like it had been in the kitchen at the café before Ava had come in. Something inside him shifted, something deep, something hot, something he hadn't felt in a long time.

Her gaze slipped to his mouth, and that deep, smoldering heat suddenly erupted into something fierce and possessive. An instinctual need to draw her into his circle, to slide his hand around her waist, and to pour his strength into her.

He might be a bastard that was shunned by the world, but there was one thing he had, and that was strength. He could be a steel wall for Hannah and her little girl, a wall that no enemy could penetrate.

Hannah caught her breath, her gaze snapping to his face. Awareness flushed her cheeks, and suddenly, tension skyrocketed between them, a heated sexual tension that pulsed through him like a hot wind on an August night.

He realized suddenly that he wanted to kiss her.

Chapter 7

N O, NOT KISS her. He wanted to *consume* her. He wanted to taste her kiss. He wanted to trace his lips down the side of her neck. He wanted to spread his palms over her hips, draw her close, and feel her body against his. He wanted all that vulnerability, goodness, and warmth to pour into him, and he wanted to give her his strength, every last vestige that he could summon. "I want to kiss you," he said, softly, keeping his voice low, so low that she couldn't hear.

But when her cheeks flushed and her eyes widened, he realized that she'd heard exactly what he said. "You do?"

"Yeah." He moved his hand ever so slightly, just enough so he could slide his thumb over her lower lip. It was so soft that he felt like the world had shifted under his feet.

Her cheeks turned pink. "I want you to kiss me," she whispered. "Is that horrible? I mean, I don't even know you—"

He laughed softly. "Yeah, it's horrible, because you should run screaming from me."

She lifted her chin. "If I should run screaming from you, why are you standing here touching me? Shouldn't your protector instinct make you want to keep me safe from you?"

"Yeah. It should." He moved closer, until his mouth was inches from her. "It always has in the past. Women run from me like their life depends on it, and I like it that way. Until I saw you sitting on that bar stool in the café, until you smiled at me. My world stopped."

Her face softened. "You never let anyone smile at you, do you?"

"I'd let you smile at me all day long." His gaze dropped to her mouth, unable to contain the rising need within him to drop his head another few inches, and take her mouth in his. One kiss. One whisper of a kiss that he could take with him into the rest of his life.

"I'm afraid of men," she whispered, even as she inched toward him ever so slightly, and rested her hand gently on his chest, barely touching him, but at the same time, sending fire streaking through his body.

"And I'm the kind of guy you should be afraid of," he said.

"So this is a bad idea," she whispered, her gaze flicking to his mouth again.

"Hell, yeah."

She bit her lower lip, settling on his face. "It's been so long," she whispered. "I don't even know if I remember what it feels like to be kissed."

It was that whisper of yearning in her voice, the way she looked at him as if he could give her something she needed so badly, something kind, something soft, something nurturing, that broke his self-control. He could offer her nothing of what she wanted from him, but the mere fact that she was looking at him with that kind of trust and acceptance, was too much. For this one second, this one moment in time, he wanted to be the guy she needed.

He thumbed her lower lip, and then bent his head and closed the distance between them. He brushed a kiss over her lips, lightly, intending it to be nothing more than a whisper in the cold, but the moment his lips touched hers, he completely forgot about being chaste.

The kiss was both pure innocence, and pure sinful heat. No, not sinful. There was nothing sinful about this woman. She was everything he wasn't, kind, nurturing, shining light into the world. Kissing her was a grasp at salvation for him, a chance to breathe in the hope that could galvanize him for another decade to keep fighting the battle against the monster inside him.

A small sigh of pleasure drifted from her, and his gut tightened. Her fingers were still resting against his chest, but he felt her fingertips curl ever so slightly, digging in, just enough to show him that he was affecting her at least on some level. Yeah, he knew he wasn't the kind of guy to pour light in anyone else. Hell, he was the guy who would strip the light out of anybody…

That thought, that brutal truth, was like an icy cold stab through his gut. He broke the kiss immediately, and stepped back, dropping his hands to his sides. What the hell was he doing kissing a woman like Hannah? He would break her. He would put out that light, and watch everything she was shrivel and die if he poured himself into her life.

There was no chance he was going to do that to her. No chance.

He shoved his hands in his pockets, but didn't go anywhere. He couldn't make himself step away. He was too entranced watching the play of emotions across her face. She was slow to recover from the kiss, her eyes still closed, her mouth still parted slightly, her breath slow and deep.

Finally, she opened her eyes and looked at him. There was so much emotion in those brown depths, so much wonder, so much softness. She smiled slightly, and touched her fingers to her lips. "That was interesting."

His eyebrows shot up. "Interesting? That's it? Like it was a piece of trivia you picked up on the Internet?"

She laughed, a low, quiet laugh that seemed to pour right into him. "Yes, that's exactly what I was thinking. The moment your lips touched mine, I thought to myself that this was exactly like surfing the Internet for random facts about kangaroos."

He couldn't keep the smile from curving the corners of his mouth. "I have to say, that this is the first time that my kissing has been likened to web searches for Australian marsupials. I'm not really sure whether or not I should take that as a compliment."

She laughed again, but this time it was more genuine and deeper, but there was an edge to it that made it sound rusty, as if it had been a long time since she had laughed. "Well, I wouldn't necessarily classify it as an insult, so, in the interest of positive and constructive self-talk, you should definitely find a way to classify it as a compliment."

Despite her humor, a little part of him couldn't help but wonder if she really hadn't responded to the kiss the way he had. But at the same time, he also felt like laughing, and that was a great feeling. The conversation was inane, and he loved feeling like he wanted to chuckle. Not much made him chuckle. "It wasn't my best stuff. I didn't want to lay my best kiss on you, because I wasn't sure you could handle it."

Her eyebrows went up this time, and she looked at him with interest. "You know, I would expect that your best stuff would probably melt a woman's brain, so I'm thinking it's a good thing that you held back on my behalf."

He didn't miss the veiled compliment in that comment. He grinned. "If you're cold, I'd be happy to do a little melting and warm you up." Even as he made the offer, he swore to himself. What the hell was he doing? He had no right to be making plays for this woman, ever. Wasn't it only a few seconds ago that he'd gallantly decided not to kiss her anymore, let alone *again?*

Before she could answer, he turned away, not giving her the chance to volunteer to test his best stuff. "I'll bring your bags in. Why don't you go find Ava, and figure out where you want me to put them?"

But before he could make it to the door, Hannah stopped him with her hand on his arm. "No, no, no. That's not necessary. I'm perfectly capable of bringing all her stuff in. I'd feel terrible if you delay your departure any further, and then get stranded in the snow. All I needed was a guide to get me here, and I'm good. So please, don't stay. You can go."

The sudden urgency in her voice caught his attention. He looked down at her hand still on his arm, then returned his gaze to her face. She wanted him to leave. He wanted to be on his way. But it was zero degrees here, and the house wasn't heated yet. What if it didn't warm up? "You need help unpacking?"

She gave him an amused look. "Do I? Who do you think packed my trailer?"

"You?"

"Of course me." Her fingers tightened on his arm. "Go, Maddox. Seriously."

He swore under his breath, sensing the genuineness

of her request. She wanted him to leave. But he wanted to stay. He wanted to kiss her again. Which meant he had to get the hell out. "Fine—" Then his gaze landed on the three pieces of wood by the wood stove.

Three pieces of wood for a week-long blizzard?

They had to be better prepared for that. He nodded at the wood. "I know where the wood is. I'll bring in enough for you to get through the week if you lose power, and then I'll leave."

"I can do it—"

"You can't do it all before the storm hits. You unload. I'll get wood." He couldn't look at her again. At the weariness in her eyes. At the lips he'd kissed only moments ago. At this crappy house she was staying in. Because if he let himself see all that, he'd just want to park his ass in their house and be guardian to protect them from everything. And if he did *that*, it would be the slow path to destroying them both, and he would never, ever destroy any woman the way his father had destroyed his mother.

"Maddox—"

"I'm getting the wood." He wasn't going to stay, but he sure as hell was going to make sure they were warm before he left.

He didn't even turn around as he opened the door, stepped outside, and headed toward the barn, using his truck's headlights to light his path. It would take less than an hour to bring in all the wood they'd need for the week. The snow would be bad by then, but he had chains in his truck. Hell, he used to drive a snowplow for extra money when he was in high school.

The snow wasn't going to stop him from getting them wood, and it wasn't going to stop him from leaving when he was finished.

But as he reached the barn and grabbed the door to open it, he couldn't help but look over his shoulder. Hannah was already carrying grocery bags into the house. He looked again at the size of the trailer, and knew it would take days for her to unload it.

He wanted to stay and help.

He couldn't.

His job was wood. Nothing else. Nothing but leaving them before he could break them.

SHE WANTED MADDOX to stay.

She wanted his help.

And she didn't like that feeling at all.

Hannah leaned on the kitchen counter, bowing her head as another wave of exhaustion flooded her. Her muscles were so weak, and her head was throbbing. How much longer could she keep this up? When she'd driven up to the house and seen how dilapidated it was, she'd almost cried right then and there. Only Ava's presence in the backseat had enabled her to put a smile on her face, and happiness in her tone.

Dear God, Maddox was right about how bad this house was. She'd wanted to get away from the big city and all the dirt, crowds, and reminders of Katie that wouldn't let them go, but this was not what she thought she would get when she rented the house. Her mom had always talked about Rogue Valley, a town she'd driven through as a kid, the one she wished she could have raised her daughters in.

Hannah had decided to make that dream a reality for the second generation of Crowley daughters...and the ramshackle cabin in the middle of nowhere was so far from what she had expected. How were they ever going to thrive here?

Hannah closed her eyes, listening to the thuds coming from the back porch as Maddox stacked wood. He'd already made a sizable pile by the woodstove, and had been adding more supplies by the back door for the last thirty-five minutes. It felt so good to hear the sounds of him moving around. She loved knowing that if the roof collapsed right now, he would be there to pull the timbers off them and make sure they were okay.

She didn't know why she wasn't afraid of him anymore, but she wasn't. Maybe it was because she'd felt a kinship with Lissa, and it was apparent how much Lissa loved him. All she knew was that she felt safer with him around, safe in a way she hadn't felt in a very long time. She had learned not to trust men, repeating that lesson so many times throughout her life, and she'd watched her own family members die because they had trusted the wrong men. She had to show Ava how to be strong on her own, so that Ava would never align herself with a man just because she thought she couldn't do it by herself.

Which meant the last thing Hannah was going to do was succumb to any wimpiness and ask some stranger to help her out. She was doing just fine. She'd even managed to find the boxes that had Ava's bedding, and the two of them had made Ava's bed, set up her stuffed animals, and started making Ava's room feel like home. The little girl had fallen asleep within moments, buried under a huge pile of blankets, clearly feeling content and safe in their new house, which made Hannah know she had made the right decision by coming here, both to Rogue Valley and to the house.

But, God, she couldn't lie to herself anymore. She missed her job. She missed her friends. She missed her condo. She missed being in a house that didn't make her wonder how long it would keep standing. She missed everything about Boston.

And most of all, she missed her sister.

Tears suddenly filled Hannah's eyes, and the most overwhelming sense of grief seemed to crush her from all sides. She braced her elbows on the counter and buried her face in her hands, trying desperately to hold the tears in, but it felt as if the dam that had locked them up for the last six months was finally springing leaks that she couldn't stop.

She bit her lip and squeezed her eyes shut, trying to breathe deeply, trying to put her grief, her loneliness, and her fears back in the box she'd kept them locked in so tightly. But there was something about being in this depressing house, with a storm raging around them, that put her over the edge. When Maddox left, it would be completely up to her to find a way to make this work.

She couldn't do it. She just suddenly knew she couldn't do this.

"Hannah?" His voice startled her, and she stiffened, horrified that he'd caught her crying.

She didn't turn around. She couldn't let him see how lost she was. People took advantage of vulnerability and weakness. Instead, she grabbed a box of cereal and put it in the cabinet. "Yes?"

There was a long pause, so long that she almost turned around...but she didn't. There were still tears glistening on her cheek.

"I've got enough wood stacked to last for a week without power. The generator looks old, and I don't like that. I'm not sure it's going to come on if you need it."

No generator? In sub-zero temperatures? Panic started to grip her, but she shook it off. They had wood, so no problem. "We'll be fine, thanks to the wood. I've built many fires in my life." She took a deep breath. "You're amazing, Maddox. I can't tell you how much I appreciate everything." She managed a weak laugh. "I hereby de-clare you at liberty to get on the road and get out of town before you're stranded here."

He didn't answer, and she glanced over her shoulder to see if he was still there. The moment her gaze met his green stare, she realized that he knew exactly how upset she was. It was the empathy and understanding on his face, the awareness in his gaze, the stubborn way his arms were folded over his chest.

Maddox knew, and he cared.

And she had no idea how to handle that.

Chapter 8

MADDOX'S EYES NARROWED, and Hannah felt his inspection as his gaze ran over her. She was still wearing her parka, because the heat had barely made a dent in the Arctic temperature in the house. Maddox had offered to set a fire, but she hadn't wanted one going right before she went to bed. She desperately needed sleep, and she didn't want to have to stay up to watch a fire.

She stiffened, waiting for his response, for him to declare she had to go to Lissa's. If he did, she wasn't sure she had the strength to refuse, even though she knew Ava needed to set down some roots and find her new place.

His gaze settled on her face again, assessing. She gave up trying to appear strong, and wiped the back of her hand over her cheeks, to try to clear the tear streaks. She shrugged. "The toughness is all a facade. Don't tell Ava."

"Tell her what? That you're fierce and strong? I think

she knows."

She sighed, too tired to fight. "I'm neither, and I think we both know it." She waved wearily at the back porch. "I can't thank you enough for the wood. Truly. You'll never know how much it matters to me."

Maddox watched her for another moment, then shook his head. "I've watched people die of broken souls because they weren't strong enough. You have a fire inside you that you won't let die. I see it."

There was something so intense about his words that she stood a little taller, suddenly wishing she was actually the woman he saw in her. "I'm not—"

"Just say thanks."

There was an edge to his voice that caught her attention. Pain. Grief. Wariness. The argument inside her died, and she simply inclined her head. "Thanks."

He nodded. "I have to go. The storm's getting pretty fierce."

Fear flickered through her, a sudden intense feeling of vulnerability at the thought of him leaving. *Don't leave.* The plea shot through her mind, silent, hidden, unacknowledged. She didn't need him to stay and take care of her. She could handle it, and she needed to show Ava exactly how capable two badass females could be. So, she nodded. "Yes, I can feel it shaking the house. How long is your drive?"

"About six hours, without snow. Tonight, it'll probably take twice that, depending on how far south the storm is stretching right now."

Guilt flashed over her. "I'm sorry you had to stay—"

"My choice. I don't regret it." He studied her face again, his gaze so intense that she felt it burning over her. "You're sure you're okay?"

"Fine. Just tired." She pushed herself off the counter. "I have all the perishables put away, so I'll head to bed when you leave."

He still didn't move from the doorway. "How much stuff is still in the trailer?"

"I got everything we need for now. The rest can wait."

He still didn't move, and suddenly, the old kitchen seemed to shrink, and she became aware that they were alone, only a couple yards apart. The brim of his cowboy hat was lined with snow, and white fluff was piled up on his shoulders and arms. He looked solid and strong, undeterred by the last hour of hauling firewood through a blizzard. He seemed to be all the strength that she didn't seem to have.

He finally levered himself off the door and walked toward her. She stiffened, drawing herself up to her full height as he neared, but she still had to crane her neck to keep eye contact. He came to a stop directly in front of her, his heated gaze burning through her. "You're shivering."

She nodded. "It's cold."

"It's not so cold in here anymore." He lifted his hand and set it against her cheek. His hand felt so cool that she almost sighed. Her eyelids fluttered closed, and she leaned into his touch, suddenly too tired to hold her head up. Just for one moment, one tiny moment, she let herself lean into him.

He swore under his breath, and set his other hand on her forehead. The cool touch felt so good. "Your skin's on fire."

His voice startled her, jerking her awake. Belatedly, she realized she'd started to doze off into his hand. Embarrassed, she tried to pull back, but her back was against the counter, and there was nowhere to go. "What?"

"You're sick. You have a fever."

A fever. Damn. That explained a lot. She was usually

good at ignoring exhaustion, and the physical demands of emotional overload, but she had started feeling so horrible in the last hour. A fever made sense. "I didn't realize that." She tried to think. "I know I have ibuprofen somewhere." She closed her eyes, trying to think of where she'd seen it, but her mind felt too weary to think.

Maddox, however, didn't appear to be burdened by the same lack of mental clarity. He swore again, this time not under his breath, using choice invectives that she hadn't heard used in quite that order before. "Why aren't you in bed?"

She laughed at his outrage, a delirious, exhausted laugh. "Why am I not in bed when I'm sick? Because I'm a mom." After six months, it still felt unnatural to call herself a mom. She wasn't a mom. She was an inadequate substitute for the mother a little girl had lost, but she was all Ava had, and she was doing her best. "Who's going to take care of Ava if I sprawl out in my bed for the next week?"

He narrowed his eyes. "You still need to take care of yourself."

The burden of six months of trying to succeed in a role she had no idea how to do, in the midst of grief, fear, and stress, suddenly took over. She suddenly couldn't pretend to be okay, or polite, or nice anymore. "I do take care of myself," she snapped. "But I also take care of a little girl, and I work. I do everything I can, so don't get on my case just because I'm not lazing about in bed just because I have a slight fever." She tried to shove past him, but just as she was making her grand exit, a wave of dizziness hit her, and she stumbled.

Maddox caught her arm, steadying her with effortless strength as she fell into him. Her legs started to shake, and she started to slide to the floor. "I just need to sit down for a second, and I'll be good," she muttered, completely irritated that her body had chosen that moment to disprove her claim of awesomeness.

"Just a second, eh?" Giving her a skeptical look, Maddox helped her ease to the floor.

She sighed as she leaned back against the cabinet, pulled her knees up, and, draped her arms over her knees. "God, this feels good. Standing takes so much effort sometimes, you know?"

"Yeah, I know." Maddox crouched in front of her, his green gaze intense.

"Do you? I doubt standing has ever been a supreme effort for you." She looked at him, and again, that little voice cried out, *don't leave.* She bunched her fists, refusing to give in to the urge to be weak. But he just looked so capable, crouching there, his forearms resting on his thighs. Did the man ever falter in his strength? God, if she could feel like that for one day, she'd take on the world. She eyed him. "How are you so capable? Do you drink some magic Wyoming potion?"

His brows shot up, and the corner of his mouth curved. "Potion?"

"Yes, like some special coffee or extract of wildflower that makes you an unstoppable physical machine of awesome? I want some."

His smile widened. "Sorry, no potion. It's just because I'm such a complete bastard that weakness and fatigue are too scared to come near me."

"Bummer. I knew it wasn't that easy. I could use easy right now." She leaned her head back against the cabinet and closed her eyes. The wind was howling more fiercely now, rattling the shutters and making hissing sounds as it whipped around the house. "You do realize that you really need to leave, right? I know you're like this glorious cauldron of capability, but at some point, nature wins, even against you."

He ignored her statement. "Want me to carry you to bed?"

She couldn't suppress the small laugh as she opened her eyes and looked at him. "What kind of question is that? Of course I do. What woman wouldn't want you to carry her to her bed? To any bed, actually. You're one of those guys, the ones that women fantasize over, aren't you?"

His brows knit. "You're delirious."

"No, I'm not. I'm just trying to summon a sense of humor. Clearly, if you think I'm delirious when I'm trying to be funny, it's one of those epic fail moments." She sighed, studying him. His face was angular and hard, and there were more than a few scars visible, little white lines that told of a dark past. She wanted to touch them, to chase away the moments that had caused them, the way she'd wanted to chase away her mother's pain, and Katie's bruises.

She hadn't been able to help either of them, leaving her with a sense of helplessness that had haunted her every minute of her life. And now, for some reason, Maddox was awakening that same need in her, that same longing to take away the darkness. Why? Why him? Why now, when she had nothing to offer, when she was living on fumes, pouring all she had into the little girl who wouldn't talk? Instinctively, not really making the decision to do it, she reached out and brushed her finger over a tiny white scar on his jaw, barely visible through his whiskers.

He went still, his eyes snapping to hers. Tension suddenly crackled between them, silence leaping between them as they stared at each other. The only movement was the slide of her fingers over the scar. "I want to erase whatever caused your scars," she whispered.

Maddox's hand closed around hers, and he drew her

hand down, away from his face, but he didn't let go. "Nothing will ever erase that," he said, his voice rough. "It would be a mistake to try."

"Why?"

He pressed a kiss to her knuckles, one at a time. "Because sometimes it's important to remember the darkness, so that it never gets a chance to surface again."

She frowned at the remark that was so similar to the one he made before. "You're not evil, Maddox—"

"Ah, Hannah," he said gently, interrupting her. "If only I could be what you see me as, but I can't. Which means that as much as I want to stay and help you guys out, that's just not an option for me." He turned her hand over, and pressed a kiss to her palm. "I'll have one of my brothers check on you as soon as the storm is over. They all have chains for their trucks, so they'll be able to get over here as soon as the storm dies down. I'm sure Lissa will want to come, and bring you enough casseroles to last you for a month."

Something tightened in her chest at his words, at the notion that there would be somebody out there looking out for her. She'd had that once, a long time ago, after she and Katie had been orphaned. She'd taken Katie to live on the streets to avoid being split up in foster homes. She remembered so clearly the day she'd met the two boys who had become their protectors.

Brody and Keegan Hart had found her and Katie living in an alley, freezing cold. They'd brought them home to a mismatched gang of homeless kids who were living under a bridge, living together as the tight-knit family none of them had. The nine kids had all taken the last name of Hart, as if that could protect them from being torn apart.

Without the Harts, she and Katie never would have made it. But even then, with her makeshift family, there'd been that constant fear that someone would find them, drag them all back to foster homes, and tear them apart. So there had been safety, but also a terrible, constant, very real terror. But with that fear, the Harts had also made her and Katie a part of a community, the kind she had come here to find. And with Maddox's words, how his brothers would check on her, and Lissa would bring her food, it made her want to cry. It was what she wanted, to find a way to give Ava a community that would hold her up if her last remaining family member died.

Maddox's comment about his brothers made her hope that she'd found what she wanted, but at the same time, doubt crept in. With the exception of her brief time with the Harts, she didn't know how to be a part of a community, of a family, to accept help from strangers like that. It made her uncomfortable, at the same time it created a deep yearning inside her. She wanted to say no, to tell Maddox not to bother asking his brothers to check on her, but the little girl sleeping in the other room kept her from protesting. Just as how she had gone with the two Hart boys that night so long ago to protect her little sister, who was shivering and hungry, she knew that she needed to accept help this time as well. She needed to create a Hart family for Ava, in case anything ever happened to Hannah.

She knew well enough by now that things happened, leaving little girls alone in life, so she had to do whatever it took to give Ava a safety net. She had to find a way to accept help, and be grateful that someone cared. "Thanks," she said. "That would relieve a lot of my worry. Just until I get a phone that works."

Maddox nodded, and her gaze fell to their hands, where he was still holding hers. Her hand looked so small in his, almost fragile, but the way he held it so gently didn't make her feel weak. It made her feel safe. "I need to go," he said.

She looked back up at him, and her heart tightened when she saw the reluctance in his gaze. "Yes, you do."

He sighed, and stood up, then held out a hand to her. She accepted his offer, sliding her hand into his. He pulled gently, drawing her to her feet. She brushed against his thigh as she stood, the brief contact sending sparks igniting through her.

For another long moment, they stood there, inches apart, tension coiling. His eyes were dark, loaded with turbulence. She wanted to touch him. To hug him. To lean into him. To use his strength, and offer him comfort.

But she didn't move, and after a moment, he stepped back. "Go to bed, Hannah. You don't do Ava any favors if you can't take care of yourself." There was an edge to his voice that caught her attention, and she studied him.

"Who do you know who didn't take care of themselves?" she asked softly.

For a long moment, he just stared at her, then he shook his head. "Doesn't matter. Just promise me."

She owed him no promise. The only one she owed anything to was herself, Ava, and Katie. But for some reason, she found herself nodding. Maybe it was because he was the only rock in this quicksand trying to consume her, or maybe it was because deep down inside, she knew he was correct. She did need to crawl into bed, pull the covers over her head, and stop trying so hard.

He nodded, and raised his hand, cupping her face with his palm. He said nothing for a moment, then he lowered his head, and she knew he was going to kiss her. Instinct told her to run, to hide, to do anything but let him get close to her. Instead, however, she felt herself wrap her fingers around his wrist, holding his hand to her cheek and lifting her face to his.

His lips brushed over hers, in a kiss so gentle and

tender that her heart ached. His fingers tightened ever so slightly on her cheek, and she instinctively wrapped her fingers more tightly around his wrist. Again and again, he kissed her, a dozen butterfly kisses so light they were like whispers on her skin, wisps of intimacy that made her belly flutter and her breath catch.

After a long moment, he pulled back, searching her face. "You make me want to be soft again," he said.

"Is that bad?"

"For me? Yeah." He rubbed his thumb over her lower lip, then dropped his hand. "Stay safe, Hannah."

She nodded, unable to stop the tightening in her heart as he turned away and headed toward her front door. When he reached it, he looked back at her as he set his hand on the knob. She wanted to tell him to wait, but the words stuck in her throat. He nodded once, tipping his hat to her, then he pulled open the door and stepped outside into the raging storm.

The wind blistered through the house, sending snowflakes dancing like angel dust across the small living room, and the bitter air knifed through her parka and jeans. Then he shut the door behind him, and all the chaos stopped. The snowflakes settled, the books on the coffee table stopped fluttering, and the wind stopped biting at her legs.

It was peace...and loneliness. She took a deep breath and looked around the small family room, scanning the faded, worn out furnishings, until her gaze settled on the wood stacked so neatly next to the stove. The door to the wood stove was open, and she could see that he had built a fire for her, ready for lighting. On top of the stove set a large box of matches, matches that hadn't been there when they had walked in, matches that she had not brought with her.

Something about seeing those matches there, matches

that Maddox had left her, made hope flutter through her. Despite his claims to the contrary, he was a good man. Maybe he was leaving town, maybe she wouldn't see him again, but in that brief moment, he had shown her a ray of hope, a glistening of possibility. Maybe there was sunlight in the darkness that seemed to follow her everywhere. At least a chance of it, maybe.

She took a deep breath, and hugged herself. Maybe it would be okay. Maybe, just maybe, the next year here would give her and Ava all the healing that they had come for.

She wanted to feel hope, she really did. But when she heard Maddox's truck engine roar to life, she was hit with the gut-wrenching reminder of the fact that she was alone, in a dilapidated house, with a Wyoming blizzard descending upon them, with a life unfolding that was nothing like anything she had ever dreamed of.

Chapter 9

ONCE HE STARTED his engine, Maddox didn't drive away. He sat in his truck, grimly studying the house that Hannah and Ava were inside. Lights were blazing through the windows, telling him that in the thirty seconds since he'd walked outside, they hadn't yet lost power.

He drummed his fingers on his steering wheel, restless, tense.

He felt uncomfortable abandoning them in that house with the storm descending upon them. But at the same time, what the hell else was he supposed to do? It wasn't as if he could walk in there and make an announcement that he was going to stay with them until the storm was over. Besides, he'd made an oath to himself a long time ago, that night when he was seventeen, to never bring anyone into the hell that was his world, especially not a woman and a child, who he could break so easily, the way his bastard father had broken his mom.

Maddox took a deep breath, reminding himself that they had enough wood in the house to last for a week, even if they had to feed that woodstove twenty-four/seven. He'd seen what she'd unpacked in the kitchen, and he knew they had enough food. They would be okay. It was time for him to go.

A bad mood settled over him as he shifted his truck into gear and swung it around to drive out. There was already several inches of new snow on the driveway, and the visibility was poor. He realized he had almost left too late. If he didn't have the tire chains in the back, he would have had to weather the storm in town.

But he had a job waiting for him, another scumbag who had jumped parole needed to have his ass hauled back in. As he drove, he hit the button on his dashboard. "Call Chase," he said.

His truck obeyed him and the phone began to ring. Chase picked up immediately, as he always did whenever one of his brothers called.

"You coming by?" Chase said without preamble. "Lissa said you were in town."

"No, I'm going to try to make it south." Maddox glanced over his shoulder as he turned the bend in the driveway, catching his last glimpse of the glow coming from Hannah's windows. And then the house was out of sight. A strange sense of discomfort settled on him, a sense of wrongness that he was driving away, but he gritted his teeth and focused on the road in front of him, which he could barely even see at this point. "I've a favor to ask, though."

"Name it," Chase said without hesitation.

"So, there's a woman named Hannah Crowley who just moved into the old Anderson place with her daughter."

"Yeah, Lissa told us about them. She and Bridgett

came over here for dinner since Travis is gone, and they both wanted Hannah and Ava to come over. Lissa was worried about them, and Bridgett was excited to have someone to play with during the storm. You bringing them over to the ranch?"

"No, Hannah insisted on staying. I set them up with firewood, but I have a bad feeling about the generator. Can you plow her out as soon as the storm eases, and check on them? She doesn't have a phone that works in the area, so she can't call for help if she needs anything." Again, tension rippled through him. What would she do if she needed something? He should've left her his phone.

"You bet," Chase said. "But the storm's going to hit hard. We're all going to be grounded for probably five days at least. The storm is bringing in more snow and higher winds than they originally predicted. It's going to be whiteout conditions for the next five days, pretty much. If you weren't heading south, I'd tell you to get your ass over here, because the driving is going to be impossible here within the hour."

Even as Chase spoke, Maddox felt his truck slide as he drove up the slight incline at the end of Hannah's mile-long driveway. Swearing, he slowed down. "I'm going to put my chains on before I get on the main roads. Just get over here as soon as you can."

"Will do, bro. Drive safe. Next time you're in town, stop by. You know it pisses me off when you swing through and don't tell me."

Maddox grinned. "I have bad guys to catch. They don't wait around so I can have family dinners with my brothers and their wives."

"That's a pathetic excuse, and we both know it. Promise me that the next time you're in town, you'll sit your ass down at my dinner table for one meal, or I won't go check on your lady friend."

Maddox laughed as he stopped his truck and set it in park. "Give it up, bro. You know you're going to go check on her no matter what I do, and she's not my lady friend." But as his laughter faded, he realized that even though he could never be a part of the life that Chase and the others had set up on the ranch, he missed them. "But yeah, I promise I'll stop by and choke down some of your home cookin'."

"You love my cooking. I'm the best in five counties, so quit blowing smoke. Catch you later, bro."

"You got it." Maddox hung up and opened his truck door. The wind was brutal, slicing into him as he slogged through the snow to the back of his truck. He had just rolled down the window to grab his chains out of the back when a viciously loud crack jolted through the storm.

Maddox instinctively dove to the side, landing beside his rear tire, using his truck to protect him.

He had barely landed when the shadow of a massive tree slammed past him, hitting the ground so hard that his truck moved. Maddox swore and leapt to his feet, shocked to see the four-foot-wide tree trunk laying less than six inches behind his rear bumper. *Hell.* The thing would've crushed him.

He quickly scanned it, trying to see how far it extended. Due to the heavy snow, he could see only about ten feet in either direction, but it was enough to know that the tree had completely blocked off the driveway. It would take chainsaws, a couple workers, and several hours to get the thing cleared.

Swearing, he slogged back to his truck and grabbed his phone again. He dialed Chase as he walked back toward the rear of his truck to get his chains.

"You coming over? Road's too bad?" Chase asked.

"No, but a tree just fell across Hannah's driveway.

The sucker is close to four feet in diameter. You're going to need to bring machines and some help to get through it." He grabbed the duffel that he kept the chains in and unzipped it.

"Man, the favors keep mounting."

"Not in the mood, bro." His bad mood was increasing by the second. He did not like the idea of Hannah being trapped there behind a blockade. "Just tell me you'll get her out of here."

"Of course I will. Did it hit her power lines?"

At Chase's question, Maddox's gaze jerked to the side of the driveway. He tried to remember which side the power lines were on, back from the days so long ago when he'd come there as a teenager. "Are they on the south side of the driveway? You remember this property?"

Chase was silent for a minute. "Yeah, I think they are. Why? Is that where the tree hit?"

Maddox grimly studied the tree, his gaze sliding along the length of it, until it disappeared into the snowy darkness. Since the tree trunk was so thick, those branches were no doubt stretching far, plenty far enough to have taken out power lines. "Shit."

"I take that as a yes."

"What?" Maddox could hear Lissa's voice in the background. "She lost power already? Tell Maddox he has to bring her here. There's no way she can last five days without power in that house. Tell him to get her and make her come."

Chase came back on the phone. "I'm with Lissa on this one, Maddox. She's got no power, no car access, and no phone. You can't leave her there, especially with a kid."

Maddox swore, thinking of little Ava and Hannah's exhaustion, and the way she'd slid to the floor in the kitchen, too sick to stand. "It's almost a mile back to the house. They can't walk out to my truck in this storm, and the tree is behind my truck. I can't drive back there." He could hear Lissa talking to Chase, and then Lissa got on the phone.

"You have to go back there, Maddox," she announced. "You have to stay there with them until the storm is over."

Maddox swore, and leaned against his truck. "That's not a good idea, Lissa—"

"It's the only option. You have to."

"I can't—"

"Maddox!" Lissa's voice was spiking with emotion. "You don't understand what it's like for her. She's alone with a small child. She needs someone to help her, and you're the only one who can do it! I don't care whether you're terrified of women and children. You have to go back there."

"Lissa—"

"Do you know what would have happened to me if the woman who owned the Wildflower Café hadn't offered me her apartment to stay in for free when I arrived in town? And then, when she let me buy the café off her for a ridiculous price that was all I could afford? She told me that the only payment she wanted was for me to pay it forward someday. This is it. This is the pay it forward, Maddox. This is who I'm supposed to help, and right now you're the only one that can do it for me. You can't leave her Maddox. You have to go back, and you have to stay there."

Sweat broke out over Maddox's brow, sweat that had no business in a sub-zero wind. He gripped the edge of his tailgate and bowed his head, fighting against the fear slamming into him. He was suddenly back in that moment when he was seventeen, staring across the back porch at his girlfriend, seeing the look of absolute horror on her face, because she'd seen the monster inside him. He would never forget that moment, when he'd finally understood that the curse of his father ran too strongly in him, and that he could never, ever take the chance of bringing a woman into his hell. "Jesus, Lissa—"

"Maddox." It was Chase on the phone again. "I know."

Maddox nodded, gritting his teeth. Chase did know. All nine of the Stockton brothers knew, because they had the same bastard father. "What the hell, Chase?"

"You're not the monster you think you are. None of us are."

"Fuck that—"

"Shut up and listen to me. This is not forever. This is a couple days. This is your moment, this is your chance to see that you're not who you think you are. You don't have a choice, and you know it. No Stockton would ever walk away from someone who needed help, especially a woman and a child."

"Dad would have."

"Fuck him. He's dead. He doesn't define us, or what we stand for. You are not him."

Maddox bowed his head. "I am him."

"No, you're not. You surround yourself with the dregs of society, so yeah, they bring that out in you. But there's a woman and a child in that house that aren't going to bring that out in you. I wouldn't send you in there if I thought it was a bad idea. I've known you for almost thirty years, and I know what you're capable of. You can handle five days without destroying everyone around you."

Maddox took a deep breath, still gripping the truck. He wanted to go back. Every fiber of his being was screaming at him to get his ass over that tree and back to the house. He knew that house was dark, cold, and getting colder by the minute.

"Okay, do this," Chase said. "Go back and check. If they have power, then they're okay for the moment. You can hike back to your truck, if you want."

"And if they don't have power?"

"Then you need to start a new chapter for what your last name stands for."

Maddox swore. "Five days."

"Maybe less. You can be a decent human being for five days. This is your call to action, bro. I had mine, and it gave me my life back. Same with Travis, Steen, and Zane. If you don't want Dad to own who you are, then you've got to do this. You'll never forgive yourself if you walk away right now, especially if I show up there in five days and find out that something bad happened during the storm and Hannah couldn't call for help. If you walk away, then, yeah, you are Dad. If you can walk back in there, then you have a chance to be you."

Maddox closed his eyes. He knew his brother was right. He had no choice. He took a deep breath, resolution settling over him. "Fine. I'm going." God, it felt good to say that. Terrifying, but also right. He needed to know they were okay. "But if the power's on, I'm not going in."

"And if it's off?"

"Fuck."

Chase laughed softly. "Call if you need a kick in the ass when you get there. Keep in touch."

Maddox heard Lissa ask if he was staying, but the phone disconnected before Chase answered.

Maddox leaned against his truck and lifted his face to the snow, letting the tiny shards of snow bite into his skin. He hadn't said a prayer in decades, maybe his whole life, but he knew he couldn't do this himself, so he asked for a little help, some kind of help, something that would keep Ava and Hannah protected from who he was.

When he finished, he didn't feel any better, because he knew exactly the blood that ran so thick in his veins. But at the same time, Chase and Lissa's words were lodged in his gut. He couldn't walk away. But hell. Five days?

Five days.

He took a deep breath, and then shook out his shoulders. He was going in, because there was no other choice.

It took only a couple minutes for him to grab what he needed from his truck, and then he turned to face the tree and the long driveway stretching to the isolated house. For a long moment, he didn't move. He felt like his boots were stuck to the snowy driveway.

He wanted to go back there. He wanted to help them. He wanted to find some fragment of sunshine in his soul, and he somehow knew that Hannah and Ava were his only chance to find it.

But he was scared shitless to try. Scared shitless of repeating the cycle that had killed his mother, and put that look of terror in the eyes of the girl he'd been planning to propose to at graduation.

But the night was dark and cold, and the storm had taken retreat away from him.

He had to face this. Not for Lissa. But for his own soul, because Chase had been right when he'd said he would never be able to forgive himself if he walked away from that little girl who had stared at him so silently, and the woman who had made his heart stop with her smile.

He took a deep breath, and started to walk.

Chapter 10

HANNAH SHOVED OPEN the back door and stumbled into the kitchen, shaking snow off her face as she leaned against the door, using her body to force it shut against the wind. She let her head rest against the wood, unable to stop the shivering deep inside her body.

She'd been outside for twenty minutes, trying to get the generator started, and she'd failed. Her fingers were numb. Her toes hurt from the cold. Her face was burning, and she couldn't stop shaking. She'd thought she was used to the cold after all the Boston winters, but even the coldest Boston weather felt like a balmy tropical beach compared to a Wyoming blizzard.

Good God. Why on earth had she held this desolate, brutal place as a fantasy for so long? She was far too warm-blooded for this. She really was. And now, she was stranded in it without heat or power, with a four-year-old, for a week. Suddenly, her brave and stubborn decision not to accept Lissa's offer seemed incredibly stupid and short-sighted.

A sliver of fear trickled through her, a deep, real fear of the impact of her decision to stay there with a small child.

She took a deep breath and looked around. The kitchen was pitch black. The only light was the faint orange glow from the wood stove in the family room. When the power had gone out, she'd been philosophical. She had pulled out her phone, used the flashlight function to make her way across the room to the stove, and lit the fire that she was so grateful Maddox had left for her. For that brief moment, she had felt resourceful and confident that she could handle it. The ibuprofen she had taken for her fever had kicked in, and she had been feeling better. Capable. Determined.

But after twenty minutes outside, everything had changed. The generator wasn't working, and she felt so sick she could barely stand up.

She closed her eyes and let the door support the weight of her body. How long had Maddox said the storm would last? Five days? Five days. She had to make it five days, then however long it took to get plowed out. Maddox had said he would call his brothers, so she knew someone would be coming for her. She took a deep breath, wanting nothing more than to slide down to the floor, wrap herself in a blanket, and curl into a ball.

But the house would be getting colder by the minute, and she had a four-year-old daughter who was sound asleep in the other room. Before she collapsed, she had to make sure they were safe.

For a split second, panic tried to grab her. Fear tried to suck away the last vestiges of confidence that she could do this. Her heart started to hammer, and weakness seemed to consume her.

She immediately opened her eyes. "No." She spoke aloud, her voice reverberating in the dark, empty kitchen. She had been in similar situations before, back in the days when she and Katie had been living on the streets of Chicago, with the Hart clan as their only support. She knew what had to be done in a situation like this. Number one was shelter. They had that. Number two was warmth. Number three was food, but they had that, as well. Clearly, they were way ahead in the game, so rah, rah, rah. All was well.

Keeping her parka on, she pulled off her gloves and set them carefully on the corner of the counter, so she would know where to find them if she needed them again in the dark. Then she pulled her phone out of her pocket and turned the flashlight on. She could only hope that the cold weather and the snow didn't keep her from getting to her car to recharge it when the battery went low. For now, it was all she had to see by.

She took a deep breath, and levered herself off the door, making her way around all the boxes on the floor toward the living room. She stepped inside the living room and slowly flashed the light around the room, using instincts learned as a teenager to assess the situation. There were three big open doorways that were letting the heat dissipate into the rest of the house. One led into the kitchen, one was going to the hallway, and one opened into what appeared to be a dining room. Except for the door into the kitchen, there were no doors between the rooms. She was going to have to find a way to tack blankets up over those openings, to keep the heat inside. Ideally, she'd like to keep the kitchen heated as well, but she'd have to see whether that was possible.

She needed a hammer. Nails. God. Where had she put those? She was pretty sure they were still in her car. Regret flooded her, regret that she hadn't done a better job preparing for the possibility of losing power in the middle of the night. She had just been so consumed with arriving at their new place, with surviving the moment, that she had failed to adequately prepare for the contingency. She felt like she was a kid again, trapped in an inadequate housing situation. First, the barely habitable apartments her mom had been able to afford, then being homeless when even those were out of reach.

Her years of living in her nice condo in Boston as an adult had put her past behind her, making her think she would never again be in this kind of situation, and now, here it was again, a repeat of the life she'd grown up with.

Well, she'd survived that, so she would get them through this.

One thing at a time. First thing, she had to move her mattress into this room, so that she and Ava could sleep together. Once she had the bed set up, she would try to move Ava without waking her up. Then she would deal with trying to figure out how to get the blankets over the doorways.

Step one: mattress, doable.

Summoning strength she honestly didn't know she still had, she worked her way across the family room and down the hall. She popped her head into Ava's room just to check. The little girl was sound asleep, the light from Hannah's phone illuminating her sweet face. Hannah piled another blanket on top of her, and gently pressed a kiss to her daughter's blond hair.

As she did so, a powerful, undecipherable emotion flooded her, a need so deep to protect this fragile little life that was all she had left of her family. "I won't let you down, sweetie. I promise." She might have lost her sister, her mother, and left the safety of the Hart clan to go to Boston, but she had one more chance, with Ava.

For Ava, she could do this.

She gently tucked the blankets more snugly around Ava, then slipped out of the room, closing the door behind her. She made it to the end of the hallway, where her room was, and stepped inside. The blankets and comforter beckoned to her, so tempting to her exhausted body and soul. She had literally just finished making her bed when the power had gone out, but going to bed was going to have to wait.

She grabbed the blankets and pulled them off the bed, her arms so weak she had to pull them one at a time. Moving the mattress felt like it would be an impossible task, but she had to find a way. She gritted her teeth, found the little handle on the side of the mattress, and leaned back, using her body weight to haul it off the box spring. Triumph rushed through her as it slid off. It crashed into one of her moving boxes, and stopped abruptly, a massive, immovable force. Tears filled her eyes, but she bent over and shoved the box out of the way, then cleared the path of the other boxes.

When she had a passageway big enough for the mattress, she went back, grabbed the handle, and hauled on it. The mattress came sliding forward, landing in a horizontal heap on all the boxes. She managed to get it across the floor, but it thudded into the doorframe. She stepped back, realizing that she was going to have to tilt it on its side to make it through the door. Obviously. She didn't need to be a math geek to realize she should have been able to anticipate that little issue.

She grabbed the corner of the mattress, and tried to lift it. She got the side of it about two feet off the ground, but the far side of it was wedged in the middle of one of her boxes, and she couldn't get the angle to move the mattress to a vertical position. She pushed as hard as she could, then paused. Letting the mattress lean against her shoulder and the side of her head, she closed her eyes. Sweat was pouring down her temples, and her arms were shaking. "It's just a mattress, Hannah," she said aloud. "You can completely handle this. You've moved plenty of mattresses down hallways in your life, and this is just one more."

But it didn't feel like one more. It felt like the one that would break her. Because you know what? Moving a queen-sized mattress out a door and down a hallway sucked on a good day. Moving it when she had a freaking fever and was exhausted? It was like a bad joke by a universe that had decided to become a bully with an obscene and rude sense of humor. Translation: it was impossible.

Except, it couldn't be impossible.

It had to be possible, because there was no other way.

"Ava needs this," she said aloud. "You have to do this for Ava." The thought of her little girl galvanized her, and she gave a mighty shove to the mattress. It finally flipped upright, even though it was still on top of the boxes. Not giving it a chance to fall back down, she grabbed the handle and hauled it fiercely toward the doorway. It slid through, coming to a stop against the opposite wall. She stumbled, and lost her balance, crashing into the wall. She landed hard on her knees, and suddenly exhaustion consumed her.

She closed her eyes, and pressed her face to her palms. One minute. She needed one minute of rest, and then she would stand up and wrestle that mattress through the doorway, and down the hall. But as she sat there, it felt increasingly difficult to summon the strength to stand up again. She had been at the end of her coping capacity many times in her life, but for some reason, in this moment, it felt like she had no more reserves left to give. She could tell the fever was getting worse, and her muscles were shaking with exhaustion.

A sudden banging from the front of the house jerked her awake. She froze, her heart stuttering as she listened to something hammering against the front door. Dear God, was that the wind? Fear galvanized her to her feet, and she grabbed the mattress again, shoving it with all her weight, trying to get it to bend around her doorframe, so she could get it angled down the hall.

It wouldn't move, the banging became louder, and more and more panic started to build. "Come on!" She couldn't stop the tears of frustration and exhaustion now, but she grabbed the handle on the side of it and literally flung herself forward, trying to free the mattress from its wedged spot against the wall.

"Hey, hey, hey. Let me help you with that."

Hannah froze at the sound of Maddox's voice. Something rippled through her, through every single cell in her body. She couldn't believe what she was hearing. "Maddox?" As she said his name, a beam of light flashed on the ceiling above her head, illuminating the hallway with light that felt so beautiful that she wanted to cry.

Maddox appeared on the other side of the mattress, looking down at her, his face truly the most beautiful thing she had ever seen. "Yeah, it's me," he said. "A tree fell over the end of your driveway. It looked like it hit your power lines, so I came back to check on you." His gaze fell on her face. "I think I'm glad I did."

"You came back?" She couldn't believe he was standing there, snowy and strong, in her hallway.

"Yeah. No one is going in or out of your driveway until the storm is over and Chase can bring some crews in to clear the tree." His eyes were dark, roving her face with such concern that something in her heart turned over. "You moving this to the family room?"

She nodded.

"Good plan. Let me grab the mattress and you can get the bedding."

She didn't move. She just stared at him, unable to grasp that he was there. Maddox frowned at her, then he grabbed the mattress and hauled it aside, shoving it as if it weighed nothing.

Once there was no mattress between them, he moved toward her and caught her chin with his hand. "You look like you're going to pass out," he said, his voice so gentle that tears filled her eyes.

She wanted to deny it. She wanted to tell him that she was strong and fierce and didn't need his help. But the words wouldn't come. She just nodded silently, unable to stop the tears from sliding down her cheeks.

"Come on." He slid his arm behind her back, and before she knew what he was doing, he swept her up in his arms, cradling her to his chest.

She knew she should protest, demand he put her down, and refuse to acknowledge weakness even to herself, but the words didn't come. She just leaned her head against his shoulder and closed her eyes, too tired even to slide her arms around his neck. His shoulder was solid and warm beneath her cheek, a feeling of strength that was so far from what she could muster on her own. She didn't even bother to open her eyes to see where he was taking her. She just surrendered to him, to his strength, to his protectiveness, to his rescuing.

She could no longer deny the truth: she needed him.

Chapter 11

MADDOX BENT DOWN, and Hannah felt a cushion sink beneath her. She opened her eyes, and saw that he was setting her on the couch in the family room. His arm stayed around her for an extra moment after she was settled, his face inches from hers. He had set his flashlight down somewhere, but the faint light still cast a glow on his face, enabling her to see the contoured lines of his cheeks, and the strong set to his jaw. "Thank you," she whispered.

He flashed her a quick smile. "Stay here. I'll be right back."

She nodded, unable to summon the energy to protest. He stood up, and she heard his boots thudding down the hall. Within moments he was back, and crouched beside her as he settled the blankets from her bed around her. He tucked them tightly against her, his brow furrowed as he watched her. "You're shivering."

"I can't get warm," she mumbled. "I was outside trying to get the generator started, and I got so cold."

An emotion flickered over his face, but it was gone before she could decipher it. "I'll work on that for you," he said. "Let me get the mattress set up first. You okay for the moment?"

She nodded again. She knew she should get up and help him, but her body felt too heavy, and the cushions felt like quicksand that was trapping her. He studied her for a moment more, then leaned forward and pressed a quick kiss to her forehead, a kiss that made her heart turn over. Before she could respond, he was gone and walking down the hall again.

She watched him through half-closed eyes as he dragged the mattress effortlessly down the hall and set it up in the middle of the family room. Within a few minutes, he had retrieved the linens from the floor of her bedroom, and had made the bed with easy familiarity that she wouldn't have expected from a rugged, scarred cowboy. In only a few more minutes, he had made the bed, using the blankets that he hadn't put on her. He made setting up the bed look so easy, a task that had nearly broken her, making her realize how truly awful she felt right now.

He finished the bed and walked over to the couch again. He crouched in front of her, his face level with hers. Quietly, he reached up and lightly moved a lock of hair that had fallen across her face. "Want me to get Ava and bring her out here?"

She shook her head. "I'll get her. It might startle her if she wakes up and finds you there."

He frowned. "Are you up for that?"

"I have to be." She tossed the blankets aside and forced herself to her feet. Dizziness assaulted her, but as soon as she started to sway, Maddox was suddenly beside her, his arm sliding around her waist.

He frowned down at her, but said nothing as they

walked down the hall toward Ava's room. She opened the door quietly and slipped inside, well aware that Maddox was still close beside her, his hand on her lower back, ready to catch her.

She knew she should push him away, but she honestly didn't know if she might fall, and it felt good to have him there to catch her if she did. She bent over the bed, and smiled at Ava's sleeping face. Her heart turned over, and she smiled at Maddox.

He was watching her with an inscrutable expression on his face...almost with longing? Then the expression was gone, and she thought maybe she'd imagined it. What would Maddox long for anyway? The open road, and a life anywhere other than trapped in a blizzard with two needy females.

Her cheeks burning with fever, she bent over Ava and slid her arms under the little girl. Even in her sleep, Ava's arms instinctively went around her, and she scooped her up, stumbling when Ava's full body weight was in her arms. Before she could lose her grip, however, Maddox's arms went around Hannah, helping her support Ava. Not trying to take her away, just helping her do what she needed to do.

With Maddox by her side, she made it to the living room, and settled Ava under the blankets. She pulled the blankets over her daughter, then stood up, bracing her hands on her thighs as she fought for the strength to stand. "So, I need to hang the blankets next."

"No. I'll do them. You need to lie down." Maddox walked over to her, frowning.

She shook her head. "It's my responsibility. You did the mattress. If you could just fix the generator before you go, that would be awesome."

One eyebrow went up. "Sweetheart, I'm not going anywhere. I missed my window."

Her heart started to pound as the implications of his words settled on her. "You're not leaving?"

"Not until the storm is over, and you're plowed out."

Suddenly, the small room felt even smaller. "You can't stay here."

The other eyebrow rose. "You want me to sleep in the barn?"

"No, but..." She looked around the tiny living room, the tiny house. How could she and Ava share a house with a man she didn't even know? Fear started to clog her throat, and her lungs constricted, making it difficult to breathe.

"Hey." Maddox moved closer to her and set his hands on her shoulders. "Look at me, Hannah." His touch was gentle, yet firm, filled with a nurturing strength that made her want to cry.

Reluctantly, she raised her gaze to his. His green eyes were intense as he studied her so thoughtfully that she felt heat rise in her cheeks. "I don't trust men," she whispered. "It terrifies me to think of having you in this house for a week."

"I know." He sighed, his thumbs tracing small circles on the front of her shoulders, almost as if he didn't even realize he was doing it. "Generally, I'm not a man that any woman should trust. I know that. But..." he hesitated, as if he were searching for the words. "You make me want to be a protector. You make me want to protect in a way I've never wanted to before. I'm not a good guy, and I carry genes so dark they would give you nightmares. But I swear on my mother's grave, that I would never, ever hurt you or Ava. And I will get the hell out of your lives, before I can destroy your souls."

She searched his face, confused by his words. "Destroy our souls? What does that mean? Are you a devil worshiper or something?" Because that would be kind of weird. Of all the things that she feared about men, being around one that would summon the devil and possess her with it, hadn't made it onto her list of things to be afraid of.

Maddox's face darkened, and he shook his head. "No, I definitely don't worship the devil. If I had a chance I'd take the bastard out, with pleasure."

There was an edge to his voice that made chills pop up on her arms. "You sound like you've already met him."

His gaze met hers. "I have."

She remembered the scars on his forearms, and suddenly she knew. The fear fled from her heart, replaced with a deep, burning need to hug him, to heal him, to clear the darkness that kept him captive so ruthlessly. "I'm so sorry."

He shrugged, but before he could say anything, his phone rang. He pulled it out of his pocket and answered it, without turning away from her. "Hey."

He listened for a second, one hand still on her shoulder, still tracing circles with his thumb. It was too intimate, but at the same time, it felt so good, she didn't want to pull away.

"Yeah, I'm at Hannah's," he said. "They don't have power. Right now, we're arguing about whether I'm staying for the rest of the week. She seems to think that me leaving is still an option."

Heat flooded her cheeks, and she instinctively tried to pull away, but his fingers tightened on her shoulder, tugging her forward into him. He caught her off balance, and she stumbled into him. His free arm immediately wrapped around her waist, supporting her against his side. Exhaustion suddenly flooded her again, and she closed her eyes, resting her head against his shoulder as he spoke into the phone, explaining the state of the house.

After a moment, he put the phone to her ear. "Lissa wants to talk to you."

Hannah fumbled for the phone, her fingers brushing against Maddox's as she took the phone from him. "Hello?"

Lissa's warmth filled her with an indescribable sense of comfort. "Hannah, are you seriously thinking of kicking Maddox out?"

She grimaced. "I just—"

"Listen to me, sweetie. This blizzard is going to be brutal, and you don't have power. You need him."

Hannah stiffened. "I don't need him—"

"Yes, you do, and that's nothing to be ashamed of. He says you're sick. Is that true?"

Maddox's arms wrapped around her, pulling her more tightly against him. She wanted to resist, but his warmth and strength was too appealing, so she closed her eyes and leaned on him, her cheek against his chest. "Yes, I have a fever."

Lissa's sigh was audible. "Don't be stubborn, Hannah. It's not a shame to admit you can't do it all on your own. That was one of the first things I had to learn when I first got here. Maddox is a great guy, despite what he thinks of himself. You don't have to be afraid of him."

Hannah grimaced at Lissa's perceptive statement. "I'm not—"

"Yes, you are. I saw it in your face, but that's okay. You don't need to be ashamed of that. My mother's string of useless boyfriends taught me that some men were to be feared, but the truth is that not all men are bad. Maddox is one of those who is worth believing in, completely. Let him help you."

Tears filled Hannah's eyes. "I don't know how," she whispered, but even as she protested, a part of her wished she did know how to let someone, to let Maddox, help her.

Lissa's soft laugh echoed over the phone. "Oh, sweetie, Maddox is a born protector. You don't need to do anything, other than to simply take a deep breath, and tell him he can stay through the storm. The rest will work out. Okay?"

Hannah squeezed her eyes shut, breathing in Maddox's delicious, masculine scent, feeling the strength of his body beneath her cheek, and in the way his hands were resting on her hips, supporting her. He felt so good standing there, enveloping her depleted body in a strength she couldn't muster on her own. She hadn't felt so overwhelmed in years, and she hated it. She wanted to be strong, to be independent, to be self-sufficient.

Then a tremor wracked her body, and she knew that this time, for once, she couldn't do it alone. "Okay," she whispered.

"Great." Lissa's relief was so evident that Hannah wanted to smile. "We'll see you after the storm. Go get some sleep and let Maddox take care of things. Bye."

"Bye." Hannah hung up and let the phone drop to her side. Maddox caught it just as it started to slip from her fingers.

For a long moment, neither of them said anything. She just stood there in his arms, leaning on him, too exhausted to pull away from him. She felt like it was his body that was generating what little strength and warmth still remained in hers, and if he moved away from her, she would have nothing left.

"What did Lissa say?" he asked softly, his hands tightening on her hips, as she belatedly realized she was starting to sway.

"She's manipulative and convincing," Hannah muttered, unable to keep the appreciation out of her voice.

Maddox laughed softly. "That she is. What's the verdict? Are we still going to argue about whether I can stay here?"

Hannah took a deep breath. Her body started to shake even more, and she wasn't sure if it was from the fever, from terror, or from a sense of relief so deep that it went all the way to her bones. Maybe all of them. "You can stay," she whispered. "I would be deeply grateful if you would."

Maddox's arms tightened around her, and he let out a deep, shuddering sigh. "Okay, then."

She felt him press a kiss to the top of her head, a kiss so gentle and tender she wanted to weep. His finger slid under her chin, gently lifting her face to his. His green eyes searched hers so intently that her belly tightened. Neither of them moved, and suddenly, she became aware of him as a man, not a man to be feared, but as a man who was pure male, pure strength, and pure protector.

A man who made butterflies leap in her belly, and longing pulse in her heart, which she had kept so carefully closed for so long.

Shock reverberated through her, shock that she was noticing him, truly noticing him all the way in her heart, as a man, shock that there was a man out there who could get through her shields. Her mind wanted her to run, to flee, to hide, but at the same time, a deeper part of her wanted to plant roots, and stay right there, to step into the moment for the first time in her life.

He smiled, a tender smile that made something inside her melt just the tiniest little bit.

He was going to be in her house for almost a week, a house that had been reduced to one room, which suddenly seemed very small, very intimate...and filled with possibilities that made it feel like the tiniest drop of sunshine had suddenly landed on her heart.

Chapter 12

THERE WAS NOTHING left to do.

Maddox stood in the doorway of the living room, watching Ava and Hannah sleep. It was almost four in the morning, and he was tired as hell, but so on edge he couldn't sit still. He'd tried to fix the generator, but it was too dark to see what he was doing. He'd started to bring stuff in from Hannah's trailer, but the bitter wind knifing through the barely-heated living room when he'd opened the door to go outside had shot that idea. He'd unpacked their kitchen. He'd hung blankets on the doorways. He'd found extra blankets for the couch for him to sleep on.

There was literally nothing left to do. There was no other room to be in, except that living room, where Ava and Hannah were tucked up beside each other under the blankets he'd heaped on them while they were sleeping.

He was restless.

Impatient.

Uncomfortable.

He was trapped in a house with two vulnerable females, against every rule that he'd lived by for years. He didn't want to be here...but at the same time, he wanted to be here so badly that he could barely handle it.

He hadn't thought that he'd wanted this. He'd walked away from any dreams like this a long time ago. He'd given them all up when he was seventeen, when he'd walked away from the girl he'd loved and all his dreams of this kind of moment. He'd forgotten how badly he had once wanted it.

Until now.

Until he was standing beside the wood stove watching Hannah and Ava sleep, while the wind howled outside and battered the house. Hannah's cheeks were flushed, and there was sweat beading on her forehead. He knew she was sick, and he didn't like it. He knew Ava wouldn't talk, and that concerned him. He knew they were in for at least five days of brutal weather, cut off from civilization, without electricity, and he didn't like that either.

He wanted both of them to be glowing, happy, and safe. For his whole life, he had believed that the key to any woman's happiness was to be as far away from him as possible. And yet, given this particular situation, he knew that his presence was necessary for their safety.

He didn't know what he thought of that. He didn't like it, for their sake, but at the same time, to feel like he was necessary for the well-being of Hannah and Ava made him feel like something beautiful was beaming down on him for the first time in his life.

Walking away from them in this moment would not be honorable, so he didn't have to do it. He could sit there, on their couch, breathing in the wholeness of who they were, and he didn't have to feel guilty that he was stealing life and hope from them. For five days, he had the gift of being able to live in their world without feeling like an asshole for taking up space in it.

He realized suddenly that this blizzard was a gift, a gift that would sustain him when he walked out the door and returned to his life of chasing down scumbags who wanted to put a bullet between his eyes.

Weariness settled on his shoulders, and he knew it was time to crash. For a brief second, he considered taking the moral road and sleeping in Ava's room to give them privacy. Then he looked at the old wood stove, and he knew that he would never leave them sleeping alone in a room where a fire was raging.

A deep sense of satisfaction settled over him, and he couldn't help the small smile that played at the corner of his mouth as he added a couple logs to the wood stove. He then crouched beside the makeshift bed, and laid his hand on Hannah's forehead. He frowned when he felt how hot it was, burning his palm. He checked Ava's forehead, but hers was cool and dry.

Something shifted inside him, something deep in his chest as he looked down at the two sleeping females. They were relaxed, utterly trusting that they were safe. They were in his hands for safekeeping, and he fisted his hands as he stood up, his shoulders tensing as he walked around the mattress to the couch.

He sat down, rested his elbows on his knees, and pressed his face to his palms. Son of a bitch. How the hell was he going to do this for five days? He didn't know how to take care of people. Shit.

With a low groan, he leaned back on the couch, and stretched his legs out. His feet hung over the arm, but he didn't care. He just grabbed a blanket, pulled it over him, and clasped his hands behind his head, staring at the ceiling, listening to their breathing.

He hadn't gone to sleep in a room with someone else present in a long time. It should feel weird, an invasion of his privacy, a threat to the sanctity of his world. But he liked it. He liked listening to the two different patterns of breathing, to the sounds of the sheets rustling when one of them moved.

He let his eyes fall shut, not planning to sleep, but so that he could better focus on their sounds, and on the feeling of deep peace that settled in him as he listened to them. He felt the muscles in his body begin to release, relaxing in a way he hadn't felt in a long time. His body felt heavy as it sank into the cushions. His shoulders relaxed, and his lungs expanded in a deep, slow breath that seemed to fill his whole body with the oxygen it was starved for.

His breathing became even slower and deeper, matching the rhythm of Hannah's breathing. Not intentionally, but because his body was reaching out for her, wanting to connect to the beautiful energy that she generated so completely.

He knew she was exhausted. She was sick because she had pushed herself too far. He wanted to know her story. He wanted to know Ava's story. He wanted to know how the two of them had wound up in a dilapidated rental in Rogue Valley, Wyoming with the rental trailer. Hannah's SUV wasn't cheap, so it wasn't because she was broke. So, why were they there? He wanted to know what happened to them, and he wanted to chase away the shadows that were in both their eyes. He wanted to bring light and happiness back into their world.

He had no idea how to do it, because he didn't even know what light or happiness was anymore. But he had five days, and he knew that was what he wanted to do.

He took a deep breath again, letting himself drift lightly off to sleep, dozing ever so slightly, not to sleep, but to restore himself so he could be there for them when they woke up.

As much as he despised the scumbags that he brought in on his runs as a bounty hunter, he always felt like he was doing some kind of good in the world by making sure the dregs of society didn't run around free, like his dad had too many times.

But as Maddox lay there, listening to the wind hammer the dilapidated house, breathing in the fullness of Hannah and Ava's presence, he realized that *now* was his actual opportunity to make a difference in the world. A real difference. A beautiful difference.

Unfortunately, he knew he'd find a way to fuck it up.

Because he wasn't the good guy.

He was his father's son.

He knew what his destiny was, and it didn't include this.

But hell, he wanted to break that cycle. For once in his life, for five days, he wanted to break that damned cycle.

THE QUICK MOVEMENT of the blankets awoke Maddox from a sound sleep. He sat up quickly, his gaze going straight to the mattress. The faint morning sun that had made it through the blizzard gave him enough light to see Ava sitting up, an alarmed look on her face as she looked around, one hand on Hannah's shoulder, as if she was trying to wake her up.

"Ava." Maddox sat up, swinging his legs onto the floor.

Ava spun around, her eyes wide as they settled on him.

"It's okay, baby," he said gently. "Your mom has a little cold. She's sleeping. She's fine."

Ava stared at him, as if waiting for more, her blue eyes riveted on him.

He recalled then that she'd been asleep when they'd moved her to the living room. "We lost power in the storm. That means that we don't have heat or electricity, until I can fix the generator this morning. We moved the mattress in here where the wood stove is, to keep everyone warm."

The wind rattled the shutters on the front of the house, and Ava jumped, her gaze snapping to the window that was rattling. Maddox could feel the fear emanating from her, and he swore under his breath. "I was going to get some breakfast. Hungry?" Food had always been a good distraction for him as a kid. He had no idea if it would work for Ava as well, but it was all he could think of. His experience with kids was limited. More than limited. Pretty much nonexistent, except for his occasional interactions with his brothers' kids.

Ava stared at him for a long moment, and then she slowly nodded.

"Great." He stood up. "You want to wait in here, and I'll bring out something? Or do you want to come in with me? It'll be pretty cold in there, so you'll need to wrap up in a blanket." He truly expected Ava to want to stay in bed next to Hannah, but she untangled herself from the bedding, and rose to her feet. She pulled a pink and white polka dot blanket around her, and held up her arms to him.

The expression on her face was so trusting, that Maddox suddenly couldn't breathe. He just went still, staring down at the little girl holding her arms up to him, as if she truly believed there was no place safer for her than in his arms.

Memories of his past raced through him, memories of a childhood hell that he'd endured, of all the lessons he'd learned about how brutal life could be. About how the only thing that ever came from reaching out to a parent was pain, the kind of pain that ate away until there was nothing left but a shell of humanity.

And yet there was Ava, holding out her arms to him, still believing in safety and goodness.

Of anyone she could have chosen to trust, the last person she should've selected was him, and yet in this moment, especially with Hannah so sick, he was literally the only one Ava had to lean on.

Resolution flooded him, a grim determination to somehow find a way to be the solid core this taciturn little girl needed. He walked over to her and crouched down. She immediately slid her arms around his neck and he picked her up, settling her against his hip. She was so light, like a feather that could get caught up in a breeze and swept away forever. His arm tightened protectively around her as he leaned forward to rest his hand on Hannah's forehead.

Her skin was hot, still burning, with sweat beading on her brow. Her eyes flickered open, fuzzy and glazed as she looked at him.

"Ava and I are going to get some breakfast," he said gently. "I've got everything taken care of. You just go back to sleep."

She nodded, mumbled something incoherent, and rolled over, closing her eyes again. His fingers drifted over her hair, noting the dampness from the fever-induced sweat. Ava's arms tightened around his neck, and he glanced down at her. Her eyes were wide with fear as she stared at Hannah, a look of such stark anxiety on her face that his heart, his long dead heart, turned over.

"Ava. Look at me."

The little girl dragged her eyes off Hannah, and stared at him, her face inches from his, her arms so tight around his neck, as if she was afraid she would get ripped out of his arms.

"Your mom is tired because she's fighting germs. It's just a cold. She will be fine, and running around the house, bossing you around in another day or two. Do you understand? She will be fine."

Ava just continued to stare at him, fear so vivid in her little face. That fear got to him, because he had seen that same kind of fear in the eyes of every single one of his brothers when they were kids, because they'd all grown up under the brutal hand of their bastard father. The expression on Ava's face was just like the ones he'd seen on his brothers' faces, and suddenly he understood. Ava had seen violence, the same kind of violence that he'd grown up with, that all of his brothers had faced before they had become big enough to fight back.

Anger burst through him, a dark, black fury that wrapped around his gut like a vicious monster. He was consumed with the need to fight back, to cut down the darkness that was so rampant, to destroy the monster that had brought violence into this little girl's life.

He swore at the sudden burst of hatred, so fierce that it shook him to his very core. Swearing, he shut his eyes, fighting to shut down the violence swirling through him. He didn't want Ava to see it on his face, to feel it in the tension of his muscles, to understand that her entire well-being depended on a man who had been born and raised in a life of violence.

Her arms tightened around him, and he felt her rest her cheek against his shoulder. His eyes snapped open, and he glanced down, something inside him shifting when he saw her resting her cheek against him, while her eyes watched her mom. What the hell? How had Ava been so close to him when the surge of violence rushed over him, and yet her only response had been to lean on him, as if he was the protection against it, not the source of it.

"Maddox?" Hannah's sleepy voice drew his attention, and he looked down at her.

Her cheeks were flushed, and something tightened in his gut. He leaned forward and brushed a tendril of hair away from her cheek. "What can I get you? Some ibuprofen? You're burning up."

She nodded. "There's some on the kitchen counter." Her gaze flicked to Ava, and he saw her notice the fear in the little girl's eyes. Resolution flooded her hazy gaze, and she summoned a smile, a brilliant, energetic smile that he knew took every core of her strength. "Hey, Ava," she said gently. "I'm going to be fine. I just have a little cold. Maddox is going to take care of both of us, okay? Everything is okay." She untangled her hand from the sheets and lifted it toward Ava.

He saw her arm was trembling, so he quickly caught her wrist and gently lifted it toward Ava's hand. Their fingers intertwined, and he had a sudden urge to wrap his hand around their joined fingers, to hold them together, to somehow let them know that he would keep them safe, no matter what it took, no matter how much darkness lived inside him.

Then Hannah lowered her hand, and the moment was over, his opportunity gone. Hannah snuggled back into the blankets, her eyelids already closing. Maddox took a deep breath, tightened his grip on Ava, and stood up. "You like cereal? I saw some sort of frosted fruit things in there. You like those?"

A tiny smile curved the corner of Ava's mouth, and she nodded. Her gaze was riveted on him as if Hannah's endorsement of him had made everything okay. She was definitely more relaxed about Hannah now, maybe reassured by the fact that Hannah had woken up enough to tell her everything would be fine. But as Maddox glanced over his shoulder at sleeping Hannah as he headed for the kitchen, his gut tightened. She looked so small and exhausted in the pile of blankets.

He needed to be there. He needed to be there for both of them.

Chapter 13

HANNAH HAD NEVER thought she would have a moment like this. Ever.

Two days after being rescued from the deadly mattress by Maddox, Hannah was happier than she ever thought she could be. With a happy sigh, she snuggled deeper into the blanket, her head resting on a throw pillow on the couch as she watched Maddox read Ava's bedtime story. Ava was curled up on his lap, pointing at the drawings on each page as Maddox read the book and talked about the pictures. Hannah couldn't get over how gentle his voice was. This big, broad, rugged cowboy, talking about a flying squirrel named Norman, as if he was in awe of every tiny, furry creature ever created.

Ava was clearly riveted by his storytelling, laughing every time he deviated from the words that she had memorized as a result of all the times that Hannah had read her that same book.

Laughter.

Hannah had feared that laughter was gone from Ava's life, but Maddox had brought them back to life. Lying there, on the couch, listening to the gurgles of hysterics from her daughter was the greatest gift Hannah had ever been given in her life. Who would've thought that a cowboy with dark, weighted shadows in his eyes would be the one to make her daughter feel safe enough to laugh again? Maybe it was all the time he'd spent reading to her. Maybe it was the hours he'd spent in the bitter cold working on the generator, until electricity and heat flooded their little house. Maybe it was the Mickey Mouse pancakes he had made Ava as soon as they had power again.

Or maybe it was just the solid strength of his presence, because that's what was doing it for Hannah.

"Okay," Maddox said, closing the book. "I think ten bedtime stories is enough for little girls who need their sleep. Time for bed, pumpkin." He kissed her forehead as Ava threw her arms around his neck, squeezing hard.

Tears blurred Hannah's vision as she watched Ava hugging him. Somehow, Maddox was giving Ava the gift of learning that not every man would harm her. It was a lesson that Hannah had never had, not until the last two days of having Maddox take care of her and Ava while the fever had been raging.

Tonight, she felt almost like her old self again, but she hadn't wanted to interfere in what had already become a nighttime ritual between Ava and Maddox. Somehow, Maddox was healing the cracks in Ava's heart, a gift Hannah would forever be grateful for.

Ava finished hugging Maddox, and then ran over to Hannah, climbing on top of her with a mischievous giggle. "Oh, you think you can pin me down, so you don't have to go to bed?" Laughing with her daughter, Hannah swept Ava up in a hug and stood up. It was amazing to feel like her muscles would hold her again, and she hugged Ava to her as she carried her to the bedroom, feeling Maddox's eyes on them.

Hannah took her time putting Ava to sleep, hugging her daughter, and singing the little songs that they had once sung together, back when she was Aunt Hannah, and not Mommy. Ava snuggled close, but her voice didn't join in the songs, and the deep sense of peace that Hannah had felt watching Ava and Maddox reading on the couch faded, replaced by the grim reality of life, of the depth of the damage that had been done to Ava's view of the world.

She rested beside Ava until the little girl fell asleep, then carefully untangled herself from the blankets. Feeling sadness in her heart, now that she wasn't too sick to remember all the things they were facing, Hannah made sure the nightlight was on before she shut the door, leaving Ava to dreamland.

She made her way back into the living room, where Maddox was sitting on the couch, watching her, as if he'd been waiting for her. He was leaning back, one arm trailing along the back of the cushions. He propped his feet up on the table, his jeans loose and low over his hips. He had on bright red socks that were much too cute for a man as rugged as he was. He was wearing a blue sweatshirt that had a loose neck that showed just enough of his collarbones to make her belly jump. He hadn't shaved since he'd been there, and his whiskers were thick and long. Not a beard. Just an incredibly masculine shadow along his strong jaw. He studied her, his gaze so intense that she felt heat rise to her cheeks. He was pure masculinity, strong and powerful, but his gentleness with Ava, and his kindness when she had been so sick were intertwined with who he was.

When he'd been so solicitous when she was so ill, she had learned to trust him, to trust that he would be there for her, to see him as her support. But now that she was feeling better, suddenly, she didn't see him only as a healer who held the weight of her burdens in his arms. He was also pure male, stretched out on her couch. With her daughter asleep behind a closed door, it was just the two of them in the small, contained space.

Her pulse began to flutter in her throat, and she stopped in the doorway, suddenly nervous. Letting him take care of her when she was sick, and allowing him to nurture Ava were completely different than seeing him as a man, a man who could reach into her heart, and make her vulnerable.

She cleared her throat, trying to distract herself from thinking about him as a man. "So, thanks again for taking care of Ava and me when I was sick. I really appreciate it."

He nodded, still studying her. "That's why I came back. To help you guys out."

Hannah shifted restlessly, torn between wanting to go over to the couch and sink down next to him, and wanting to flee to her bedroom. "Well, I appreciate it." Unbidden, her gaze drifted to his shoulder and his upper arm. The way he was sitting made his right biceps flex, and her belly jumped at the reminder of how strong he was. Strong enough to hurt her, if he wanted.

The thought made her flinch, and she took a step back, her need for safety suddenly overwhelming her attraction to him. She was frustrated by the way her old thought patterns had sprung up, but grateful at the same time, because she was terrified by the direction of her thoughts, seeing him as a man, a deliciously sexy man. She cleared her throat. "I'm going to head to bed now. I'm feeling so much better, but I'm super beat. So, I'll just—"

"I made some hot chocolate. Want some?"

She hesitated. "You mean, the kind that Skip's wife used to make for you? The kind with melted chocolate and cream?" He had already treated them to the hot chocolate a couple times, mentioning briefly that he and his brothers used to spend a lot of time on a ranch owned by a man they used to call Ol' Skip. Apparently, it was the ranch that his brother Chase currently owned, that some of his brothers had built houses on with their wives.

It was *really* good hot chocolate. The thought of snuggling down next to Maddox on the couch with a mug of it in her hand sounded infinitely better than sneaking off to her room because she was too afraid of her own feelings to be with him.

Maddox nodded. "The milk should be hot by now." He stood up. "Sit. I'll bring it out."

He was past her and into the kitchen before she could reply, leaving her standing there.

She could either duck back into her bedroom and leave him with two mugs of hot chocolate when he walked out, or she could summon the nerve to go sit on the couch.

She wanted to sit on the couch with him. She really did. But, God, she wanted to almost too much. What was she doing?

Hannah closed her eyes, trying to calm the pounding of her heart. It was suddenly racing, because she was re-membering the two times he had kissed her before she had gotten sick. Nothing else had happened since then, partly because they'd been sharing the room with Ava, and, of course, because she had felt like she was dying.

But Ava wasn't in the room with them, and her body no longer felt like ten thousand pounds of lethargy.

She took a deep breath, trying to think rationally. She could sit on the couch with him, and that would be purely platonic and safe, right? Right.

But what if something happened with him? What if he tried to kiss her? What if his arm was too tempting for her not to run her fingers over it? Her heart started to pound even harder. *What if he tried to kiss her again?* She didn't even need to ask that question. She knew she would kiss him back. Despite all her determination not to get involved with a man, not to trust a guy, and not to bring one into her and Ava's life, she knew that the last two days of Maddox's caretaking had whittled down the wall she kept erected so carefully around her.

She wanted desperately to sit on the couch with him. To spend one evening wrapped up in him, before he left. The snow had stopped that morning, and the wind had died down. Maddox had talked to Chase, and it sounded like they would probably be plowed out tomorrow, which meant this might be her last opportunity with Maddox, her last moment to breathe in how he made her feel.

The kitchen door opened, and she jumped, startled as he appeared next to her. He had a mug in each hand, with steam spiraling off them. His eyebrows went up, and his gaze settled on her face. She knew he was reading every emotion she was feeling, because she had no ability to hide them.

Silently, he set one of the mugs in her hand. Her fingers closed around the handle, brushing against his palm. Electricity jumped in her belly, but before she could panic, he slid his hand along her jaw, and bent his head.

Dear God. He was going to kiss her, and they weren't even on the couch yet. How could he want to kiss her? She hadn't showered in two days, she was wearing baggy jeans and a sweatshirt, she had no makeup on, and her hair was a disaster. There was nothing remotely sexy or appealing about her right now. There was no possible way he actually wanted to kiss her—

His mouth paused a breath from hers, his lips hovering just over hers, teasing her, but not touching. "I've been wanting to kiss you for two days," he whispered.

He wanted to kiss her. Her stomach leapt, and her fingers curled, the urge to touch him almost too much to resist. She swallowed. She wanted to say yes. Desperately. But fear clamped around her chest, and she couldn't get the words out. She simply couldn't say yes, and tell him it would be okay for him to kiss her.

For a long moment, they stood there in silence, and then he pulled back, searching her face. "You're a wise woman," he said softly.

As he moved past her to the couch, she wanted to grab his arm and pull him back, to ask him to pose the question again, to give her another chance to answer. But she didn't. She just stood there, clutching her mug, like some panic-stricken fool who couldn't function in the presence of a man.

Maddox sat down at the end of the couch, his forearms braced on his thighs, his fingers wrapped around the mug of hot chocolate. He bowed his head, so she couldn't see his face, but his shoulders were tense, and his grip on the mug was tight.

Suddenly, she forgot to be afraid of him. She saw only a man who'd given all of who he was to her and Ava for the last two days, a man who she'd just insulted by being terrified of him. Maybe she didn't want to get romantically involved with him. Maybe he did have shadows that were very dark and haunted. But the truth was that she had never felt as safe in her life as she had these last two days. Never. And she had thanked him by making him feel like she saw him as a monster.

With a nervous sigh, she walked over to the couch and sat down beside him. Not at the far end of it, but in the middle, close enough to let him know that she wasn't trying to put a chasm between them. "Maddox?"

He didn't look up. "Yeah?"

"It's not you. It's not you that I'm afraid of. It's...an

instinctive reaction that grabs me, I don't know how to stop it. But the truth is, I've spent my whole life feeling unsafe. Pretty much every minute of every day has been overshadowed by a need to keep looking over my shoulder, to keep people at a distance, to protect myself."

He looked up at her then, not moving, except to turn his head to look at her. There were so many shadows in his eyes, so much darkness, like the nightmares that chased her all the time. He didn't say anything. He just looked at her, waiting for her to finish.

"But..." She hesitated, unsure how to articulate what she wanted him to know. "These last few days with you, even when I was so sick, trapped in the storm, without electricity..." She shrugged, tracing her finger over the rim of her mug. "I just..." She finally looked up, needing to see him, to meet his gaze as she spoke. "These last few days," she whispered, her voice almost breaking, "I felt truly safe for the first time that I can remember. I will never forget that gift you gave us, that ability to let go, and stop flinching at every shadow. I haven't heard Ava laugh for a long time, and I know that you have made her feel safe as well. It's a gift, Maddox, a gift that I could never repay you for. It gives me hope that maybe some time, someday, Ava could live in a world where she feels brave and confident, not the world that I grew up in."

Maddox studied her for a long moment, his stare so intent that it seemed to penetrate the deepest, coldest recesses of her soul. "What happened to you? What happened to Ava? What are you running from?"

Hannah's throat tightened at the gentleness in his voice, at the raw caring in his eyes. Tears swam in her eyes, and she had to look away as she fought for composure. "I don't like to talk about it—" She froze when she felt his hand in her hair.

She closed her eyes, desperately focusing on the feel

of his fingers in the strands, ever so gently tucking her hair behind her ear, pulling it away from her face. His finger traced along her jaw, a touch so tender that she held her breath, unable to focus on anything but the way her entire body reverberated in response.

"Tell me." His voice was gentle, but there was an urgency to it, almost as if he needed to know for his own survival.

Her eyes opened, and she looked at him. His face was inches from hers, his eyes turbulent and dark. There was anger in there, a controlled, suppressed anger, which should have scared her. Somehow she knew that anger was on her behalf, and would be harnessed only to protect her and Ava. A strength that would be wielded in her defense.

Suddenly, a need to tell him welled up inside her, an almost desperate need to unload it into his strong, capable being, as if telling him would somehow pour his strength into her, and make her better able to face it, and triumph over it.

She swallowed. "Six months ago—" She stopped when he shook his head. "You don't want to know? I thought you—"

"Tell me from the start," he said. "The shadows in your eyes are much older than six months. I want to know it all."

The genuine need in his voice made tears swim even more fiercely in her eyes. He cared. He wanted to know. She could tell he meant it. And suddenly, she wanted to pour it all out to him. She wanted to unload everything onto his capable shoulders, as if putting it into words would give her the answers that had evaded her for so long. She managed a small smile. "It's a long story," she said. "Complicated, boring, and in the past."

Maddox searched her face, and she could almost see

the wheels turning in his mind, as he sorted through everything that she had mentioned to him in this conversation, and during all the other times that they'd been together over the last few days. Finally, he spoke. "Tell me what happened six months ago, then. One sentence. Put it into one sentence."

One sentence. Surely, she could handle one sentence, right? She swallowed, and looked down at her steaming mug of hot chocolate. It felt so incongruous to be sipping the most delicious hot chocolate, while ugly images formed in her mind. She took a deep breath. "My sister..." Tears started to fall down her cheeks, and suddenly she couldn't speak. God, she had kept it in for so long, that merely saying those two words made the grief tear through her, grief she had refused to acknowledge, because she'd been so focused on survival, and trying to make things right for Ava.

With a low sigh, he took her hot chocolate from her hands and set it on the table next to his mug. Then he wrapped his arms around her, and pulled her against him. She squeezed her eyes shut as she pressed her face into the curve of his neck, fighting against the sobs trying to take her. His body was so warm and strong, somehow holding her up as the memories came flooding back, every little detail that she had forgotten for so long, filling her mind in the most horrible of ways.

He pressed a kiss to her forehead, his arms tightening around her, like steel shields protecting her from the world. "Tell me, sweetheart. Get it out of your heart, so you can live again."

Hannah took a deep, shuddering breath, her chest so tight she could barely get the oxygen into her lungs. Maddox's words settled into her, and she knew he was right. She had to tell someone, and that someone was him, and the time was now.

Chapter 14

ANTICIPATION HUMMED THROUGH Maddox as he saw Hannah settle. *She was going to tell him.* For two days, he'd wondered about the little girl who wouldn't talk, who always had to be near him or Hannah, who cried out in her sleep and clung to him when he comforted her. He'd wondered about the fiercely courageous woman who had been so exhausted she'd spent eighteen consecutive hours pretty much asleep. He wanted to know what nightmares haunted them, and he wanted to make their pain go away.

Hannah lifted her chin, and he saw the determination in her eyes. His heart softened. "So courageous," he said softly, fingering a lock of her hair as she looked at him.

She was so close to him, only inches away, and her hand was wrapped around his wrist. He didn't think she was even aware that she was holding onto him, but he knew. He liked it. He knew he shouldn't be getting involved with them, but he was stuck there, and while he was there, he was going to bask in every moment he had with them.

Hannah sighed. "Not so brave," she said softly. "Just a survivor."

"It takes courage to survive," he said. "What happened six months ago?"

Tears swam in her eyes, tears of such grief that something inside him turned over. It made him think of the day he'd found his mother dead on the couch. He had shut down his tears that day, and never let them come back. But the vulnerability Hannah was sharing with him made him want to be soft for her, to somehow be what she needed.

"My sister, Katie, was murdered by her ex-boyfriend. Ava is her daughter. Mine, now."

Shit. His fingers tightened in her hair, and his jaw tensed. He wanted to rage. He wanted to shout. He wanted to fight against how brutal the world was. But Hannah was watching him as if he were her only source of strength to keep going, so he took a deep breath and shoved his rage deep inside, as he had so many times during his life. "What happened?"

"She had broken up with Rick a few months before, because she was getting the sense that he was...unstable. Aggressive. He hit her once, and I talked her into leaving him. Of course, he didn't want to let her go, and he started pressuring her to come back. He was devastated by her leaving, and Katie felt bad." A tear spilled down her cheeks. "I tried to keep her from going to see him, but she felt terrible that he was suffering. He promised he would change, and he kept saying that until she believed him. She wanted to help him, because she was that kind of person. So, she left Ava with me and went to his apartment to see him. It was just supposed to be a quick dinner, but she didn't come back."

Maddox swore silently, but he stayed still, aware of how tightly Hannah was gripping his wrist.

"When she didn't return, I knew something was wrong, but I couldn't take Ava over there, you know? So, I called the police and reported a domestic disturbance at his address. They got there just as Rick was... God... just as he was carrying her down the back stairs to his car. She was already unconscious, and she never woke up. She died three days later in the hospital. Rick said she'd fallen down the stairs and he was trying to help her, but I know he was lying. She was too bruised and battered for a simple fall down the stairs." Hanna's voice shook as she replayed that story. The grief from those three days, the terror of how she could go on without her sister, her fear for Ava, the loneliness, the emotions she'd fought to suppress, that she'd fought to ignore. "I took Ava to see her, to say goodbye. I didn't know if I should, but I felt like she needed to see her mom one last time, you know? How could I deprive her of that? But now...God...she hasn't said a word since." She looked up at Maddox, the grief tearing through her. "I don't know how to help her. I don't know how to fix things for Ava. I don't know... God, Maddox, I miss my sister."

Maddox swore under his breath, and reached out, drawing her into his arms. She collapsed into him, burying her face in the curve of his neck, letting the strength of his arms surround her.

"I made a mistake," she whispered, barely able to talk through her tears. "I shouldn't have let Katie go see him, and maybe I shouldn't have let Ava see her mom in the hospital. They're all I have, all that matters to me, and because of my mistakes, Katie's dead, and Ava lost her mom and won't even talk." Her voice shook desperately, and grief assaulted her.

Grief.

Guilt.

Loneliness.

The deep anguish of loss that ripped away at her shields and left her gasping for air, for life, for some sliver of hope that would get her through the next day, and the day after that. "I tried to fix it. I pressured the police, and they eventually arrested him for voluntary manslaughter. I stayed in town long enough to testify last week, and then we left. I wanted to do that for Katie, but God, seeing him in that courtroom..." She shivered, remembering the look of pure venom on his face. "He's sitting there, alive and smug, and blaming *me,* while my beautiful sister is gone, and her daughter, God, Ava...I don't know how to help her."

Maddox had never wanted to be more than who he was than he did in that moment. He wanted to ease her pain, to somehow pry her from the grip of her grief and guilt. He wanted to save her and Ava, to somehow spare them from the violence that had found them...but he couldn't. He was just a piece of shit born from the same violence that had stolen everything from them.

But there was one thing he knew for absolute certain, and he needed her to understand it. He knew he could give her this much. He slid his fingers through her hair as he brushed a kiss over the top of her head. "Listen to me, Hannah," he said, his throat raw with emotion he wouldn't allow himself to feel. "There's only one person responsible for what happened to Katie, and that's the bastard who hurt her. No one else is to blame. Not Katie for going there, not you for not stopping her. Only him. You live with the purest beauty in your soul, and you can't let some piece of shit take that away from you—"

She sat up, tears streaming down her face. "How can you say that? How can you say that it's not my fault, when I could have made different choices that would have meant Katie would still be alive?"

Darkness settled inside him, a dark ugly truth that

made his skin crawl. "How do I know? Because my father killed my mother, and I didn't save her. I blamed myself for her death for years until I finally figured out that the only one who did something was him. He did it. He killed her. *He is responsible.*"

Hannah lifted her head, searching his face desperately, as if hoping that somehow, someway, he had the key to save her from the haunting guilt and pain inside her.

He slid his hand along her jaw, his fingers brushing over the softness of her skin. "Sweetheart, I've lived in the shadow of his poison my whole life, and I've lived the carnage of what he left behind. If there is one thing I know, the only one responsible for his actions is him. No one else. Not ever. Sometimes we get lucky, and we can interfere and protect others from bastards like that, but if we *can't* find a way to stop them, to save those they hurt, it's not our fault. *It's not our fault.*"

Hannah stared at Maddox in shock, stunned by his story, by his guilt, by his loss, by the fact he'd faced the same kind of death that she'd dealt with. She'd lived her life trapped by the darkness of what had happened to Katie, and to her mother before her, but she'd lived in silence, afraid to talk about it, afraid to look it in the face and acknowledge how much it scared her... and yet here was Maddox, who had experienced the same thing. Suddenly, for the first time since Katie had died, she didn't feel so alone. "After a string of abusive boyfriends, my mom was killed in a car accident when her drunk boyfriend crashed the car," she whispered. "I was sixteen, and Katie was twelve. How old were you when your mom died?"

Maddox's face softened, and he touched her cheek. "Seven."

"Seven," she whispered. He'd only been *seven.* "Who did you live with then?"

"My dad."

She stared at him in shock. "I don't understand. Why didn't they take you away from him?"

"Because that wasn't how this town worked back then," he said. "Besides, I had eight brothers around to support me, including my twin brother, Ryder. They were my family, and I'd rather have stayed there with them and my dad than to try to fend for life by myself. I needed my brothers." He studied her. "Where did you live?"

"They split us up in foster care, so we ran away. After a few months, we hooked up with a group of kids living under a bridge in Chicago, and they took us in. There were nine of them, all runaways. They'd all taken the last name of Hart, creating the family that none of them had. We stayed with them for about a year, but as soon as I turned eighteen, I moved us to Boston and started college, working during the day and taking online classes until she was big enough to stay home alone at night while I went to school." She bit her lip, remembering those first nights when she and Katie had been living on the streets. "I never would have made it without them," she said softly, tears burning in her eyes. "Life was so much better sleeping under that bridge with the Harts, than it was living in foster homes without Katie."

He understood exactly what she meant, because he'd experienced the same thing with his brothers. He trailed his finger along her jaw. "Where are they now? Those kids?"

"The nine of them who took the same last name bought a ranch in eastern Oregon. There are also a few of us scattered around who never took the last name Hart, but all of us spent time living together when we were homeless. That creates a bond, you know?"

"I bet it does." Maddox studied her. "They all live on

a ranch together, huh? They're like Chase, who wants us to be a happy family on his ranch." He laughed softly. "Sounds like they stick together. I'd like to meet them someday. Loyalty is the foundation of what matters."

Hannah tensed. "I don't keep in touch with them anymore."

Maddox frowned. "Why not?"

"Because..." Hannah bit her lip. "I don't like to think about that time in my life. I need to feel brave and strong and successful. If I think about them, I think about how scared I was, and how desperate. I...I don't want to be that girl anymore."

Maddox sighed, stroking his finger along her arm. "I get that. That's why I will never live on the ranch. We did a lot of riding on that ranch when we were kids. It was our salvation when life was shit at home, which was almost all the time. Even though Chase and the others live there now, every time I step on that ranch, I feel like that kid again, hated by the town, feared by others, treated like scum. I felt powerless back then, and I never want to feel like that again."

She nodded. "Yes, that's exactly it. As a kid in a bad situation, you aren't allowed to take control of your life. You have to survive what you've been dealt. It's a feeling of being powerless and dependent." She shook her head. "I never want to feel like that again, either." She couldn't believe he understood, but he did.

Maddox nodded. "If it weren't for my brothers living here, I'd never come back to this town. Ever. Neither would Ryder. Each time I walk back into town, I feel the darkness gripping me, both of my past, and what's inside me. I come back only for them, but not that often. It's just not where I want to be."

Hannah stared at him, the tight edge of guilt that she lived with starting to ease its grip on her heart. "I always feel so guilty when I don't return their messages. Brody is the oldest. He was the protector of the group. He calls me every month, and has since the day I left. I..." She grimaced. "I haven't taken his call since Katie died. I don't know how to tell him."

Maddox raised his brows. "They don't know?"

She shook her head again. "If I tell him...it makes it real," she whispered.

Maddox took her face in his hands and lifted her face so she was looking at him. His heart broke for her, but at the same time, he knew that hiding from the pain didn't make it go away. "Hannah, sweetie, you have to look at it. It is real. Katie died. If Brody and the others are the kind of family you described, they have a right to know, and I promise you'll feel better if you tell them, and let them support you."

Tears filled her eyes, and suddenly she couldn't breathe. "Don't say that it's real—"

"I have to say it." He stroked his fingers over her cheeks, wiping away the tears she didn't even realize she'd shed. "Katie's gone, honey. You have to accept it."

She shook her head. "No, I don't want to—"

"Baby, you're not dead. Do you understand that? You're here. Ava's here. Katie lives on in both of you, so you have to let yourself live."

Grief filled her, and she tried to pull away. She didn't want to have this conversation. She didn't want to have to tell Brody what had happened. He'd be on the first plane out there to help in whatever way he could. She hadn't seen him or any of the Harts since she'd left. She didn't want to go there again. She didn't want to be the girl who needed to lean on him, or anyone else. She glared at Maddox. "Don't tell me what to do. You don't know what it's like—"

"I don't? Really?" He held out his arm, showing her

the scars. "I know darkness, honey. You know how I know it? Because my father was a violent alcoholic who beat the hell out of us kids, and my mom. She was seventeen when she met him, and she came from a hellish situation. She wanted to be saved, and she fell for him. She was eighteen when she married him, and had me and Ryder six months later. She was young, and scared, and fragile. He was an asshole who broke her spirit, which was already in shatters when she married him. She died of a broken soul, even more than a broken body, Hannah. Even her own sons couldn't give her enough of a reason to survive."

Hannah stared at him, her heart breaking for the anguish she felt in his voice, for the pain on his face. "I'm so sorry, Maddox—"

He shook his head, cutting her off. "When I was sixteen, I fell in love," he continued. "She was the daughter of the town's minister, with the purest spirit I'd ever met. I honest-to-God, thought she was an angel sent to save me. I worked my ass off, saved money, and bought a diamond ring to give her at graduation. I was going to marry her, and walk away from my hellish life."

Dread filled Hannah. "What happened?" She was afraid to ask, afraid to open that door, but she needed to know, and she knew Maddox needed to tell her.

Maddox dragged his gaze off Hannah, staring past her shoulder at a blank spot on the wall as memories of that night flashed through his mind. He was suddenly back in that moment, that moment when he finally had to stop lying to himself about what he was. "Her name was Beth. My dad was out binge drinking, so I'd made a candlelight dinner for her on the back porch. I had just taken the ring out and gone down on one knee when my dad came home." He could still smell the acrid scent of burning rubber as his dad had careened into the driveway. He remembered his heart freezing in horror as his dad stumbled out. He recalled with perfect clarity that he'd gone absolutely still, praying that his dad wouldn't see them out back. He remembered the flash of absolute fury at himself that he'd been stupid enough to think it would be okay to have the dinner at home.

"My dad came home. He saw us as soon as he got out of the truck, and stumbled over. He saw the ring in my hand and started yelling at me, cursing me to hell and back, cursing my mother, shouting about how love would destroy everything, and I was a stupid fool to think I could be anything more." He pulled away from Hannah, needing space as all the old emotions came flooding back.

He stood up, pacing away from her. "Beth was horrified. She knew he was a bastard, but she'd never seen him in a rage. I was watching her face as she watched him, and I knew it was too much for her. She was too pure—" He stopped, trying to stay hard, to shut down his emotions, but the images were too powerful, coursing through him. "Then my dad came on the porch. He... fuck..." He looked at Hannah, who was still sitting on the couch, her face stricken as she listened. "He hit her. He just slammed the back of his hand across her cheek and knocked her down."

Hannah sat up straighter, looking at him, and suddenly, Maddox didn't want to say anymore. What the hell was he saying? He didn't want to bring that darkness into this room. And he didn't want Hannah to see the rest of the truth, the truth that defined *him*, not just his father. "So, yeah, I get it," he said, abruptly cutting off the story. "I get how you can have a past that is so dark that you want to rage whenever it comes near you. I know how being with people from that time can bring it back." He turned to face her. "But I also know that without my brothers, I'd be in jail now, or dead, or something worse. Yeah, they're from my past, but having anchors who know the darkness you come from, can anchor you. My brothers are my rock, and if you've got someone willing to be yours, hang onto it." He strode back across the room and sat back down. "Don't hide from Brody and the rest of the Harts. They can help you. Think about it."

She searched his face for a long moment, then finally nodded. "I'll think about it."

"That's all I ask." He sat down next to her, relieved to know that she would consider reaching out to her family. He needed to know she had a support team when he left... fuck. *When he left.*

He didn't want to leave. At all.

Shit. How had that happened? But it was true. He didn't want to leave her. Or Ava. Not just today. Ever.

Chapter 15

"WHAT HAPPENED NEXT, Maddox?"
Hannah's question jerked him back to the present. For a split second, he didn't realize what she was talking about...and then he realized she wanted to hear the rest of the story after his dad had hit Beth. He glanced over at her, at her beautiful, trusting face, and his heart tightened. He didn't want her to know the rest. He didn't want her to look at him the way Beth had. He needed her to look at him like there was hope for his soul. He needed it so badly that it actually hurt. So, he shook his head. "I don't want to talk about it."

Hannah sighed and wrapped her hand around his arm. She set her head on his shoulder, and snuggled up against him. Maddox froze at the intimacy, his entire soul screaming out for her. He was caught in such darkness that Hannah's touch felt like a salvation, a breath, a chance not to fall into the endless chasm. But he couldn't drag her into it. *He couldn't do it again.* But he knew he couldn't stand up and walk away, not from this moment, and not from the house when they were finally plowed out. He needed the connection with her too much.

It had to be her who pulled back, because he couldn't do it. She had to make the choice for him. She had to choose to push him away, and for that to happen, she had to understand how bad he was.

Hell. He didn't want to do this, but he had to. He swallowed hard, his skin ice cold as he realized there was only one way to make Hannah protect herself from him. The truth. Maddox bowed his head and closed his eyes, his forearms braced on his quads. He didn't want her to know the truth about him. He didn't want to ever see her looking at him like she saw the monster inside.

But he also knew that for her sake, he had to show her, because he wasn't going to be strong enough to walk away. She was making him want something he hadn't dared want since Beth, even though he knew better.

"Maddox?"

He didn't look at her. He just began to talk, his voice ragged as he began to strip away the image she had of him, the one he wanted her to have forever. "When my dad hit Beth, something inside me snapped. I went after him, and my only goal was to kill him. I unleashed seventeen years of hate and fury onto the drunken bastard. I couldn't even think, or see, or even hear anything. I was in a blind rage, and all I wanted was his death." Maddox fisted his hands, remembering that day, that horrific day when he became like his dad. "My brothers dragged me off him. I was still screaming, trying to get free of their grip. My hands were bloodied from punching him, my knuckles torn. I'd even broken my thumb from hitting him so hard. I fought like hell against my brothers, but six-on-one wasn't in my favor. They got me off him, and Chase was shouting at me to look at Beth. So, I did...and everything stopped for me."

God, he'd never forget the look on her face. "She was

back against the railing. She was screaming, her hands clutched over her heart. Tears were streaming down her cheeks, and she had blood spattered on her nice white dress. My dad was on the ground at her feet. His nose was busted, there was blood everywhere." Maddox wanted to look at Hannah, but he didn't dare. He couldn't handle the expression he knew would be on her face. The disdain. The disgust. Maybe even hate or fear. "My dad was long past being able to defend himself and I was still attacking him. I would have killed him that night with my own fists if my brothers hadn't stopped me. I would have killed him in cold blood. Beth looked at me, and I saw the absolute horror on her face, and that's when I knew. My dad was a monster, yeah, but *so was I.* She knew it, and we both knew right then that it was over between us. She grabbed her purse and ran, and we never spoke again."

Maddox remembered that moment when she'd backed away, a look of terror on her face, as if she were afraid Maddox would come after her next. "I let her go," he whispered. "And I never forgot that lesson." He bowed his head. "I still have that ring." He hooked a finger around the collar of his shirt and pulled out a silver chain. Dangling from the end of it was that engagement ring he'd once been so proud of, a ring that had once symbolized his foolish belief that he had a right to believe in hope and light and goodness. Today, the ring had a different purpose. "I still wear the ring as a reminder never to trust myself, never to get too close to a woman, never to let myself feel too much. It reminds me to protect others from the monster that lives within me." He dropped it back under his shirt, but as he released it, Hannah caught it and drew it free.

His heart started to pound, but he didn't look at her. He just stared at the wall on the other side of the room, his vision blurring. Even though he wasn't looking at her, he was aware of every move she made, of the brush of her fingers against his chest as she lifted the ring to look at it.

"This is quite extraordinary," she said softly. "How could you afford this as a seventeen-year-old?"

"I found it in an old thrift shop. The guy held it for me for eight months while I earned the money." He laughed softly, remembering the number of hours he'd poured over the counters at the assorted thrift stores in the area, borrowing his brother Zane's motorcycle to head to nearby towns in his search for a ring worthy of Beth. He knew exactly what the ring looked like without even looking at it. The center solitaire. The six smaller diamonds set on the platinum band. The intricate carvings that wrapped around each stone, almost as if the setting was embracing each stone. "I liked that it was old, that it had a history, that someone had loved it before. I thought the love it carried would protect us." Shit. He couldn't believe he'd said that aloud.

Her fingers closed around the ring, hiding it in her fist. He looked down at her hand, her small, delicate hand, holding so tightly onto the ring that had once been his beacon of hope and faith in the darkness of his life. No woman had touched it since he'd bought it, and seeing her holding it made something inside him turn over. Silently, unable to stop himself, he wrapped his hand around her closed fist, holding her fingers tightly around the ring.

"That's beautiful," she whispered. "You're such a romantic."

"I was, but not anymore." He couldn't take it anymore. He had to know what she was thinking. Slowly, unable to stop himself, he turned his head just enough to see her face...and then froze in shock.

The expression on her face was such warmth, such kindness, such *empathy*. She was looking at him as if she wanted to take him in her arms and hold him until his past vanished. There was no judgment, no fear, no disgust...just...God...caring...almost love...

Yearning pulsed through him, a raw, visceral ache to reach out and draw her into his arms, to lose himself in the energy she was pouring into him. So, he shook his head. "Don't look at me like that, Hannah. My dad's monster lives inside me, and I will destroy any woman I love, just like my dad killed my mom, and I broke something inside Beth that day."

She shook her head. "Don't do that to yourself, Maddox, You're wrong—"

"No." He squeezed her hand more tightly, more urgently, almost desperate to make her stop talking, stop saying things that his soul was crying out for. "Never forget what I am, Hannah. I would have killed my own father with my bare hands if my brothers hadn't stopped me." He held up his hands to her. "Never forget the blood that was on these hands, the blood that will be on them again if the monster ever wins again." He looked at her. "My brothers are all that have kept me from adding to the stain on my soul. You have family that will do the same for you. Don't let them go."

Longing flashed across Hannah's face, a yearning so achingly heart-breaking that he couldn't help but reach out and grasp her hand. "I don't know how to connect with them," she whispered. "I don't know how to trust anyone. I don't know..."

She was so lost and so vulnerable that something inside him snapped. He'd admired her fierceness and her courage. It made him feel safe to be around her. After his mother and Beth, he was terrified to be around women who were soft, who he could break emotionally, so the vulnerability on Hannah's face should make him want to run away... but it didn't.

It made him want to be her strength, to hold her, to protect her, to make her strong again.

Silently, unable to stop himself, he traced his finger along her jaw, staring down into her upturned face. "I know what it's like not to trust," he said softly. "But if you pick the right people, it's worth everything."

"I trusted my mom and Katie. I don't know how to trust anyone else." She searched his face, her dark brown eyes so rich with emotion. "But you make me feel safe," she whispered. "For the first time since my mom died, I feel safe. Is that trust? Do I trust you?"

Her words touched a chord deep inside him, a chord that was so beautiful that it seemed to swell up and resonate through every cell of his body, breaking through years of rust and shadows until his entire body was vibrating. "You trust me?" He knew it was wrong. He knew he shouldn't allow it, but it felt so good, so incredible.

"I don't know. I just know that I feel safe with you, and that is the most incredible feeling." She laid her hand along his jaw, her gaze steady on his. "Thank you for that, Maddox. Thank you for making us feel safe. We needed it so much, and I didn't even know it, until you gave it to us."

Warmth flooded him, a deep, longing that came from a place inside him that he'd crushed so long ago. A longing to connect with her, to kiss her, to lose himself in the softness that could come from only one place: her. "I need to kiss you," he whispered, thumbing her lower lip. "Tell me not to."

Hannah's cheeks flushed, and she met his gaze. His heart seemed to stutter when he saw the longing on her face. Heat rushed through him, and he knew what she was going to say before she said it.

"Kiss me, Maddox. Kiss me, now."

Emotions plunged though him, intense longing, need, heat, desire...everything that he'd shut down for so long. His fingers tightened on her jaw, and he bent his head until his lips were no more than a whisper from hers. "If I kiss you," he said softly, "I'm not going to stop. I need you too much."

Hannah slid her hands into his hair. "Kiss me, Maddox," she said again. "Kiss me with all you have."

He had no chance to resist. No chance at all. The only path he could take was the only one that would keep him alive.

He kissed her.

THE MOMENT HANNAH felt Maddox's lips on hers, everything inside her came roaring to life. All the darkness, all her protective shields, everything that she had locked down inside her for so long suddenly exploded into a cacophony of color, energy, and light.

Desperate for more, for him, for what he made her feel, she surrendered completely to him. Need filled her, the most beautiful, most alive, most glorious need for this amazing man who had taken such care of her and her daughter. She reached for him, drawing him more tightly to her, and kissed him back. She'd never considered herself passionate, but apparently, she'd just been waiting for the right man, the right moment, the right emotions.

She kissed him back, greedy for the taste of his mouth on hers, for the way he made her feel, the way he unleashed the deepest part of her that was so powerful, and so vivid, and so vibrant. She wanted more of what he awakened inside her.

Maddox, with his kisses, his honesty, and his caring, made her feel bold. He made her feel alive. He made her feel safe enough to forget to tread carefully. He liberated her to live so fully in the moment that she felt as though she would never be contained again. Joyfully, she flung her arms around his neck and dragged him down to her, basking in feelings and freedom that were unlike anything she had ever experienced before.

Maddox growled low in his throat and his arms locked around her waist, dragging her against him as if he too had unlocked the door to something he had no control over. His kisses were so tender, and yet filled with passion and vitality at the same time.

Hannah knew that he perceived himself as dark and dangerous, but everything pouring out of him into her since the day they had met contradicted that perception. He was made of kindness, warmth, love, support, and understanding. His nature as a protector was evident. She loved his protective instincts, and, at the same time, was completely overwhelmed by the sheer beauty of what it felt like to be surrounded by so much strength and safety.

She needed more of him. More of his kiss, of connection with him, both physical and emotional. Restlessly, barely aware of what she was doing, she slid her hands under his shirt. The moment she spread her hands over his bare stomach, palming his torso, a sense of absolute rightness filled her. She needed to be close to him, to touch, to feel him against her.

Then he slid his hands under her shirt, spanning her lower back, and she forgot about everything but the feel of his hands on her skin. Pure gentleness. Heart-melting tenderness. And beautiful strength.

There was something so incredible about the feel of his strong hands palming her waist. He encircled her with his arms, his muscles flexing against her, even while he deepened his kiss, his tongue going deeper and deeper, drawing her out of her cocoon and into the light of radiant colors and brightness.

Suddenly desperate for more, she pulled her sweatshirt and sports bra off over her head, unable to stop herself, unable to walk away from the need he was stoking inside her. Somehow, despite a lifetime of not trusting men, she felt safe with him, gloriously, wonderfully safe, so safe that she surrendered to all she was feeling, not trying to hide from it or shut it down. She embraced her desires to open herself to the strength he was giving her, to surrender to the passion and need spinning through her like a whirlwind of fire.

With a low groan, Maddox locked his arm around her lower back and bent his head, taking her nipple into his mouth and sucking. Hannah gasped and clutched at his shoulders, her body shaking as he grazed his teeth across her nipple. Vibrant sparks of passion and desire shot through her like fireworks, breaking through barriers that would no longer be contained.

She found herself dragging his shirt free of his jeans, and when he raised his arms to let her pull it over his head, she did so without reservation, desperate for more skin and more connection. The moment they were both naked from the waist up, he pulled her back on the couch, bracing himself over her as he showered her with kisses along her neck, on her sternum, and over her breasts.

Hannah had never felt like this before, so safe, so free to tap into the strength and desire within her, to listen to the fire burning within her. Maddox sank between her hips, his pelvis against hers. It was a position of pure domination by him, a position that gave him complete control of her...but she felt no fear. Just an amazing sense of safety, of glorious delight in putting herself in a vulnerable position with him, knowing that she was completely safe and protected.

She locked her feet behind his back, pulling him more tightly against her. She could feel his erection pressing against the juncture of her thighs. The sensation was erotic and powerful, and she loved knowing that he was hard because of her, because of her kisses, because he wanted *her.*

The knowledge that she was affecting him as much as he was affecting her ignited the desire already pulsing through her, increasing her level of need exponentially.

She wanted to be naked with him. She wanted him to make love to her. She wanted to lose herself in all that he was, and somehow find a way for them both to escape from the darkness, and together, somehow find their way to sunshine, sunshine so bright that it would dissolve the shadows. She gripped his shoulders, pulling back to look at him. "Make love to me," she whispered. "I need you. I need this. I need how you make me feel."

She saw the look of surprise and awe on his face, and her heart softened at his inability to believe that she could see such beauty in him, that she could trust him, despite the stories he'd told about his past. She knew then that Maddox was the man her heart had been waiting for. He was the man meant to show her what it was like to live again. He was the man to show her that not all men should be feared. He was the man to teach her that some men used their strength in the most beautiful of ways when it came to women.

Despite her need for him, she could see the resistance on his face, his need to protect her from the monster he perceived himself to be. She knew he was too honorable to ever cross that line, so she didn't give him a chance to stop. She just went for the waistband of his jeans, sliding her fingers around the button, and unfastening it, her fingers moving with astonishing dexterity given how badly her body was trembling with need for him.

The moment she slipped her hands beneath the front of his boxers and wrapped her fingers around the steely hardness of his cock, she knew she'd won the battle. Maddox whispered her name, a heart wrenching, guttural cry of need, desperation, and complete surrender. He rolled off her, staggering to his feet as he yanked his jeans off. She was still trying to unfasten her own pants when he was back, helping her unfasten her jeans and pulling them over her feet. It took only moments before he was back on top of her, his hips settling between hers...but this time, there was no fabric between them, a glorious sensation of skin against skin.

She felt the tip of his cock pressed against her entrance, nudging gently, asking, inquiring, probing, but not taking or demanding. He was going to make her take the initiative and be in control, which was both scary and exhilarating.

She locked her feet behind his butt, lifted her hips to him, and dragged his head down for a kiss, a deep kiss into which she poured every emotion that was dancing within. Glorious need, breathtaking desire, liberating safety, and the deepest soul-to-soul connection.

With a low groan, her name entwined in a gasp of desire, he capitulated to her demands and slid inside her, a beautiful, incredible sensation made her heart fill with more hope, more love, and more freedom than she'd experienced in her whole life.

"God, Hannah," he whispered, his lips brushing against her ear in an intimate confession. "This is the most beautiful thing I've ever experienced in my life. I didn't know this kind of perfection existed." He framed her face with his hands, staring down at her with the most incredible, unguarded look of awe, tenderness, and love.

Seeing that expression on his face, directed at her, made something inside her open completely to him, physically, emotionally, and spiritually. His face softened in recognition, and he smiled.

She smiled back, her heart filling with joy at the sight of his dimples. "God, you're beautiful," she whispered.

"Nothing compared to you, Hannah." With the guttural moan of deep, pure desire, he plunged deep inside her, catching her cries with deep kisses designed to safeguard her most hidden desires. He thrust again, and she gasped as he moved again and again, stirring her into a passionate frenzy that obliterated everything but him. His thrusts became deeper and faster, as he switched position and angles, working her into a state of trembling need until she was at the peak of desire.

As he moved, Maddox kept whispering her name over and over and over again, saying it with so much emotional intensity, and reverence, and nurturing, that her final shields fell, and she gave herself completely to him. The moment she surrendered to him, an orgasm exploded over her, starting deep inside her belly and spreading like rushing water mixed with fireworks through her belly, down her legs, to her heart, and along her spine.

She gasped, clinging to him, her only foundation. Maddox shouted her name, and then, with one final thrust, he poured himself into her, surrendering to his orgasm. It shot through him, his body shaking as he held himself over her, his gaze locked on hers as ecstasy overtook him. His muscles trembled violently, as if his orgasm was going to tear him apart just as hers was. They clung to each other, gloriously trapped by the grip of the orgasms, before they were sent over the precipice with the last final gasp. He collapsed against her, his face buried in the crook of her neck, his breath rasping in his chest. She wrapped her arms around him, holding him close, while their bodies shook with the intensity of what had just happened between them.

She knew in that moment, she would never, ever, be the same.

Chapter 16

H E WOULD NEVER forget this night.

Maddox pulled the blanket more securely around Hannah, being careful not to wake her. She was using his chest as a pillow, her hands tucked up under his chin, her legs tangled with his. They'd gotten dressed after making love, as a precaution against Ava walking in, but when he'd walked her to her bedroom, somehow, he'd ended up following her onto the bed after a kiss good night that neither of them could stop...

And now it was almost two in the morning, Hannah was sound asleep, wrapped around him, and Maddox was lying there, listening to the silence of the night, and the steady rhythm of her breathing.

He hadn't slept in the same room as another person since he'd moved out of his dad's house and stopped living with his brothers. He needed his space, the space he'd never gotten as a kid, until now, until this moment, until Hannah.

Maddox closed his eyes, breathing in the subtle scent of flowers that seemed to cling to Hannah all the time.

He turned his head slightly, so that his cheek was resting against her head, strands of hair tickling his cheek.

Sex had never meant anything to him. It had been a way to...he didn't even know. A way to hide from the darkness haunting him?

Tonight, everything had changed. Tonight, he'd made love to the woman who had awoken his heart for the first time in a very, very long time, maybe ever.

But sometime during the evening, the wind had stopped blowing. The storm had moved on. By morning, Chase and the others would plow them out, and there would be no reason for Maddox to stay, and every reason for him to leave.

How in God's name would he ever make himself walk away tomorrow? But he had to. He knew he did. But—

He suddenly heard the sound of tiny feet padding in the hallway, and he froze, swearing under his breath as he listened to Ava pause outside the door. What the hell had he been thinking, sleeping in Hannah's bed when Ava was around? What kind of message did that send to her?

The door opened and Maddox went very still, allowing the shadows to swallow him as Ava pushed the door open and peered inside. She was wearing her girl power superhero nightgown, and she was holding Alfred tightly in her arms.

He watched as Ava padded over to Hannah's side of the bed. She patted Hannah's arm, but her mom didn't move. Maddox knew Hannah was exhausted from the lovemaking, which had stripped her of what little energy she'd begun to regain after being sick. Ava tapped Hannah again, and he saw the glisten of tears on her cheeks.

Maddox swore under his breath, barely able to contain the instinct to reach out to the little girl, as he'd done so many times over the last two days when Hannah had been so sick.

Ava bit her lip, and looked up, her eyes meeting Maddox's. Instantly, her little face morphed into a smile, and she held up her arms.

Maddox's heart softened, and he leaned over Hannah, and picked up Ava. To his surprise, the moment she was on the bed, Ava burrowed against Maddox's side, tucking herself between the two adults.

Maddox stretched out on his back, one arm still around Hannah, and the other one around Ava, as she squirreled down between him and Hannah, moving incessantly until she found her spot, which resulted in her face pressed against the crook of Maddox's neck, breathing heavily on him.

After a long moment, he felt her fingers tracing his beard, tapping gently.

He laughed softly. "Are you scared, baby?"

He felt her nod against his neck, and he tightened his arm around her. He hated that she was afraid, that she and Hannah had to live in fear. He wanted to free them from the grips of fear. He knew what it was like growing up scared, and it sucked. "Do you want a story?"

She nodded again, and wiggled closer to him, still tapping his chin. She held up Alfred, and he smiled. "A story about Alfred?"

She nodded for a third time, and then snuggled contentedly down beside him with a deep sigh.

Maddox sighed, trying to think of a story that might help her, one that might chase away the fears. "Did you know Alfred used to be afraid of the dark?"

Ava shook her head, and propped herself up so she could see his face. It was dark, but the light from the hall gave him enough light to see her face watching him so carefully.

Maddox paused, trying to think of a place to start. "When Alfred was a puppy, he lived on a street where a big, mean dog lived. Alfred was scared of the dog, because he thought it might hurt him."

Ava's eyes widened, and she sat up, clutching Alfred to her chest. For a moment, Maddox hesitated, unsure whether to continue. Then he saw Hannah roll over and face him. Her eyes were on him, and she nodded slightly, encouraging him.

Shit. He had no idea what the hell he was doing. He had no experience trying to make up stories that would make a traumatized four-year-old feel better. He raised his eyebrows at Hannah, asking for her to finish the story, but before she could say anything Ava tapped his chin again, drawing his attention back to her. She held up her hands, palm out, in an entreaty for him to continue.

He realized then that it wasn't just a story she needed. She needed a story from *him*, because for some reason, she trusted him. Damn. It had to be him.

Resigning himself, Maddox sat up with a groan, leaned against the headboard, and held out his arms. Ava scrambled onto his lap, tucked her feet between his thighs, and leaned her head against his chest. Maddox wrapped his arms around her, and rested his chin on her head, watching Hannah, a small smile playing at the corners of her mouth while she listened to them. "Did Alfred have trouble sleeping at night?" Hannah asked.

Maddox nodded. "Yep. At night, he would hear the big dog barking, and Alfred would lie in bed listening, being a little bit scared." He paused. This wasn't a good story. Now he was creating new things for Ava to be afraid of. By the time he finished the story, she would probably be afraid of dogs, too.

He had no idea how to help a kid. He raised his eyebrows at Hannah, again asking for her help, but she just smiled at him and patted his knee, as if he would be fine with a little reassuring pat.

The next time he and Hannah were alone, he was going to have to point out to her that he was not a puppy dog, but a bumbling, idiot male who had no idea how to help a little girl. But for the moment, since she was intentionally ignoring his pleas for help, it was up to him to figure out how to make this better. He'd grown up scared, but at some point, he'd stopped being afraid. He thought for a minute, trying to think of what happened in his life when he had stopped being afraid, when he had begun to sleep at night and stop listening for his dad's footsteps in the hall.

It was when he had become strong, when he'd started believing he was strong. And that had happened when his youngest brother Travis had moved into the house, at which point Maddox and his brothers had realized that there was someone weaker and smaller than them that needed their protection. Keeping Travis safe had forced Maddox to find his strength.

Galvanized by the idea, he thought fast. "One day, Alfred's owner, who was named Susie, brought home a tiny kitten." He lightly rubbed Ava's back as he spoke. "Have you ever seen a tiny kitten? Do you know how little they are?"

Ava lifted her head to look at him, and she shook her head.

Maddox took her hands and cupped them together, making a little basket of her tiny hands. "A baby kitten would fit right here." He tapped the bottom of the basket. "It would fit right in your hands. Much smaller than Alfred."

Ava stared at her hands for a moment, then she looked back at him and nodded.

"The kitten was so little that it could barely walk

without tripping on her own feet. Susie loved her so much, and named her..." What name would a four-year-old girl respond to? "Fluffy. Susie named the kitty Fluffy." He glanced at Hannah, and relaxed when he saw her smiling. Okay, so he got that part right. "When Susie went to school that day, she asked Alfred to take care of Fluffy and make sure she was safe. Alfred, of course, agreed to watch Fluffy, because he loved Susie, and because Fluffy was really, really cute. She was also really, really little, and Alfred could see that she definitely needed someone to watch out for her. Plus, how hard could it be to watch a little kitten, right?"

Ava grinned, and bounced on the bed.

"Exactly." Maddox warmed to the story, the ideas beginning to flow now. "Of course, as soon as Susie left, Fluffy slipped out through the screen door and bounded straight into the yard."

Ava rolled her eyes and shook her head, grinning.

"What do you think Alfred did?" Maddox asked.

Ava made a running motion with two fingers, and Maddox nodded. "Exactly. He ran after her, but she was already down the street, checking out everything. She ran right into the yard of the mean dog."

Ava went still, staring at him, her eyes wide. She clutched Alfred to her chest tightly, and Maddox was pretty sure that she didn't even realize she was doing it. He glanced at Hannah, and she nodded, urging him to continue.

Hoping he was doing the right thing, he went on. "Alfred was terrified. He ran to the hole in the fence and started barking at Fluffy to come back, but she ignored him. She just ran right across the yard to play with a dandelion under the window. Just when she reached the dandelion, the mean dog came around the side of the house. It saw Fluffy, and stopped, staring at the kitty."

Ava moved closer to Maddox, her eyes wide as she stared at him, riveted by the story.

"The mean dog was so much bigger than Alfred, and Alfred was terrified. He barked at Fluffy, and she looked up and saw the dog. She froze in terror, unable to move, even as the mean dog started running towards her. Alfred realized that Fluffy was too scared to run. She couldn't get away. There was no one to help her...except for Alfred. He didn't have time to be scared anymore. He had to save her! So, he squeezed through the hole in the fence and raced after the mean dog, who was thundering toward Fluffy. Just as the big dog reached Fluffy, Alfred got close enough. He lunged after the big dog and bit him right on the end of his tail!"

Ava put her hand over her mouth, her eyes wide.

Maddox grinned. "The mean dog was so startled when he felt Alfred's little teeth poke him in the tail, that he jumped straight up in the air yelping in absolute terror. He jumped so high that he banged his head on a tree branch."

Ava giggled, her eyes twinkling as she watched him.

"When the big dog landed and saw little Alfred standing there growling, he realized that the tiny dog had bitten him. He realized that the little tiny dog was so powerful that he'd made the big dog smash his own head into the tree just with one little bite!"

Ava burst out laughing, a beautiful, heartfelt laugh that he had never heard from her before. It made his heart leap, and he grinned at Hannah, who had tears in her eyes. He held out his hand to Hannah, and when she slipped her hand in his, he squeezed it before turning his attention back to Ava. "The big dog decided right then and there that little dogs were much scarier, and much more powerful than he had ever realized, especially Alfred. He immediately backed up, then turned and ran around the side of the house, and hid under the rosebushes. Alfred was so surprised, that he stood there for a full minute, waiting for the big dog to come back, but he never did. Finally, Alfred realized that by simply pretending to be big, brave, and strong, he had convinced the big dog that he was more powerful. All it took to make the danger go away was for Alfred to believe he was strong. That was all it took. Just his belief."

Ava was riveted, her gaze steady on his face, listening to every word.

"Alfred went over to Fluffy, picked her up by the back of her neck, and carried her out of the mean dog's yard. From that day on, every time Fluffy and Alfred passed the mean dog's yard, the mean dog always ran around to the back of his house, and hid under the rosebushes. Alfred became the hero of the neighborhood. Each time another dog had to pass the yard, Alfred would walk with them to show the mean dog that Alfred was their friend. Whenever the mean dog realized that that dog had Alfred's protection, he would stop bothering that one, too. Eventually, the mean dog had no one left to bark at, and he gave up. He decided that life was more interesting lying in the sun, and enjoying the roses, than it was scaring everybody else. He was happy, everyone was safe, and it had all happened because Alfred had decided one day to be brave, even though he didn't feel brave, and that was all it took for everything scary to simply disappear."

Maddox finished the story, and silence fell in the bedroom. Ava studied him, and he could almost see her processing the story, and making it her own. After a moment, she nodded and looked down at Alfred. She lifted him so they were eyeball to eyeball, and she studied him carefully. Maddox saw her lips moving, and he knew that Ava was having a discussion with the dog. He glanced at Hannah, and saw her watching Ava with an expression of such love and emotion on her face, that his throat tightened.

Ava might be scared, but she had a mom who loved her more than words could ever express, love which would always wrap around her and provide a buffer against all the crap that the world would throw at her.

Ava finished her conversation, then snuggled back down in bed, nestling against Hannah. Hannah wrapped her arm around her daughter, kissed the top of her head, and then looked up at Maddox.

He shifted, knowing that his role in the moment had ended. It was time for him to get up, and let the mother/daughter bonding happen. His chest tightened with regret as he reached for the blankets, surprisingly sad at having to extricate himself from the situation. He didn't want to get up. He wanted to stay there, in a world he didn't belong in, in a situation he was too rough for.

But just as he went to flip the blankets back and get up, he felt a small hand wrap around his little finger. He looked down and saw Ava was holding onto him. His heart turned over. "I'm sorry, baby, but I need to go—" He stopped when Hannah encircled her fingers around his wrist, and he looked quizzically at her.

She smiled gently at him. "Stay, Maddox. We both need you."

He wanted to stay. He wanted to stay badly. But he couldn't mislead them. He couldn't make them count on him when he wasn't dependable. "Chase will be here in the morning. I'll be on my way after that."

He didn't miss the flash of pain across Hannah's face, and guilt tore through him. What the hell had he been thinking, to make love to her the night before he was going to leave? Guilt ripped through him, and he rolled onto his side to face her, careful not to squish Ava, who was still between them. He stroked his fingers down Hannah's jaw, searching her face. "I didn't mean for last night to happen," he said. "It was selfish and cruel to make love to you when I knew I had to leave. I don't want to make it worse by staying here with the two of you, knowing that I have to leave."

Hannah put her fingers over his lips, silencing him. He glanced down at Ava, and saw that her eyes were closed, and her breathing was steady and even. She was already asleep, her fear eased by his story. Somehow, that made a little bit of the tension in his chest ease. Yeah, maybe he'd been a selfish asshole to make love to Hannah, but by giving Ava peace, he'd done something right, at least *one* thing right in his life.

"Maddox." Hannah's soft voice drew his attention back to her, and he dragged his gaze off the sleeping child to look at the woman he'd already betrayed.

"I'm so sorry," he whispered. "I didn't mean to make love to you. I have no excuse, but if it's worth anything to you, making love to you was the most beautiful moment I've ever had in my life. I will hold it in my heart forever, as a gift, as a moment when I was able to experience the beauty in life that I don't deserve. I will treasure you always, and I will treasure that moment, and the memory of it always. You are an incredible woman, and you deserve every happiness, every gift, and every moment of joy that exists in this world."

Tears filled Hannah's eyes, and she smiled, a smile so heartfelt that something inside him twisted. He didn't deserve to have her look at him like that, like he was special, like he was worthy. He didn't understand what she was seeing that made her look at him like that. "Hannah—"

She put her fingers back over his lips and shook her head. "Listen to me, cowboy. I wanted tonight. I needed you. I needed to lose myself in your tenderness, your strength, and your kisses. You might not have had many beautiful moments in your life, but I haven't either. I know the blizzard is over. I know you will never let yourself stay. I understand you, Maddox, and that's why I will never regret what happened."

His throat tightened. "You deserve so much more than what I gave you—"

She raised her brows. "More than beauty? More than reverence? More than the gift of feeling so safe that I could completely lose myself in what was between us? More than that?"

He hesitated, unsure of himself in the shadow of such poetic words. "I did that for you?"

Hannah sighed, and nodded at the sleeping child. "You do that for both of us, Maddox. I know you still see yourself as a monster, but you're not. You're that bright light of warmth that we both needed so desperately."

He didn't know what to say to that. He truly had no idea how to respond. He wanted to be that for them. He'd stayed because he'd wanted to help them, but he hadn't really believed he could make a difference for them. "I helped?" He could barely even choke out the words, so desperate was he for the answer to be yes.

Her face softened. "Yes, Maddox. You helped."

He nodded, turning his head away at the sudden tightness in his throat. "I need to go."

She stopped him with a gentle hand to his forearm, a touch that he could break away from so easily, and yet, at the same time, a touch that trapped him completely. "You don't need to leave yet. Stay with us the rest of the night. Give us both the gift of being able to sleep soundly for one night, one short night."

He looked at her, and saw the earnestness on her face, the genuineness in her voice, and he realized then that he was truly able to offer them something beautiful, simply by his presence. His chest tightened, and before he even realized he was doing it, he nodded. "I'll stay."

The smile that his response generated was so beautiful, that for a moment he forgot to breathe. He slid his hand through Hannah's hair, and leaned forward pressing a tender kiss to her mouth. Her lips tasted like an angel's whisper, and he knew he would never forget the sensation for as long as he lived. When he pulled back, his eyes flickered open, and their gazes met, held together by something so powerful that he knew he would be tied to this woman and her daughter for the rest of his life.

For a split second, a fraction of a breath, he wondered what it would be like to wake up with them every day, and not return to his life. The image was so startlingly awe-inspiring that he immediately shut it down. As quickly as he had the thought, he let it go. He wasn't meant for this life. It would shatter him forever, completely, if he ever broke the trust of Hannah and Ava, and he knew that if he stayed, eventually his true self would come to light. It might be a nightmare that ripped him ruthlessly from his sleep. It might be some drunken bastard on the side of the street that triggered an old memory. It might even be something as simple as some asshole looking at Hannah the wrong way. He didn't know what it would be, but he knew that at some point, the darkness inside him would win, and he would see on Hannah and Ava's faces the same expression that he had seen on Beth's.

There was no chance in hell he was doing that to them, or himself, because he knew he would never survive it.

So, it would be just tonight. Just one, special, amazing night, with two incredible females who had fallen into his life so he could protect them during this little window of time during which fate had brought them together.

With a deep breath, he allowed himself to slide back under the covers and stretch out on his side, facing Ava and Hannah. Ava rolled over and tucked her face against his chest. Hannah scooted after her daughter, nestling against Maddox, using his shoulder as a pillow, and entangling her legs with his, creating a cocoon around Ava with their bodies.

Maddox pressed a kiss to Ava's head, then slid his finger under Hannah's chin and kissed her, this time, long and deep, until the emotions threatened to overwhelm him. When he finally released her, she smiled at him, then snuggled up against him and closed her eyes. Maddox encircled both of them in his arms, using his body to protect them from the outside world.

He closed his eyes, listening to the sound of their breathing, feeling the warmth of being wrapped around them. They were relaxed, and Hannah was asleep within moments. The two of them, deeply asleep, completely trusting him to keep them safe.

Maddox sighed deeply, unable to stop a feeling of deep, penetrating contentment from settling in his bones. His father may have been a bastard, and his childhood may have sucked on a lot of levels, but one thing it had given him were the skills to protect and guard those who needed him. He knew he was physically capable of defending Hannah and Ava against any threat that came their way, and he whispered a promise to both of them he would do whatever it took to keep them safe, to honor their faith in him.

He had only a few hours before the sun would rise, snatching this moment away from him. But that meant that he had those few hours ahead of him, hours that would last him a lifetime.

He took a deep breath, determined to etch every single second into his soul, so that he would remember it for the rest of his life.

Chapter 17

S HE WAS AN idiot.
Seriously.
Of course, if there was anyone for her to be an idiot about, it was Maddox, but that just made it worse.

Hannah sat at the kitchen table, her chin propped up on her hand, as she watched Maddox teach Ava how to make pancakes that looked like Alfred. He had made her a stool with a railing and pulled it up next to the stove, so that there was no way for her to reach the stove, or fall into it. But she was right next to him, watching what he was doing, pointing to the chocolate chips when he asked her what he should use to make the eyes.

Hannah could not believe how kind he was. She had never met a man like him. Yes, the Harts had always taken care of her and Katie when they were young, but they had been homeless teenagers, not exactly the same as a man like Maddox. Watching Maddox take care of Ava made Hannah think of her time with the Harts. It had been the only time in her life, besides now, that she had felt the security of knowing that someone was there to protect her. If anyone from foster care or child services had come after her and Katie to separate them, and drag them back, the Harts would have found them, and helped them get away again. Even as kids, the Harts had been dangerous, loyal, and absolutely relentless in their protection of each other.

She sighed, watching Maddox's smile as he followed Ava's directions on where to put the strawberry for the nose. Yes, Maddox definitely reminded her of Brody, with his quick smile, and his kindness, combined with his strength. Of course, a significant difference between them was that she had always thought of Brody as her brother, and never had the least bit of attraction to him on a physical level…but the same could not be said of how she felt about Maddox.

Heat pooled in her lower body as she thought of last night with Maddox. Making love with him had been the most incredible experience of her life. He had freed her to completely open herself to what she was feeling, and what she wanted. He made it safe for her to reach out, to take what she wanted, and to turn herself over to him. She had loved every moment of it. And then the finale had been sleeping, with both her and Ava wrapped up in his incredibly strong arms. She had known then that the universe had given her that moment to help begin to heal the broken pieces of her heart, the pieces that had been broken for so long, that she hadn't even realized there were cracks.

And now, the sun was shining. The blizzard was over. Real life was creeping back, inch by inch, minute by minute. She glanced out the window at the brilliant white snow glistening across the property. Even the ramshackle barn looked charming and wonderful when it was covered in all the snow. The sky was a brilliant blue, without a cloud to be seen, and all the branches of the trees were bent under the snow, making it look like a Christmas card from some fantastical, small New England town, where neighbors were best friends, children ran around outside without fear, and you were never alone, even if you wanted to be.

In the distance, she could hear the low hum of a chainsaw, and she knew that Chase and probably his brothers were working on the tree that protected her, Maddox, and Ava from the real world. At any moment, all this would be only a memory. And that was why she was an idiot, because she didn't want it to be a memory.

Somehow, her heart had forgotten that this was temporary. It had forgotten that she didn't trust men. It had forgotten that she was all about girl power for her and Ava. Her heart wanted the moment with Maddox and Ava to be her life today, tomorrow, and the day after that, continuing on indefinitely, creating a cocoon of safety and tenderness in which she and Ava could heal and thrive.

That was exactly what she had wanted when she had chosen Rogue Valley to settle in. She had thought it would come from the neighbors, but it hadn't. She looked over the stove as Maddox lifted the spatula to move Alfred from the griddle to Ava's plate. All the feelings she had craved for so long, had come from one man, a man so haunted by his own demons that he could not even see what he brought into their lives.

"Go show your mom," Maddox said. "I'll make a few more for the grown-ups." He winked at Hannah as he ladled some more batter onto the pan.

Hannah's heart tightened at his private intimacy, and wrapped Ava up in her arms as the little girl bounded up onto the seat next to her, her face glowing as she held up Alfred the pancake to show her. "It's beautiful," Hannah said. "It looks just like him."

Ava nodded happily, and poured syrup over the pancake, her face glowing as she watched Maddox cook.

Hannah glanced over at him, and her heart tightened when she saw the yearning on his face as he watched them. Suddenly, her heart started to pound. There was no mistaking the expression on his face. He was feeling the same thing she was feeling. *He didn't want to leave.* If that was the case, maybe he didn't have to leave. Maybe she could make it safe for him to love himself, the way he had made her feel safe to simply be.

Her heart pounding, she stood up and began to walk over to him. It wasn't something she would ask in front of Ava, because she already knew how much Ava would want him to stay. But she had to let him know how she felt. She had to say something. He would never believe that he deserved to stay. It would never occur to him to insert himself in their lives, so it was up to her to show him that he was welcome, and that he was worthy.

His eyes darkened as he watched her approach, a sultry, heated expression that was so similar to how he had looked at her the night before when he had been making love to her, claiming her as his own.

"Hey gorgeous," he said, as she approached him. He slid his arm around her waist and pulled her up against him, planting a decadent, delicious kiss on her that sent ripples of excitement and desire through her body.

The moment he ended the kiss, she gripped the front of his shirt, her fingers clenching the soft fabric of his T-shirt. "Maddox."

He grinned and kissed the tip of her nose. "Hannah."

"Do you hear the chainsaw?"

His smile faded. "Yeah."

"How long do we have?"

"Not too much longer." There was an edge to his voice, a sense of regret that she recognized, because it was the same one that gripped her own heart.

She took a deep breath. This was her moment. He'd probably say no. He would probably tell her he had to leave, for the safety of her and Ava, but she had to tell him that she wanted him to stay, if for no other reason than to give him the gift of knowing that she believed in him, and she saw the beauty in his soul. Maybe he wouldn't be ready to accept that about himself now, but she could at least plant the seed, and she could at least open the door for him to decide to stay if there was any chance of that possibility. "I was thinking—"

His cell phone rang, making them both jump. He swore and glanced over at the counter, where his phone was sitting. Hannah followed his glance, and saw the name Chuck Williams on the screen. Maddox silenced the phone, and turned back to face her. "Sorry. Tell me what you were thinking."

His cell phone beeped, and they both looked over as a text message from Chuck Williams popped up on his phone. *Maddox. When are you back in town? I'm overloaded with cases right now, and I need you back on the job.*

Hannah looked up at him, her heart pounding with the reminder that Maddox had a life outside this little cabin. "Is he your boss?"

Maddox shrugged. "I take the cases I want. I wouldn't call him my boss." He shrugged, but his face had become hard again. "I'm not very tolerant of people who try to control me and dictate my actions. It doesn't bring out my best side."

Hannah's determination faded as Maddox's tone shifted from soft and nurturing, to one more defensive and protective of himself. "Do you like being a bounty hunter?" It wasn't what she had meant to ask, but for some reason the question popped out, maybe because she didn't want to see him as a man who worked with criminals, carried a gun, and was willing to shoot people if he had to.

She wanted him to be the man who had been so tender, kind, and nurturing for the last few days.

Maddox met her gaze, and something flickered in his eyes, something that told her that he understood why she was asking. "I believe that bad people shouldn't be allowed to hurt other people. Someone has to drag their asses back to the jail they're supposed to be in, and I'm good at it." He met her gaze. "I'm good at it, because that's my world. Darkness. Violence. Staring death in the face. It doesn't bother me. And I have no problem dishing it out. That's the real me, Hannah." He gestured toward Ava, who was happily munching her pancake. "I can't keep this up," he whispered, his voice low. "I can't keep being this person."

Frustration gripped Hannah. "I don't understand. Are you miserable? You seem happy here, with us. Is it all just a lie?"

He swore and ran his hand through his short hair. "No, dammit. That's not what I'm saying. Right now, we're living in this little cocoon, but life isn't like this. Life is going to get shady. It always does. And that's going to bring out the side of me that neither of us wants to see."

Hannah felt like stomping her foot. "How do you know what I want to see? With all that I've been through, don't you think that I know when someone is a good person, and when someone isn't? You bring peace to my soul, Maddox. For the first time ever. My soul couldn't possibly trust you if there was anything about you that would endanger me. Don't you understand? Just because you can bring in criminals, and because your dad was a jerk doesn't mean you're destined to destroy everybody."

She stepped back and held her arms out to her side. "Look at me," she demanded. "Just look at me. Do you honestly think that you could hurt me? That you could destroy me? Is there any part of your soul that could bring harm to me? Or to Ava?"

Anguish flashed across Maddox's face, anguish so deep that she felt the ache in her own heart. "Yes," he said, his voice hard and flat, almost dead. "I would, if I stayed around you long enough. Someday, something is going to set me off, and that will be the end. I will not stay around long enough to do that to you."

The truth of his words. He believed everything he said, all the way to the depths of his heart. "I don't understand," she whispered. "Why can you not see what a good person you are?"

He raised one eyebrow. "And I don't understand," he said. "How can you be given the gift of a family like the Harts, and shut them out of your life? How can you be so consumed with loss and darkness that you can't let in the sunlight that the universe gave you so long ago?"

Her mouth dropped open in shock at his words. She stepped away from him, her heart clenching painfully. Loneliness assaulted her, a deep sense of fear, fear of reaching out, fear of going back to who she'd once been, and a fear of more loss. "They aren't my family," she whispered. "They're teenagers who saved me many years ago."

Maddox walked over to her and caught her chin, lowering his voice so quietly that Hannah could barely hear it. "That's bullshit, Hannah. Family isn't about blood. If it was, my dad wouldn't have been such a son of a bitch. Except for Ryder, each of my brothers has a different mother than I do. You could call them my half-brothers, except that would be a lie. Each one of those men is my brother in every part of my heart and soul, including Dane Wilson, the Rogue Valley sheriff. There isn't a drop of blood that Dane and I share, but he is my brother in every way possible. I'd be dead by now if it wasn't for them. I may be fucked up. I may be a bastard. I may be a demon waiting to be unleashed. But I also know that without my brothers, I'm nothing. You have that kind of support with the Harts, and you know it." He met her gaze. "So why are you walking away from them, if you know how important they are?"

His words made her heart cry. There was no way for her to deny his truth. The Harts were her family, and she had walked away from them so many years ago. "I don't know." It was the truth. Maddox was wrong. He wasn't the broken one in this room. It was her.

"I didn't mean to make you sad, hon." His face softened, and he took her hands, holding them to his heart. "The truth is, sweetie, that we all have baggage from our pasts. It defines who we are today, and it drives our actions every moment of our lives. Because of your past, you can't reach out to the Harts. Because of mine, I am forever burdened with the darkness inside me. Yeah, it sucks on some levels, but protecting those we love makes it worthwhile."

Tears filled her eyes. "Are we really protecting those we love? Or are we stabbing ourselves in the heart?"

He sighed and slid his finger over her cheek. "It might be both, but I'm okay with that. I'd stab myself in the heart a thousand times a day if that's what it took to keep you and Ava safe."

She stared up at him through tear-blurred vision. "What if keeping me and Ava safe meant you staying with us? Could you find a way to do that?"

Regret filled his face, and he sighed deeply. "Sweetheart, there's nothing more dangerous to you and Ava than me. So, no, I wouldn't stay with you."

"But—" She stopped when she heard the loud roar of an engine coming from the front of the house. Her heart seemed to freeze when she realized it was the sound of a snowplow. They had broken through. The protective shield around their enclave had been broken.

She looked at Maddox, and gripped his shirt. "It's too soon," she whispered. "I'm not ready."

Maddox wrapped his hands around hers, dwarfing her fists in his hands. "I will never be ready to walk out the door and leave you and Ava behind," he said softly. "It will always be too soon."

She searched his face, trying to understand. "Then why do you have to leave? Tell me whatever it is you haven't told me. There has to be more than what you've said."

He frowned, and then sighed. "There is."

Chapter 18

MADDOX'S SOUL FELT like it was being pierced in a thousand places with Hannah looking at him like that, trying to understand why he had to leave. He couldn't believe what it felt like for her to look at him with such faith. She honestly believed in the goodness in him, and that made his throat tighten, and his chest ache. "Hannah," he said softly, stroking his finger along her cheek. "You have no idea how badly I want to be the man that you see when you look at me. The only way I know how to do that is to walk away."

He heard the engine of the snowplow pause, and he swore silently, realizing that at any moment someone was going to knock on the front door, or even just walk right in. He couldn't leave Hannah looking at him like that, with hurt in her eyes, unable to understand why he was the way he was.

He knew there was only one way to do it. Only one way to show her what he was. Gritting his teeth, he pulled his wallet from his back pocket and flipped it open. He paused for a moment, his heart pounding, then he took a small, yellowed piece of paper from behind his credit cards and he handed it to Hannah. "After the incident with my dad and Beth, I put the engagement ring in her locker at school. I wrote a note and said that I had bought it for her, and I still wanted her to have it. I told her I wanted her to keep it, so she would always know how deeply she was loved. I told her that she had been the only bright light I'd ever had in my life, and I appreciated all that she had done for me. I also wrote that I would never bother her again, because I understood that she could never trust me to keep her safe."

God, he remembered those words he had written. His hand had been shaking. His eyes had been blurred with tears, a seventeen-year-old boy who had given up on dreams before he had even become an adult. But even then, he'd learned what his limits were on what he deserved to hope for or ask for in life. "I wanted to do right by her. I wanted to somehow find a way to wipe away the trauma from that night, the heartbreak of finding out that the man she loved, that she had been willing to marry, was nothing more than a monster, and that she had failed to see it."

Hannah stared at him, her lips slightly parted, her dark brown eyes riveted to his face. Her fingers were loosely clasping the note, but she wasn't looking at it. She was just watching him, and the empathy in her eyes was almost too much for him to take.

He nodded at the note in her hand. "I found that note from her in my locker the next day, along with the ring. That letter is my curse. It's my destiny. It's my reminder of what I can't allow myself to want or have. I want you to read it."

Hannah looked down at the paper in her hand, staring at it for a long moment. Maddox felt himself tensing, knowing that she was going to read the words that he had made his mantra for so long, words that had literally broken him when he had first read them.

She finally looked up at him. "Why on earth does it matter what a seventeen-year-old girl thought of you fourteen years ago? Why would I care what she thought? I know what I see today. That's the truth. That's the reality."

Maddox swore. "You should care because she saw what I'm capable of. You haven't seen it. I have. I've lived it. I feel the darkness fermenting inside me. I feel the need for violence. I feel the hate. I feel it. She saw it. She knows." He pulled the paper from her hand, his hand shaking as he took it. He needed Hannah to understand what he was. He simply could not walk away until she knew. He didn't know why, but he needed Hannah to see the real him.

He stepped away from her and unfolded the paper. "Ava, hon," he said as he turned toward the little girl. "Mommy and I need to talk in the living room for a sec. Is that okay with you?"

She nodded and gave him a thumbs up and a smile. She looked so happy and peaceful, sitting at the table that his heart turned over. She pointed to the snow and made a patting motion with her hands.

He raised his brows. "You want to make snowballs later?"

She grinned and made a throwing motion.

"A snowball fight?"

She nodded again, smiling more widely.

He nodded. "You and your mom against me. Sound good?"

She clapped her hands, her eyes dancing.

"As soon as I get done talking to your mom." He walked over, gave her a kiss on top of her head, then grabbed Hannah's hand and walked out into the living room, leaving before he could let himself think about how sweet and adorable Ava was.

He shut the kitchen door and then took Hannah to the far side of the room. When he turned to face her, she was staring at him as if he were insane. He frowned. "What?"

"How on earth can you consider yourself a monster when you treat Ava like that?"

He didn't answer her. He unfolded the note and began to read it.

Maddox. I have never seen anything like I saw last night.

Everyone in town talks about your father, his drinking, and his violence. I knew the kind of home you came from, or I thought I did. I had no idea what your life was really like. I can't believe your father punched me in the face. That isn't violence. That's sick. Your father's sick, not the kind of sick that can be helped with treatment. The kind of sick that belongs in a horror movie.

But you··· You're so much worse than he is. Your father doesn't pretend to be anything other than what he is. No one trusts him. No one cares if he lives or dies. No one is surprised when he gets put in jail for be-ing a drunk. But you. You're the real demon. You pretend you're kind. You pretend you're sweet. You pretend you're worth trusting. You make people believe that you're a good guy, that you'll keep them safe, that you'll use your strength, and your heart to weave a cocoon of protection around everybody that you care about.

Damn you, Maddox. Damn you!

You're a liar and a cheat. You betrayed me, and everybody else in the school and this town who sees any kind of goodness in you. Anyone can protect themselves against the threat they see coming. But no one can protect themselves against the hidden threat, a threat shrouded in the disguise of a friend, a lover, and a protector.

You took my heart, you made me trust you, you made me love you, and you made me believe in you. My parents didn't believe in you, and I fought against them in support of you. I gave everything to defend you, because you made me believe in you, and you made me love you. And it was all a lie. A lie!

You are so much more of a monster than your father ever will be. He's an old man. A drunk. A loser. One punch, and you had him on the ground. One punch had ended it, but then you attacked him like a rabid animal, salivating for the taste of his blood. I can still hear the sound of his nose crunching under your fist. I can still hear his groans as you kicked him in the ribs. I can still hear that horrible scream tearing from your throat, like a wild animal attacking its prey. I will never forget watching the man who won my heart turn into a monster right in front of me.

I don't want this ring. I don't want this note from you. All I want is to find a way to wipe you from my mind forever, so that I never have to think again about the fact that I live in a world that is also occupied by you. Stay away from me. Stay away from my family. Stay away from my friends. Stay away from my town. Do everyone a favor, and just die. Beth.

Maddox took a deep breath as he finished the letter, trying to slow his racing heart. He hadn't read it in several years. He'd forgotten exactly how bad it was. He could still remember the stark shock that had reverberated through his body as he read the words of the girl he had built all his dreams and all his love on.

He looked up at Hannah, and her face was white, sheet white. "When I read her note, I realized she was right," he said. "Every time I was with her, I had made sure to show her only a nice guy. I was considerate, kind, understanding. I pretended that I was fine. I pretended that my father hadn't affected me at all. I pretended that I was worthy of who she was, with her protected life, her happily married parents, and her Sunday mornings at church. I never once let her see what was inside me. So, she's right. I did betray her. I did lie."

He folded the letter over, the creases well-worn from years of living in his wallet. "I learned a lot from that. I learned that I'm a monster. I don't remember kicking my dad. I don't remember screaming. I don't remember feeling my fists sink into his flesh. All I remember is rage, so much rage. But her letter is the play-by-play that I don't recall. I lost control because I loved her, and that love made me vulnerable. When my dad hit her, I had no ability to control myself."

He met Hannah's gaze. "Love turned me into the demon. I won't do that again, especially not to you and Ava. You guys have had much too much violence and

175

loss in your life. Do you really think either of you could handle it if I became violent in front of you? This is why it's so important to me that you understand who I am. No more misrepresentation. No more pretending I'm something that I'm not." He held out his hands, palms up, in surrender. "This is what I am, Hannah. And we both know that you and Ava need so much more than a ticking time bomb that will explode at some point."

As Hannah stared at Maddox's face, she finally understood. She understood why he saw himself the way he did. She also understood, for the first time, the side of him that he had kept trying to explain to her. Her heart bled at the words Beth had written to him. She'd felt his pain while he read them, and she'd felt the way he raised his barriers, shutting down his emotions.

How could he possibly believe in himself after that?

And, how could she possibly believe in him after that? Could she?

She did. She still did. Why?

Silently, she took his hand, and turned it over. There were scars on his knuckles, the kind of scars that came from punching things. His dad? The criminals he tracked down? A tree? She thought of the scars on the hands of the man who'd killed her sister. On the hands of the boyfriends who had hit her mother. Men with scars on their knuckles had always made her want to run, to hide, to protect herself. Why wasn't she afraid of Maddox? Was she stupid? Desperate for love? Or able to see a truth that only she could see?

She looked up at Maddox, searching his face, trying to see the truth in there.

She saw his pain. She saw his anguish, years and years of anguish. But she also saw the violence, beat into him by a childhood of hell. She thought of how he had showered her and Ava with kindness, genuine kindness, affection, and warmth. He made them safe. Was he right that his darkness would win? Or would his goodness and beautiful heart triumph? She was afraid of men. She didn't trust them. One bad experience would destroy her forever.

But as she looked into Maddox's haunted eyes, she knew that he was wrong. He would never break her or Ava. Ever. She knew it all the way to the depths of her soul, through all the broken pieces of her heart that lay scattered around her. "I believe in you," she whispered.

Pain flashed across his face. "No, Hannah, don't—"

She laid her hands on either side of his face. "Ava and I have both seen darkness. We've seen the worst kind of men that walk this earth. I see the scars on your hands, and I see the scars in your heart. I know what you have done. I know what you are."

He went still, watching her, like a cat poised to spring away.

"But I'm not afraid, and neither is Ava."

He closed his eyes, and tipped his head back, as if fighting off a surge of emotion that was too strong for him to cope with. Then suddenly, he opened his eyes, slid his hand behind the back of her neck, pulled her against him, and kissed her.

It wasn't a sweet, tender kiss. It was a kiss of desperation, the kiss of a man drowning in hell, fighting for breath, for air, for salvation. Hannah flung her hands around his neck and pulled him close, kissing him back just as fiercely. She accepted all of his turmoil, taking it into her, and giving him all the peace and love she had to offer. She rode the tide of his frenzied kiss, of the desperation eating away at him, of the need raking through him with such agonizing ferocity.

He angled his head, deepening the kiss, taking, taking, taking. Except she knew that it was more than that.

He was offering her his pain. He was surrendering his fear and his self-hate to her. He was trying to find his way through the darkness to the light that she was offering him.

So she held him tight, allowing him to pin her against his body with such strength that he almost took her breath away. His legs were strong, braced on either side of hers, a fierce warrior made of both the hardest steel, and the most tender, fragile threads of hope.

It was hope she felt in his kiss. The hope that maybe the words on that folded sheet of paper that he'd lived by for so long weren't actually the end of his story. God, she needed hope, too. She had left Boston to escape from the memories and the oppressive hopelessness and fear that had been crushing both her and Ava. In a few short days, Maddox had changed all that for her. He had shined sunlight onto them, beautiful, nourishing sunlight, and then he'd enabled them to feel it.

His darkness was worse than hers, in some ways. More personal. More internal. She was afraid of the world. He was afraid of himself. She broke the kiss, pulling back just enough to be able to speak, her lips still against his. "I love you, Maddox. So does Ava."

He sucked in his breath, his arms tightened around her, and he froze. She could feel his heart thundering against her chest, a frenzied, almost out-of-control rhythm. He whispered her name, a low, guttural groan of anguish, and then he swept her up in another kiss, this one a thousand times more desperate and agonized than the one before.

His kiss was frantic and deep, so deep, as if he was trying to lose all he was in their connection. His arms were so tight around her, and she could feel his chest trembling against her. Tears filled her eyes at the realization that the strong, capable, modern-day cowboy was actually trembling because she had told him that she loved him. Because it meant something to him, and because it terrified him.

She held him tight, accepting the desperation of his kiss, his frantic need, his shields, meeting each kiss with her own, of equal strength, equal passion, equal need. "I need you, too, Maddox," she whispered.

He broke the kiss and stared at her, searching her face. "Hannah—"

There was a loud knock on the front door, making them both jump.

Neither of them moved. They just kept staring at each other. Hannah's heart was pounding, and her cheeks were flushed with heat. Why had she just told him she loved him? Did she really need to have her heart completely broken right now?

Maddox ran his finger along her cheek, as he had done so many times in the past few days. "I will treasure you forever, Hannah. You and Ava have given me something so beautiful that I didn't even know existed."

"You're still leaving?" She didn't need to ask. As soon as he'd started reading the letter from Beth, she'd known he was going to leave. Beth's accusations had become embedded on his soul, and she knew the resulting scars would never leave, no matter how much she offered of herself, and no matter how much she loved him. And yet a part of her had hoped that he would step into the sliver of sunlight she was offering him.

He nodded. "I'll stay for the snowball fight, and then I have to hit the road." He sighed, searching her face.

She nodded. "I know." She did know. And she also knew that as much as she loved Maddox, and she did, that she needed him to love her right back, and so did Ava. Simply staying there, but not loving them, wouldn't be enough. Maddox had taught her about love. She wasn't afraid anymore, but at the same time, he'd awakened a longing in her for love, real love, the kind of love that would battle through any obstacle, no matter what.

Maddox couldn't go there...or rather, he wouldn't. He could. Anyone could. But he wouldn't. And she needed that from him, and so did Ava.

Which meant he wasn't right for them...but if that was so, why did everything feel so good when he was with her?

Chapter 19

MADDOX LOVED HIS family, but he had never wanted them to disappear more than he did right then. He wasn't finished with Hannah. He had more to say. He wanted her to say more. He just didn't know what it was that he was searching for, what words he wanted to hear, what words he wanted to say. It was so close, almost accessible to him, but he couldn't quite find it.

And no one was giving him time to find out.

A cheerful knock sounded on the door again, Lissa's voice echoed through the door. "Hey, guys! I have food!"

Maddox's irritation faded immediately. Lissa was bringing them food. Damn, she was thoughtful.

Hannah glanced toward the door, and Maddox saw the surprise on her face at Lissa's comment. "Food? Why did she bring food?"

Maddox smiled, his heart softening at the confused expression on Hannah's face. "Because you have been officially inducted into the Stockton circle of protection. That includes food, especially pies." The fact that Lissa had brought Hannah food struck deep inside Maddox.

When he left, his family would make sure she was taken care of. He didn't need to do it. She didn't need him.

Hannah didn't need him anymore.

That truth sat like a weight on his chest.

They'd needed him for the last few days, but now? His family would take care of them. They weren't alone. They were safe and protected.

He had no excuse to stay.

Hannah glanced toward the door, a look of stark, vulnerable longing on her face. "Really?"

"Yeah, really. You've got your posse now, sweetheart." He stepped back, forcing himself to release her. "Go let her in. She's got to be freezing out there."

Hannah didn't move for a moment. She just looked at him. Maddox managed a grin. "We can talk again before I leave. Go ahead." He kissed her quickly. "Go!"

A grin flashed across her face, a heart-melting grin of pure joy, and then she ran across the room and opened the door. Maddox stepped back into the shadows, watching as Lissa bound into the room, sweeping Hannah up in a bear hug worthy of long-lost sisters. To his surprise, his throat tightened as he watched Lissa unload several casseroles into Hannah's arms, and then grab some pie boxes that she'd set on the floor.

Hannah was smiling. Lissa looked happy. It was a perfect moment...the kind of moment he'd once dreamed of being a part of. The kind of moment he had to keep himself far away from.

Why was he the way he was? Why the hell couldn't he walk into that life, like Chase and his other brothers had? Why wasn't there a path for him into that life?

Chase appeared in the doorway, and his gaze went straight to Maddox, somehow finding him, even in the shadows. He whistled low under his breath. "You got it bad, bro, don't you?"

Maddox looked at his brother, the one who had lived through the same hell that he had. Chase had actually been the one to kill their father, but he'd done it to save the life of their youngest brother, Travis. It had been self-defense, not an assassination. "How do you do it?" he asked, as the women headed into the kitchen with the food. "How do you not let the monster inside you win?"

Chase stomped the snow off his boots, and then walked in. "There's no monster inside any of us, Maddox. It's just shadows from Dad. Let the old stories go."

"No monster? I wish." God, he wished. He realized that he really did wish that. For years, he'd convinced himself that he didn't care. That it didn't matter. That it was fine that his job was to haul assholes back to jail, not to sit around at family dinners. But now, it was a lie. He wished like hell that he was someone else.

Chase hung his jacket up by the door, and walked across the small living room, coming to a stop in front of Maddox. "Listen to me, bro. Dad was a bastard. He's dead. When he died, he took all of himself with him. All that's left is who we are. The shadows inside you are just shadows. They're not him."

Maddox silently handed him the letter from Beth. Before today, he'd never shared it with anyone, ever. He'd been too ashamed of what he was. Now, he needed them to know.

Chase frowned, but he took the creased paper without question. He unfolded it and silently read it. Maddox waited, his muscles taut as he watched Chase read. His brother read to the end, and then swore under his breath. He looked at Maddox. "This is how you define yourself? Because of her?"

"Did I really kick him?" Maddox had never asked what had happened that day, even though Chase had been there and pulled him off.

"Come on, Maddox. Dad had just punched the woman you loved in the face. The fact you attacked him made you a hero, not a monster."

He wanted to know. "Did I kick him after he was already down? After he couldn't hurt her anymore?" He *had* to know. "Did I scream like a crazed fucker?"

Chase sighed and crumpled the letter in a ball. He tossed it on the coffee table, then faced Maddox. "I was the one who killed him. You remember that, right? I *killed* him."

"You killed him in defense of Travis. A fight that got out of control. You didn't stab him in cold blood after he was already unconscious." As he spoke, Maddox's gut sank. Chase's avoidance of the question was enough of an answer. He *had* kicked his dad when the old man was down. He had beat the hell out of him when he was already down. He had screamed like a fucking lunatic.

He suddenly felt exhausted. Beyond exhausted. Like he needed to sit down before he collapsed. His head started to pound, and he felt sick to his stomach as the truth settled onto him. "As long as I never showed you that letter, there was a chance Beth was exaggerating. There was a chance she wasn't telling the truth. There was a chance I wasn't that bad." He looked at his brother. "But seeing your face as you read it...it all happened like she said, didn't it?"

Chase swore again. "Tell me, Maddox. Do you think I'm a monster for killing him?"

"No." Maddox didn't hesitate. "It was the only way to stop him from killing Travis. But I'd already stopped him when I attacked him, so it's not the same."

"Fuck that, Maddox! It is the same!"

Maddox had no idea how Chase could believe that. "How? How the hell is it the same?"

"Both you and I faced a situation where he attacked

someone we loved, who was defenseless. We both carried scars from his abuse, and we both knew exactly what he was likely to do if we didn't stop him and protect Travis and Beth. We both knew the truth, Maddox. The fucking *truth*. We weren't making this shit up, bro. We *lived* it. So, hell yeah, we took him down. It's our job and our duty to protect those who can't protect themselves."

Maddox stared numbly at his brother, still reeling from the truth that he was exactly what Beth had described. "If I was a hero, why did Beth call me a monster? Why didn't she throw herself in my arms, thanking me for saving her life, and calling me her hero? Because she didn't."

"Hey!" Chase interrupted him, an edge to his voice. "Fuck Beth."

Maddox stiffened. "Shut the hell up—"

"No, I'm not going to shut up." Chase glared at him. "Who cares if she couldn't handle you? That's her problem, not yours. Yeah, none of us are well-adjusted choirboys. Who the hell cares? We're loyal, we work our asses off, and we stand by those we care about, no matter what. I'm proud to be a Stockton, and I'm proud to be your brother." He held up his hand as Maddox started to argue. "Yeah, we don't fit in mainstream society. Yeah, you're not a fit for a minister's daughter who wants to believe the world revolves around church potlucks and swear jars. Who the hell cares? The world already has plenty of uptight pretty boys who don't know how to throw themselves into life and live, for real. We don't need to be that."

Maddox stared at him. "I'm not saying I want to be a choirboy—"

"Yes, you are. If you're letting Beth's opinion define you, then that's exactly what you're saying. The truth is, bro, we're fucked up, yeah, but all it takes is the right woman to love the hell out of us despite all the crap, and then all that bullshit we're saddled with just fades away." Chase's face softened, as it always did when he talked about his wife. "Find the woman who loves you exactly as you are, bro. And from the way you were looking at Hannah, it looks like you found her."

Hannah. Just hearing her name made Maddox's gut clench. He shook his head. "I don't want to be who I am. I don't need a woman to love me as I am, because who I am will eventually destroy her. I want to get rid of the curse of who I am. That's what I want."

Chase swore. "Come on, Maddox, you aren't cursed—"

"How do I get rid of it, Chase?" He searched his brother's face. He'd seen Chase with his wife and infant son. His brother had become soft in a way that Maddox had always believed he could be...until that night with Beth. But Chase had found a way. "You don't worry about killing anyone now. How do you get rid of it?"

Chase sighed and ran his hand through his hair. "Love, I guess."

Maddox frowned. "Love? Love is what made me go after Dad in the first place. Love is what gave him the power to destroy my mom. Love makes it worse."

"Not the right kind of love."

Maddox sighed. "Talking with you is like chasing my own tail. Forget it." He grabbed the wadded ball off the table. "I have to go have a snowball fight. I'll see you later."

He didn't wait for Chase's reply. He had to get out of there. He had to get out of the living room, and the entire house.

Because when Chase had said that maybe Hannah was the one he'd been looking for, something deep inside his soul had agreed.

Chapter 20

T HE DAY WAS magical.

Hannah had never felt as happy as she felt in this moment, stomping the snow off her frozen feet, laughing at the sight of Maddox dancing around the living room, trying to get the snow out from the back of his shirt that Ava had slipped in there when he'd sat down to take off his boots.

At one point, Hannah had never thought that she would hear Ava laugh again, and yet now the little girl was laughing so hard she had fallen down onto the floor and rolled onto her side clutching her stomach. It was the kind of heartfelt, uncontrolled, belly-deep laughter that only a child could do, the child that Ava had once been.

She felt a trickle on her cheek, and absently wiped her fingers across it, surprised when she found that she was crying. Not from sadness, but from absolute contentment and joy. The snowball fight with Maddox and Ava had been more fun than she had had in forever, pure laugh-out-loud hilarity. She couldn't remember the last time she had laughed like that, and Maddox's laugh had been so warm and engaging that her heart had melted just a little bit more.

Chase and Lissa had left several hours ago, and the sun was beginning to set. The day was almost over, and her heart couldn't stop remembering that Maddox was planning to leave at the end of the day.

She sighed as she watched Maddox begin to build a fire in the wood stove, explaining what he was doing to Ava, even as he made her stand far back out of range. Hannah took a deep breath and watched him. She really, really watched him, trying to see the man beneath the tenderness and the humor.

Was there really someone in there that she was supposed to be afraid of? Was she a fool not to believe him? Because she knew that if he ever showed any kind of violence, even anger, against her or Ava, neither of them would ever recover. They were both so fragile when it came to men, the kind of fragile that would shatter with a touch lighter than a butterfly's wings.

Maddox looked up at her, and his smile faded. Pain flashed across his face, the kind of deep, personal anguish that made her heart tighten. She knew in that moment, that no matter how happy he ever was, his past would always be a part of him. He would always be a man who had grown up with violence.

Was she really the one to save him? Beth, a minister's daughter, had been so traumatized by that night that she'd tried to shut him out of her life forever. Was Hannah so much braver than that? Was Ava? Or was it Maddox's darkness that made them feel so safe, because they both knew that he was strong enough to protect them if bad things ever came calling?

She didn't know. But what she did know is that she could never, ever take a chance with Ava. She had to make the right choice for that little girl, regardless of what she wanted. But knowing what to do for Ava was impossible, because there was no doubt that Maddox was awakening her personality again in a way that nothing else had. Would he also be the trigger to something worse?

Dammit.

Hannah wished she knew what to do. All she knew was that her heart wanted him to stay, but Katie's heart was what had made her go back over to that apartment when she wasn't supposed to. But was she really so much smarter than her sister? Did she know so much more about who to love, and who not to love?

She didn't know. How would she know? How would she ever know whether her heart was right?

She felt Ava tugging on her hand, and she looked down at her daughter. "What's up, pumpkin?"

Ava rubbed her belly.

Hannah managed a smile. "Ready for dinner?" At Ava's nod, Hannah looked over at Maddox. He was watching them with a wistful smile on his face. It was a smile that said he knew this was one of the last moments he would have to watch them. "Will you stay for dinner?" She asked, trying to keep her voice cheerful, trying to keep the tears out of it.

He hesitated. "I should probably hit the road. The roads are still going to be tough, and it's going take a long time to get home."

Ava let go of Hannah's hand, and ran across the room to Maddox. She threw her arms around his neck and buried her face in his shoulder. Tears burned Hannah's throat and she had to look away as Maddox's arm went around the little girl. Dear God. Why was it so hard to know what to do? "I'll just whip up something quickly. It will be faster for you to eat here than to try to find a place to eat on your way."

Before he could answer, she darted past him into the kitchen, being careful to close the door behind her. She reached the counter and leaned on it, her fingertips digging into the old wood. She took a deep breath, and then another one, fighting against the tears. The thought of Maddox walking out the door was so painful that her chest hurt. How would Ava be able to handle it? But even as she thought about Ava, she knew that it wasn't simply her daughter who would be upset.

A part of her would break into a million little pieces the moment that Maddox walked out of their lives. She didn't know how she became so dependent on him so quickly, especially since she was so afraid of men. But the truth was, he lit her up in a way that she'd never felt before. And it wasn't simply that he made her feel good because of how wonderfully he treated her. He also made her feel safe enough to be herself. She wasn't the best cook, and he had been fine with that. He had done most of the cooking, and also the cleaning. Nothing about her bothered him, and she knew that he wasn't faking it. He truly accepted her the way she was, and she knew that nothing she did would ever chase him away.

The only thing that would chase him away was himself.

She took a deep breath, and saw his phone sitting by the counter. When he left, he would be taking their only lifeline to the outside world. She would have to get a new phone on Monday, but the closest drive to a phone store was almost two hours away. Wi-Fi wouldn't get installed for another two weeks.

Sighing, she picked up his phone and unlocked it, using the password that he'd freely given her on their first night, so that she could check her messages from his phone. There had been no messages, nothing, because she had left behind everything that mattered to her. Her job. Her friends. But still, maybe someone would call.

She dialed her voicemail, then frowned when she found she had two messages. Something inside her eased, at the reminder that there were other things in her life besides Maddox. That she had an existence and identity outside this tiny little house, in this microscopic world that the storm had forced them into.

She tensed, when she heard the first message was from a phone number she knew, one from Western Oregon. She took a deep breath as she waited for it to play. Within moments she heard the familiar sound of Brody's voice. "Hey, Hannah. It's Brody. Can you call me back? When I hadn't heard from you or Katie in so long, I got worried. I Googled you guys." At his words, tears burned in Hannah's eyes, because she realized what he was going to say. "I'm so sorry, Hannah. I'm so sorry about Katie. Please call me back. I want to be here for you and Ava. Come stay at the ranch with us. We have plenty of space. You don't need to stay forever, but we're always here for you. All of us. Hang on." There was a moment of silence, and then she heard the whisper of voices.

Then, to her surprise, someone else came on the line, someone she hadn't spoken to since the day she had left so long ago. "Hannah? It's Elle. I'm so sorry about Katie. I can't believe you've been going through this all by yourself. We miss you so much. We think about you every day. Please come back home. We're here for you."

Hannah leaned the phone against her forehead, tears trickling down her cheeks. God, how long had it been since she had talked to Elle? Elle had been only a couple months older than Hannah, but she'd been like a big sister to her, making her laugh, despite the toughness of their situation. Elle, who had been so passionate and so vivacious, a brilliant and effervescent personality no matter how depressing their situation had felt.

There was another shuffle, and then someone else came on the line. "Hey, Shorty. It's Keegan." The image of Keegan's brilliant green eyes, and dark brown hair flashed through her mind. Even at sixteen, Keegan's shoulders had been wide, and his muscles had been defined. He was the one who always carried the others when they were too tired and too worn out to keep going. He had always been the physical strength of the group, always willing to do whatever it took to help the others out when things had gotten too tough. "That completely sucks about Katie. What happened? We saw the news today that the guy who killed her was acquitted today."

Hannah sucked in her breath. Acquitted? Rick had been acquitted? A cold sweat broke out on her forehead, and she sank to her knees, gripping the phone. She'd left town after she'd testified, before the trial had ended, but she'd had no doubts that he'd be convicted for at least voluntary manslaughter, if not murder. How had a jury decided he was innocent? *God, Katie, I'm so sorry. I failed you.*

"That's bullshit, and we all know it," Keegan continued, his voice hard. "You doing okay? The article said you testified against him. The guy sounds like a psychopath, and we're concerned that he's going to come after you. Call us. Either you come to us, or we'll come to you, but there's no way we're letting that piece of shit take you, too. You're our sister, Shorty, and you always will be. Call us."

The air left Hannah's lungs. Dear God. Would Rick come after her? That hadn't even occurred to her. But as the thought settled in her mind, she thought of the way he'd stared at her in the courtroom with such hatred. Did he hate her enough to come after her?

Brody came back on the phone. "Hey, Hannah. Call me back. No messing around this time. We need to hear from you. It doesn't matter what time it is when you get this message. I'll be waiting. We love you. Bye."

He hung up, but Hannah didn't move. She just sat on the floor, trying to breathe. She felt like the room was closing in on her. Rick had been acquitted. Hearing Keegan's voice, and Elle's. So many things to try to process, and it was too much—

Her voicemail began to play the next message. It was Justine Smith, her old boss. Hannah sighed and closed her eyes, dreading another plea for her to give up on her Wyoming plans and come back. "Hannah! God. Why aren't you answering your phone?"

Hannah bolted upright at the tension in Justine's voice.

"Listen, Rick was acquitted today. Less than an hour later, he was at the office, looking for you. God, Hannah, he was cold. He scared the crap out of me. That man's evil. But it was bad. There was a temp receptionist on duty, and he talked her into giving him your new address. I got out there too late. I called the cops, but they said there was nothing they could do, because he was acquitted. I saw the look in his eyes, Hannah. He's coming for you. Please call me back."

The phone slipped out of Hannah's fingers, and suddenly she was back in that hospital room with Katie. She could see those bruises on her throat. The black eye. Her broken nose. Her hands went to her own throat, and sudden panic hit her. Dear God. Rick was coming for her.

She had to get Ava out of there. They had to leave. They had to run. They had to—

"Hannah?" Maddox's voice broke through her fear and she shot a terrified look at him.

He was standing in the doorway, Ava in his arms. The moment he saw her face, he swore. His entire body changed, shifting from relaxed to rigid with tension.

"Ava," he said gently, not taking his gaze off Hannah's face. "Can you go in the other room for a second? I need to talk to your mom."

But Ava didn't let go of him. She was also staring at Hannah, her eyes wide, her face ashen. Her arms tightened around Maddox's neck, her fingers gripping tightly, her eyes wide as she stared at Hannah.

Dear God. *Ava.* Where would they go? Where could they hide? Where—

"Hannah." Maddox walked into the kitchen and crouched in front of her. "What happened?"

She looked at Ava, who looked terrified, and then shook her head at Maddox. "Nothing. Everything's great. I just...was trying to remember my recipe for meatloaf."

His eyebrows shot up, then his gaze slid to his phone, which was resting on the floor at her feet. Understanding dawned on his face. "You checked your voicemail?"

She nodded once, managing a smile. "Yes, just a call from my old boss." She grinned at Ava. "She wants me to come back to work for her, but I told her we liked snowball fights, don't we, pumpkin?"

But Ava just stared at her, her eyes wide, her arms still tight around Maddox's neck, not believing her. God, she'd thought that look was gone from Ava's eyes, but it was back, as much as it had been before they moved. She shot a desperate look at Maddox.

Maddox picked up the phone, and she saw that the call was still active. He noticed as well, and silently moved the phone toward his hip. "How about we show your mom how to make the Stockton mac and cheese, since that's Alfred's favorite. You can show her the special Stockton recipe."

Ava's face lit up, and she loosened her grip on him just enough for him to slide her into Hannah's arms. "What do we have for cheese in the fridge? Can you check, Ava? I need to check the wood stove, and then I'll be right back." He gave Hannah a long look, then stood up and strode out of the room with his phone, pulling the door shut behind him.

Hannah hugged Ava, fighting to slow her racing heart. Maddox would help her. Maddox would know what to do. It wasn't just them. She knew he wouldn't leave her, not right now. "Want to make macaroni and cheese, sweetie?"

Ava shook her head. She just stared at Hannah, and put two fingers on her chin. It was the sign they'd created for Ava to tell Hannah when she was scared. She hadn't used it at all since they'd arrived in Wyoming...until now.

Ava was too perceptive. There was no way to lie to her and tell her that everything was okay. It wasn't, and Ava knew it. Hannah mustered a smile, though, and set Ava on her lap so she was facing her. "I know you're scared, baby, but Maddox is here. He's going to help us."

Ava shook her head and pointed to the front room.

"I know he said he was leaving. I don't think he's going to, though." Hannah hesitated. How much could she promise? "But if he has to leave, his brothers will help us. We're not alone anymore, pumpkin. We have help."

Ava put her fingers on her chin again.

"You want Maddox, don't you?"

Ava nodded.

"Me, too. But we'll find a way, I promise." She pulled Ava into her arms, hugging her tightly, while she started counting how many hours they had until the man who'd murdered her sister would show up at their house.

THE ANGER WAS back.

It was the same boiling anger that had surged over him when he'd seen his dad hit Beth, an anger that he had crushed ruthlessly for so long. And now...it was back...

And it was a thousand times fiercer.

Swearing silently, Maddox closed his eyes, his hand balling into a fist as he listened to Hannah's messages for a second time. Son of a bitch. His muscles twitched with the need to react, but he stayed still, utterly still.

For the third time in his life, a violent bastard was after someone he loved.

First, his mother.

Second, Beth.

Third...Hannah and Ava. Only this time, the *goal* of the bastard was to kill them.

For a split second, Maddox couldn't think. All he could see was Hannah and Ava, lying in that same casket that had taken his mother from him. "No!" He let out a roar of denial, then strode across the room, took a deep breath to make sure he stayed calm, and then opened the kitchen door.

Ava and Hannah were still sitting on the kitchen floor, their arms wrapped around each other. The relief at seeing them safe and unharmed was staggering, so overwhelming that he literally went down on his knees in front of them. Unable to speak, he wrapped his arms around them and pulled them both against him. Ava's arm snapped around his neck, and Hannah leaned into him. For a long moment, none of them said anything. He was aware of Ava's soft breathing against the side of his neck, and the tension in Hannah's body. He focused on the warmth of Hannah as she pressed her body against his, on the feeling of her, solid and alive.

It took several minutes before his heart stopped pounding, and the tension eased from his body. They were both safe. They were in his arms. And there was no threat to them, not right now. He took another deep breath, then pulled back slightly, enough that he could look at Hannah's face. Ava's arms were wrapped so tightly around his neck that there was no chance that he could pull away from her.

He met Hannah's gaze. "I'm staying."

The relief on her face was so tremendous that he felt his throat tighten. He had never had anyone look at him like he could save their world, but Hannah was looking at him that way right now. Her eyes glittered with unshed tears, and she nodded. "I was really hoping you would say that," she said. "I'm really not that good at asking for help, or even accepting help, but I really need it this time."

He sighed, feeling calmer now that she had agreed to let him stay. He slid his hand under her jaw and leaned forward, kissing her gently. "Sweetheart," he said. "There isn't a chance in hell I would walk away from you and Ava right now."

She nodded. "Thank you."

Ava pulled back then, and she searched his face, her vibrant blue eyes fastened to his as if he were the angel she'd been waiting for.

Maddox took her hands and folded them in his, looking right at her. "Ava, pumpkin, I know you're scared, but I'm really, really good at protecting people. I promise you that I will stay in this house, with you and your mom, for as long as it takes to make sure that you both are completely safe forever. Do you understand?"

Ava nodded, staring at him. She looked back at Hannah and made a gesture with her hand.

Maddox didn't understand the gesture, but Hannah glanced at him, and then back at her daughter. "Sweetie, Maddox and I have to talk about some things, before we tell you what's going on. But I promise you that we're all going to be okay, and that we're all safe." She leaned forward until her face was only inches from her daughter's. "I promise you that nothing is going to happen to me. Do you hear me? Nothing bad is going to happen to me. You aren't going to lose me. I promise."

Ava let go of Maddox and crawled onto Hannah's lap. She wrapped her arms around Hannah and pressed her face against Hannah's throat. Hannah hugged her tightly, so tightly that Maddox's throat ached. There was so much love between them, so much trust, so much need. There was no way in hell he was going to let any harm come to them, no matter what it took to keep them safe.

"I'm going to go in the other room and call Chase," he said to Hannah. "And I'm going to call the sheriff, Dane Wilson. I'd trust him with my life. I want to get some more information, and get some help. Okay?"

Hannah nodded. "We need to leave."

Maddox wasn't so sure about that. He'd seen people like Rick before. If the son of a bitch was willing to track her to Wyoming, he'd keep on looking until he found her, even if it took months. But Maddox had caught plenty of bastards in his life, and he was catching this one. "Maybe." He looked at Ava. "Pumpkin, I'm starving, and we both know your mom isn't the best cook. Do you think you can remember the ingredients for mac and cheese? Help her out while I call my brother? I thought I might invite him over for dinner." He winked at her. "Did you know Lissa has a daughter? She's a little older than you are, but she's super cool. Maybe she'd come over and hang out, too. Would you like that? And my brother Zane has two boys. The younger one is about your age. Maybe they can all come? Does that sound good to have some friends?"

Ava stared at him, then slowly nodded.

"Awesome. Let's start cooking. We'll need it. I have a big family." He glanced at Hannah. "Cool with you?"

"Do you really think you should bring everyone here?"

He thought about that for a minute. He'd been thinking that hosting a family dinner would create safety in numbers. Even a fool wouldn't attack with a houseful of people, but maybe Rick would. "You know, you're right. Let's go to Chase's for dinner. He's an amazing cook. Grab your boots, kiddo. It's cold out there."

Ava brightened, and she stood up and tugged on Hannah's hand. Hannah rose to her feet, managing a bright smile for the benefit of her daughter. "Maybe you should call ahead to tell them we're coming?"

Maddox nodded. "Trust me, I'm going to make a few calls."

He waited until Hannah and Ava were out of the room, then he made a quick call to Chase. He made another call to Dane, who agreed to meet at Chase's. Then he paused, debating. He knew Hannah would kill him. He also knew he'd never forgive himself if he didn't use every resource possible to keep her safe. After a long moment, he made a decision and dialed one more phone number.

A man answered on the first ring. "Brody here."

"Hey, Brody. My name's Maddox Stockton, and I'm calling about Hannah."

Chapter 21

HANNAH HAD NEVER felt so uncomfortable in her life. And, at the same time, she'd never felt so tantalizingly close to absolute peace...but that chasm was so large that her chest actually ached with yearning.

The gathering of the Stocktons in Chase's house was almost too much for her to handle...both because she ached so badly to be a part of that kind of family, and because she had absolutely no idea how to ever let herself get that close to people. Ever.

It was a cruel tease, showing her what she wanted, when she knew she was incapable of ever being a part of anything like that.

She was sitting on Chase's couch, tucked up against Maddox, his arm locked around her shoulder. Spread out around the room were his brother Zane, who looked seriously scary in his leather jacket and earring. Zane's wife, Taylor, however, looked insanely happy as she leaned against him, wearing jeans, pink fuzzy socks, and a hooded sweatshirt. Also present were Lissa, whose fiancé

Travis, was still out of town on tour. Hannah still couldn't believe that the country music superstar, Travis Turner, was Maddox's brother.

Chase was sitting on the couch, while his wife, Mira, sat on the floor playing with their toddler, JJ, who was immersed in assembling a miniature horse ranch on the carpet. Steen was leaning against the breakfast bar, his arms folded across his chest. His wife, Erin, was also leaning on the bar, standing just close enough to him that their shoulders were touching. Every man in the room had positioned himself just close enough to his wife to be able to touch her easily. Chase was sitting close to Lissa, and it was apparent that all of the brothers were watching out for her since Travis wasn't present. Dane Wilson, the sheriff, was also there, and it was clear from how the Stocktons treated him that he was family, just as how the Harts had all been family, despite not being biologically related.

The rest of the kids were playing in a newly built family room off the back of the house. She could see Lissa's lovely daughter, Bridgette, showing Ava how to play air hockey, while Steen and Taylor's boys, Toby and Luke, took them on. There was a lot of laughter, and a lot of teasing, and Ava was grinning widely. It was evident that playing with the other kids had completely taken Ava's mind off everything.

It made Hannah realize that she alone was not enough for Ava. Her daughter needed friends, and a community, and the Stocktons had welcomed both of them in with open arms.

It reminded her of her first night with the Harts. It had been raining and cold, and she and Katie had been hiding in an alley, trying to use a fire escape for shelter. Brody and Keegan had found them, and when Hannah had refused to go with two unknown boys, they had returned with Elle, who had convinced them that the boys would be their defenders, which they had.

Like the Harts back then, tonight, the Stocktons made Hannah feel safe, like she didn't have to face this all by herself. At the same time, she felt wildly out of place. All of these people were a family, and they clearly lived by that credo. She wasn't one of them, even though they were all sitting around talking about her problem as if she were.

So, yeah, she felt both more uncomfortable and happier than she'd felt in a long, long time.

Dane ended the call he was on. "Rick got on a plane at nine o'clock. He's scheduled to arrive just after midnight. It'll take him about four hours to drive to Rogue Valley from the airport, if he leaves right away."

Hannah let out a breath. "So he's really coming." She had been hoping that it had all been a false alarm, that he wouldn't make the effort to track her down, so hearing confirmation that he was on a plane, in the air, on his way to Rogue Valley made fear grip her spine.

Maddox tightened his arm around her. "We got this, sweetheart," he whispered. "You're not alone."

She nodded, too tense to answer.

"Yeah, he's coming," Dane said. "He's flying with a guy named Roger Cochran. You know him?"

"Roger?" Her skin went cold. "That's his older brother." She'd met Roger several times, and he had made her skin crawl, the way he'd looked at her, the way he'd held her hand too long when they'd shaken hands. The way he'd watched her with such cold cruelty during the trial had been completely unnerving, making her glad she'd been leaving town. She had no doubt that Roger had a string of crimes against women behind him, crimes that his family's money had hidden. And he was coming *with* Rick? "He's...God, he's terrifying."

Maddox pulled her closer. He pressed a kiss to her cheek, and leaned down so his lips were against her ear. "I promise we'll keep you both safe," he said firmly. "We're good at this."

Mira, Chase's wife, looked up from the floor. "Maddox is right," she said. "They all came to my defense when I needed them. I didn't even know them at the time. They were morally opposed to Chase getting tangled up with a woman, but they came rushing to my defense like a bunch of denim-wearing superheroes." Amusement flickered in her eyes, as the men groaned at her description. She winked at Hannah. "Fortunately, most of them have evolved to the point of realizing that falling madly in love with an awesome woman makes their lives better, not worse, right, Chase?"

"You got it, babe. You're my world." He bent over and gave her a tender kiss, clearly not the least bit reluctant to show affection in front of his brothers.

The affection on Chase's face was so genuine, so warm, and so beautiful, that Hannah's heart expanded simply by being in the vicinity of such love. She had caught an expression similar to that on Maddox's face a couple times when he'd been looking at her, but it had been so fleeting, chased away intentionally before he allowed himself to feel it.

She sighed and pulled her gaze back to Dane as he continued to talk. "I'll hang around the main road into town and watch for his arrival," he said.

Hannah knew what he wasn't saying. "You can't detain him, though, can you? Because he hasn't broken any law, right? He can just drive right past you to my house, and no one can stop him."

"Hey." Maddox took her hand. "Rick will make a mistake, and Dane will be there to catch him. We just need to create the opportunity."

"Create the opportunity?" she repeated, dread settling in her gut as she realized what he meant. "You want to *let* him get close?"

"Hell, no. He's not getting anywhere near you," Maddox snapped, his voice unyielding. "You and Ava will stay here with my brothers. They'll be ready in case somehow Rick figures out that you guys are here. More likely, he'll go to your place. I'll go to the house and wait for him."

She sat up, not liking that plan at all. "You'll wait for him alone? But he and Roger are together. They'll team up against you. That's not okay. "

At that moment, Maddox's cell phone rang. He answered it before she could see who was calling. "Maddox here." He paused for a second, listening, his gaze flicking toward Hannah with what almost looked like a guilty expression. "Great," he said. "You're all set on directions?" He paused. "Okay, see you in fifteen minutes."

He hung up the phone, and glanced at his brothers. "You guys ready?"

Chase nodded. "Ready."

Hannah frowned at Maddox. "Who's coming? Another one of your brothers?"

Chase swore under his breath. "Shit, Maddox. You didn't tell her?"

Maddox stood up, and took her hand. "Come on, Hannah. We need to talk for a moment."

"Talk?" Her heart started pounding as she rose to her feet. "What did you do?"

He said nothing as he led her out of the living room and down the hall to a guest bedroom. He walked inside, shut the door, and then turned to face her. Her stomach knotted when she saw the grim expression on his face. "What happened?" she whispered. "How could things be even worse than what they are? What didn't you tell me?"

He ran his hand through his hair, his gaze steady on hers. "When I listened to your messages, I knew we didn't have much time. I made some choices, choices that I should've asked you about first, but I thought you would say no. I didn't want to give you that chance, because I felt like I needed to do it. But in retrospect..." He grimaced. "I think I made a mistake not telling you first, even if I was going to do it anyway."

Hannah stared at him, her chest constricting. Here was the man she'd told she loved only a few hours ago. What had he done? She trusted him, she had trusted him not only with her heart, but with her daughter, and her body, and her dreams. But from the way he was talking, it felt like he was going to confess he'd done something terrible. "Tell me."

"I knew we had to get you and Ava out of the house. The only place I could think of taking you was Chase's house, but you need protection here as well, in case Rick figures out where you are."

She nodded slowly. "Yes, that makes sense."

He didn't look relieved by her agreement. "I needed a team to go with me to your house to lay a trap, but I wanted Chase, Steen, and Zane here with you. None of my other brothers could get here in time. There's no one else I trust. So, I made a call."

"You made a call?" She stared at him blankly, trying to understand who he had called, and why she would care... Then realization hit her. Reeling, she stepped back, her hands clutched to her heart. "You called Brody? You got his number from my messages, and you *called* him?"

Maddox nodded. "It turns out they have access to a private plane. They just landed at the local airport, which Dane had cleared by the town plows when I called him. They'll be at the house in a few minutes."

Hannah felt like she couldn't breathe. "I haven't seen them since I was eighteen years old," she whispered. "I told you that I left that part of my life behind. I haven't even called Brody back for months. I don't want to be a part of that!" Dear God. She had no idea what to say to him...Maddox's words suddenly flashed through her mind. He hadn't said "him." He'd said "they" were going to be at the house in a few minutes. "'*They*?' Who's coming? What do you mean by 'they?'"

"Brody is coming. He's also bringing Keegan, Jacob, and Lucas."

Hannah stared at him, her throat constricting as he named the boys from her past, the ones who'd wanted to be her brothers, who she had severed from her life when she had walked away. "You don't understand," she whispered. "They offered me the last name of Hart, and I said no. I said no, and I left with Katie. I rejected them, Maddox. They were all mad at me. Brody was the only one that kept in touch. I don't...I don't even know what to say to them. I haven't seen them or talked to them in ten years. How could you ask them to come? I owe them now. I—"

"You don't owe them anything. Their love is unconditional."

She bit her lip, tears swimming in her eyes. Guilt tore through her. How could they want to come save her when she'd ignored them for a decade? And how could she not talk to them when they showed up at Chase's house? "I don't know what to say to them," she whispered. "I don't know how to act."

Maddox swore. "I'm sorry. I knew how you felt, but I couldn't take a chance with your life. I had to do it."

"Maybe you feel you had to do it, but did you have to do it without telling me? Was that part so important to you as well?" Tears filled her eyes and she wrapped her arms around herself, a cold ache settling in her gut. "I know you have your family, Maddox. I sat there in that living room, and I saw how much they love and support each other. The Harts are like that, too. *But I'm not.* Don't you understand? *I'm not like that.*"

Maddox sighed. "Sweetheart, you have a tremendous heart. You don't need to do anything. Just let people love you. That's all it takes. You can do that—"

"I can't!" She balled her fists in frustration "I don't know how to be a part of a family like that. I don't know how to trust a bunch of people with my safety." She stared at him, unable to keep the accusation out of her voice. "You're the only one that I've trusted in my whole life besides my sister and my mom. That's it, Maddox. That's all. I don't have the capacity to open myself up to all these people. They're going to walk in this house, and they're going to want explanations. And I'm going to have to admit to them how completely damaged I am." She stumbled back, barely able to breathe. "Damn you, Maddox! How could you do that?"

"Hannah, I'm sorry—"

"No!" Tears burned her eyes, and she spun away, fumbling for the door. She would grab Ava and they would leave. They would just get in the truck and drive and—

Maddox braced his palm on the door above her head, holding it shut. "Hannah."

"Damn you." She spun around and faced him, slamming her hands into his chest. "You're right, Maddox. I shouldn't have trusted you. I thought that you saw me as a human being, not as some pawn for you to exercise your badass masculine protector persona." She couldn't keep her voice from breaking. "But I'm not, am I? I'm just...I'm just—" God, she didn't even know what she was to him.

"Hey." Maddox felt like his heart was being sawed in half as he watched the tears glisten on Hannah's cheeks. He felt that darkness surge inside him, that deep, self-hate of who he was. He knew she was right. He was an autocratic asshole. "I'm sorry."

She stared at him. "No, you're not. I can see it in your face."

He swore under his breath. "I'm sorry that I upset you, but yeah, I'm not sorry that I called them. I'll do whatever it takes to make sure you're safe, including taking action that makes you hate me."

She closed her eyes, refusing to look at him, a cut that burned so deeply he could barely breathe. "Hate you? You want me to hate you?" She opened her eyes. "Is that why you did it? To drive me away? To convince me not to love you?"

"Shit, no—" But he stopped. Maybe he had. Maybe she was exactly right. He had gotten what he wanted: Hannah finally seeing him for what he was. It was what he had been trying to get her to see since the first moment they had met, but now that he had accomplished it, it felt like absolute shit. "Hannah." He kept his voice low and tight. "You don't need to say a word to them. I'll meet them outside, and we'll go to the house. But before we do, I want you to know something."

She opened her eyes and looked at him, but there was so much hurt in her eyes that he wanted to scream, to shout, to punch something. Son of a bitch. All he had wanted to do was protect her and Ava, but he had broken her heart, the same way his dad had broken his mom's heart. He had never believed that he would ever strike her, or any other woman, let alone one that he loved. What he *had* believed was that he would destroy her soul, that he would strip from her that which gave her meaning, that which gave her a reason to live. He had seen it with his mom, he had seen it with Beth, and now he saw it in Hannah's eyes.

His legs suddenly felt weak, and he wanted to sink to his knees, bow his head, and ask her for forgiveness. "I…" He had to stop and clear the hoarseness from his throat. "There is no way in hell that I could let anything happen to you and Ava. I knew you would be pissed when I called Brody, but I also knew that I would rather go to hell for eternity than to make a choice that resulted in that bastard so much as breathing on you."

Hannah pressed her lips together, but she didn't take her gaze off him.

He knew he had to go, so that he could catch the Harts outside, before they entered the building. But he couldn't go until he said one more thing, until he told her that one thing. "After we take care of Rick, I'm going to turn him over to Dane, and I'm going to leave town from there. Dane will come back and get you, and tell you that it's safe. So this is my goodbye."

Unlike when he had been leaving her house before, there was no sadness in her eyes at the mention of him leaving. She just stared at him, her face so impassive that he wanted to beg her to say something, anything. Except he didn't really want her to talk. He knew he couldn't handle the words coming out of her mouth that would be like the ones Beth had written to him. "I know I betrayed you in the same way I betrayed Beth. I played the role of the good guy for the last few days, but in truth I'm not. I broke your confidence when I called Brody. But, here's the truth…" He paused, replaying the words that he had been about to say. He had been about to tell her that he'd done it because he loved her, because loving someone turned him into a monster, the kind of monster that would rip out her heart. He wanted her to walk out of there, understanding that there was at least one person in this world who loved her in an absolutely pure and beautiful way.

But the words wouldn't come. All he could think of was Beth's reaction, and how she was disgusted by the thought of him loving her.

He didn't want to make Hannah's life worse by telling her that he loved her.

So instead, he sighed. "You will always have a home here with Chase, Lissa, and the rest of my family. They'll take care of you. You're an incredible woman, Hannah. Your kid is amazing, and she's going to be okay. I'll deflect the Harts, and you won't have to talk to them. And you won't have to deal with me again either. I promise you that I'll stay out of your way." He knew that when he walked out, he wouldn't return. If Hannah became friends with his brothers and their wives, he didn't want to ruin that for her by showing up from time to time. "I give you my family."

Then, before he could say anything else to make things worse, he reached past her, opened the door, and walked outside.

Chapter 22

HANNAH STOOD STOCK still as Maddox closed the door behind him. She could barely breathe. Her head was spinning, and her heart ached. *I give you my family.*

He wasn't coming back. Not only to her house, but to his brother's ranch.

She thought of how Lissa's face had lit up when he had walked in the café. She remembered how Lissa had said how much they all wanted him to move onto the ranch. She recalled so clearly his protectiveness of Lissa. The love he and his brothers had for each other was so evident in every interaction they had, including the discussions in the living room about how to protect her and Ava.

And he was going to walk away from all of that, because his brothers had taken her into their circle of protection, and he didn't want to interfere in her ability to move forward.

Tears filled her eyes, and a gaping sense of loss seemed to crush down upon her. She was the one who didn't want a family. She was the one who didn't know how to relate to a whole bunch of people wanting to be close to her. And yet he was the one that was going to walk away from it all for her.

There was only one reason he would do that.

He loved her.

He loved her.

Dear God. He didn't just love her in some superficial, shallow way. He loved her so much that he was planning to walk away from what little goodness he had in his life, on the slight chance that it would make her happy.

Maddox.

She heard a car door slam outside, and she raced to the window. The inside light reflected on the window, making it impossible for her to see what was going on outside, so she ran back to the door, flipped the light switch off, and then hurried back to the window.

It was dark outside, but the spotlight above the front door cast a warm, yellowish glow on the driveway. Her heart seemed to stop as she saw Maddox jog down the stairs, wearing his parka, his cowboy hat, and his heavy gloves. He looked strong, confident, and dangerous. She couldn't take her eyes off him as he walked over to the men climbing out of a large, black pickup truck that had Stockton Ranch written on the side.

She realized that Maddox must have arranged for the truck to be waiting at the airport for the Harts when they arrived. She kept her gaze on Maddox, unwilling to look at the other men standing there, the men who had been boys the last time she'd seen them. Looking at them would make her think of a time when she was a victim, when she was lost, when she had a little sister to take care of, a sister she would never hug again.

Maddox shook hands with them, and she could hear the low rumble of their voices. What would they say when Maddox told them she wouldn't see them? God, she felt so stupid, hiding in that room while they talked outside.

The conversation went on for several minutes, and she kept her gaze riveted on Maddox, needing to see his face, knowing it would be the last time she would ever see him. God. To never see Maddox again? Somehow, after his declaration that he was giving her his family, she couldn't find the anger and betrayal that had gripped her so tightly when he had first said that he'd called the Harts.

There was a burst of laughter, and her heart catapulted at the sound of Brody's laugh. Instinctively, her gaze leapt to the man facing Maddox. The world seemed to stand still as her gaze settled on the face of the boy who'd been her salvation that night in that dark, rainy alley.

She gripped the windowsill, her face pressed against the glass as she stared at Brody. He was taller than he had once been. His shoulders were so much wider. He held himself with the fierce arrogance of a man who knew his strength and his power. There was nothing small or tentative about him. He was pure strength, pure man. But his face, God, his familiar face. She'd recognize him anywhere.

His jaw was more angular than it had once been. There were the heavy shadows of thick whiskers lining his jaw. He was pure man, but at the same time, he looked exactly as he had when he was seventeen. She couldn't see the color of his eyes from where she was, but she could picture the exact shade of green, like the color of moss on a rainy spring day. His nose was still slightly crooked, as it had been way back then, from some accident that he had never explained. His hair was even the same length, just long enough to curl over the back of his collar, that same light brown that had always reminded her of the puppy that she had tried to get her mom to let her keep when it had followed her home one day when she was ten.

She remembered the way he'd made Katie laugh, when her sister had been so scared that she couldn't stop crying. He had made Katie smile, and for that, Hannah had always loved him.

But now Katie was dead, and she was the one crying.

"Brody." She whispered his name, unable to keep the tears from drifting down her cheeks. Her gaze slipped from him to the others, all of whom had become men, but who were the same as the boys she had once known.

Keegan, with his dark hair and dark eyes. Jacob, who had made her laugh so many times. And Lucas, who had fought the hardest to convince her not to leave. God, *Lucas.* She'd been so close to him. They'd sat up for hours under the bridge, talking when everyone else had gone to bed.

She pressed her hand to the windowpane, as if she could reach out and touch them...but she had no idea how. She hadn't known how to connect with them when she'd lived with them. And now? They were strangers.

Strangers who had dropped everything to fly to Wyoming to help her. Why? Why had they done that? Why were the Stocktons gathered in the living room to protect her and Ava? Why was Maddox willing to give up his family for her? She didn't understand why everyone had come together to help her and Ava. Why would they do that?

The Harts turned back to the truck and got in. Hannah gripped the windowsill tighter, her heart pounding as the men who had once saved her life disappeared from sight.

Maddox swung into the passenger seat, and a small cry of protest escaped from her throat. "No! Don't leave!"

Maddox paused, staring straight at the window, and

she realized he had known the whole time that she was there. He stared at her for a long moment. Her fingers pressed into the glass, as if she could reach through it and touch him.

He gave her a brief nod, then climbed inside and shut the door. The sound of the door closing made her jump, and she stayed glued to the window as she watched the pickup truck do a three-point turn, and then head back down the snowy driveway, carrying five men she loved away from her.

Forever.

To face a murderer on her behalf.

While she stood in that room by herself, shutting out everyone who was trying to help her.

Silently, she leaned her forehead against the glass, unable to stop the tears from sliding down her cheeks. What was wrong with her? Why was she so unable to reach out to all these people who wanted to help her? What was so broken inside her that she chose to stand alone in the darkness, instead of in the light with the Harts, with the Stocktons...with Maddox.

He loved her.

He loved her, and she'd told him that he'd betrayed her by doing whatever it took to keep her safe?

Dear God. She'd treated him just like Beth had, seeing his love as a sign of something being wrong with him, exactly as he saw himself.

She closed her eyes, suddenly feeling more alone than she had in her whole life. Katie gone. Her mom gone. Ava in the other room, lighting up in a way that Hannah hadn't been able to do herself. The Harts, so close and already gone. Maddox, gone. All she'd had to do was open her hands and reach out and they all would have taken her hand...but her hands were fisted in tight balls by her sides, trapping her.

So, here she stood. Alone in the darkness. Hiding while everyone else took care of her problems. Maddox and the Harts facing a man who wanted to kill her. The Stocktons making Ava feel safe. She stood there alone, just as she'd stood there alone when Katie had gone off to meet Rick, just as she'd stood there alone when her mom had gone off in the car with her drunk boyfriend. She'd run from Boston. She'd run from her job, from the memories, from the past, from her own guilt...

She'd spent her life on the outside, trying to protect her heart by staying isolated and alone, and yet, despite all of that, her heart hurt more than it ever had in her life.

Chapter 23

SEVERAL HOURS LATER, Hannah sat at the end of the couch, her arms wrapped around her belly, a soft blanket over her lap. It was after midnight, and all the kids were in sleeping bags, watching a Disney movie she had seen way too many times.

Everyone was camping out in the family room for the night. Chase had decided that he could protect everyone best if they were in the same room, and no one had argued. The mood was tense, because Dane's contact from the airport hadn't been able to locate Rick or his brother. They'd been on board when the plane had landed, but no one had been able to track them since.

Where was he? On his way? Passed out drunk in the airplane bathroom?

Nausea churned in Hannah's belly as she thought of Maddox and the Harts sitting in her house, holding themselves out as bait to the man who had already murdered her sister. She saw Ava glance her way, and she managed to smile. Ava smiled back, then returned her focus to Bridgette, Lissa's daughter, who was lying next to her, and had instantly become Ava's idol.

The couch moved as Lissa sat down next to her. "They look like they're best friends already."

Hannah shifted uncomfortably, but there was no way to move away from Lissa without making it obvious. "Ava needs a friend. It's beautiful to see them together."

"Seems like her mom needs one as well."

Hannah's cheeks heated up, and she suddenly felt like the pathetic loser she'd been as a kid, the one she had fought so hard not to be anymore. "I'm fine, thanks."

Lissa sighed. "Hannah. It's not a crime to need help. It's not a crime to need friends. It's also not a crime to admit that you're barely hanging on by a thread."

Hannah stiffened, and didn't take her eyes off the children. "I know it's not a crime."

"Do you? Do you really?"

There was something in Lissa's voice that drew Hannah's attention. Slowly, almost painfully, she pulled her gaze off the kids and looked over at the woman sitting beside her. Lissa smiled right away, a warm, kind smile that made Hannah's heart tighten. "You remind me of Katie," Hannah whispered. "She was always so nice to everybody. She had more friends than anyone I had ever met in my life."

Lissa raised her brows. "Remember how I told you that I got pregnant when I was seventeen? My boyfriend ditched me, my sister had already died in a drunk driving accident, and my mom had had such a miserable life. No one even wanted me in the same room as them for fear that I would contaminate them and ruin their lives forever."

Hannah's eyebrows shot up, because she heard the ring of truth in Lissa's words. "Really?"

Lissa nodded. "I left town when I was seventeen and pregnant, because the town basically exiled me. I had absolutely nobody, and I was about to become a mom. It was the absolute lowest time in my life, so I know what it's like to feel alone, lost, and have no idea how to ask for help. I know what it's like not to believe that anyone would actually hold out a hand to me, and that it would be offered in genuine kindness, with the honest hope that I would reach out and take it."

Tears suddenly flooded Hannah's eyes, and she pulled her gaze away, fixing her attention on a blank spot on the wall across the room. "I'm sorry you had to go through that," she said softly. "It sucks."

"Yes, it does."

Lissa didn't say anything else as silence settled between them. Hannah shifted restlessly, uncomfortable with the silence, needing to fill it. "Are you happy now?" As she asked the question, she snuck a sidelong glance at Lissa. She knew that Lissa had seemed happy, but somehow, she needed to hear it from her. She needed to hear that somebody who had once been completely alone, without any family, had truly found her way out of that darkness into light.

Lissa's face lit up. "Every single day I wake up with a smile in my heart. I'm engaged to the most amazing man, who loves me and my daughter with every last bit of his soul. I'm part of his extended family, who would do absolutely anything for me or my daughter, no matter what the cost to them. It is the most beautiful thing to be part of this community. I didn't even know what it meant to have a family, until I met Travis and became part of the Stockton clan."

Envy flickered through Hannah, a deep, painful yearning, not only for the family that Lissa had, but for the ability to embrace it and let it into her heart. That envy was quickly followed by a slash of guilt, because she knew that Maddox wasn't coming back, and his family would be deprived of him because of her. "I have to tell you something."

Lissa's eyebrows went up, and she nodded. "You're in love with Maddox, right? I knew it."

Hannah's mouth dropped open. "What? I didn't say—"

"You didn't have to say anything." Lissa beamed at her. "He so needs you in his life. I never thought he would let himself fall in love, but when I saw the way he kissed you when you guys were sitting on the couch, I knew that it had happened. I'm so happy for you both. I love watching him with Ava. He loves your little girl the same way Travis loves mine. I'll tell you, the Stocktons make the best dads—"

"Stop it!" Longing shot through Hannah, a longing so intense she could barely breathe. She'd seen Maddox with Ava as well, and she knew exactly what kind of a dad he would be. "He doesn't believe in himself," she said. "And I made it worse. He called the Harts, and I got mad. He's not coming back, Lissa. He wants to give his family to me, and he's not coming back."

Lissa frowned, and sat up. "Slow down. Explain to me exactly what happened."

The story quickly poured out of Hannah, faster than she would've expected. She wasn't used to confiding in anyone, but this woman who was so kind, who had come from such a dark place, who somehow understood where she was, asked just the right questions, with no judgment, only caring. Sentence after sentence tumbled out, until Hannah was crying, barely able to explain everything that had happened over the last few days between her and Maddox. By the time she finished, Lissa was hugging her, holding her as tightly as she used to hold Katie when they were little.

"Hey, hey, hey." Lissa's voice was gentle, not judging. "It's not your fault, sweetie. It takes a lot to get one of these Stockton men over their past enough for them to be willing to take a chance on a woman. The fact he was willing to walk away from his brothers tells me exactly how much he loves you."

Hannah nodded, exhausted from crying. "I know he does, and I thought that I could get him to give me a chance, but I blew it when I got mad at him. I said things that I can never fix."

Lissa laughed softly. "Of course you can fix them. But, I agree, that it's not going to be easy to make Maddox come around. I don't know what to tell you."

"I do." They both looked up to find Chase standing over them. He was frowning, his brow furrowed.

Lissa glared at him. "How long have you been listening?"

"As soon as Hannah started crying, I came over." Chase looked at her, empathy on his face. "It's not easy to love a Stockton. Maddox is especially difficult. He's got a lot of baggage."

Hannah shrugged. "I know that. And I made it worse." She looked at Chase. "He's not coming back to the ranch. It's my fault. I know you just want your brother around, and I drove him away."

Chase sighed and sat down on the coffee table, bracing his forearms on his quads. "You didn't drive him away. He just used you as an excuse to do what he's been planning to do for a long time. He told me how you've shut out the Harts. It's the exact same thing he's done to us."

The couch on the other side of Lissa shifted, and Mira sat down. She smiled at Lissa. "Chase has worked hard to get Maddox more involved with the family for years, but he won't do it. He only comes back into town for brief visits, and he only stays as long as he needs to get something done. I don't think he was just giving his family to you. I think he was giving you to us. I think he figured by giving us something he loved, that it was almost the same thing as if he stayed with us."

Hannah looked around at the three people gazing at her, their faces full of kindness, warmth, and understanding. There was a complete lack of judgment on their faces. They weren't blaming her for Maddox's decision, and they also weren't blaming Maddox either. "But I drove him away."

"Because he was falling in love with you," Chase said. "That's scary as hell to all of us." He grinned at Mira. "Scared the hell out of me when I fell in love with you."

She smiled. "I remember." She looked at Hannah. "The only reason Chase stayed was because he had made a promise he couldn't break. Otherwise, he would have left." She leaned forward. "Maddox believes he's a monster, Hannah. You're the only one who can prove to him he's not."

Hannah looked around at the small gathering. "How? I told him I loved him—" Her throat tightened, and she had to pause to gather herself. "And he was still going to leave. And then, I told him..." She didn't even want to say the words again. "I was hurt and scared to see the Harts," she whispered. "I struck out at him because I was terrified."

"And the bastard used that as an excuse to walk away." Chase sighed, his voice understanding. He pulled out his phone and handed it to Hannah. "Call him. Tell him that you love him. Tell him to stop the bullshit and come back here."

Hannah stared at the phone, her heart pounding. Could she really do that? Could she really just call Maddox and tell him that she loved him? What about the Harts? What about them?

Chase's phone suddenly rang, startling her. She jumped when she saw Maddox's name flash across the screen. Frozen, she stared at the screen, afraid to answer it. Lissa grabbed the phone, answered it, and then held it out to her. "Talk to him. He won't ever come back on his own. You have to reach across the chasm to get him."

Hannah closed her eyes and took a deep breath. What was she supposed to say to him? Give him the same speech she'd already given him so many times, about how she believed in him? How many more times was she supposed to say the same thing, and get rejected? She shook her head. Her heart ached, but she knew she couldn't do it. "No. I can't."

Lissa sighed in frustration, and hit the speaker on the phone. "Hey, Maddox. What's going on over there?"

There was a long silence, too long. Chills suddenly crept down Hannah's spine, and she looked sharply at Lissa, who was frowning.

Then a voice came on the line, a voice that made fear grip her chest. "Put Hannah on the phone."

Rick. Fear gripped her so tightly she couldn't breathe. God, she remembered that voice, that chilling voice as he'd threatened her when he'd passed her in the court-room after her testimony. Why did he have Maddox's phone? *Maddox.* Her heart thundering in terror, she snatched the phone from Lissa. "Rick?"

Lissa sucked in her breath, and Mira leapt off the couch, racing across the room to get Chase, who had walked off to talk to Steen.

Hannah just sat there, gripping the phone so tightly her hand cramped.

"Get the fuck over here or your boyfriend dies."

She swallowed, her mouth so dry she could barely talk. "Over where?" she whispered hoarsely. "Where are you?"

"At your fucking house. You sent your boyfriend and four other assholes to take care of your problem? Well, guess what? They are now your problem. If you don't get your ass over here in twenty minutes, I'm going to start shooting them."

Hannah went cold. "Rick, don't—"

Chase crouched beside her, bending his head to speak into the phone. "Put Maddox on the phone."

"Sure." There was a scuffling sound, and then Hannah heard a grunt of pain. Then she heard Maddox's voice.

"Keep Hannah away from here—"

There was the sound of a fist hitting something, and then Maddox grunted.

Hannah gasped. "Maddox—"

"He's not available at the moment." Rick came back on the line. "Twenty minutes, Hannah. If you bring anyone else, they will all die, and you can blame yourself. If the cops show up, they die. But you are all I want, so if you get over here, I won't hurt them. Twenty minutes, bitch." Then the phone went dead.

The only sound in the room was the television blaring. The kids were oblivious, watching the movie, but the adults were all staring at her. Hannah handed the phone back to Chase. "I'll go."

"Fuck that." Chase shook his head. "No way. We're all going—"

"And then what? Maddox and my brothers were waiting for him, and he still took them all by surprise. There were five of them, and there are only three of you. What if you leave here, and he comes after the kids?" She shook her head. "No. No. *No.* This is my problem—"

"No way." Chase's voice was low and hard. "There's no chance that we're leaving Maddox to handle this on his own." He grabbed his phone and called Dane, talking low and quickly.

But Hannah knew there was no other way to save Maddox and the Harts. Rick wanted her. *Her.* Maddox's only chance was if she showed up there. But Rick wanted to kill her. How could she walk in there?

She pictured herself walking into that cabin, into Rick's trap. Into a cabin that held five men she loved dearly, men who meant everything to her, a realization she'd understood too late, so achingly late.

Five men who had grown up rough and rugged, surviving against odds that no one could defeat...except them. Men she believed in. *Men she believed in.*

She suddenly stood up, shooting a quick smile at Ava as she walked over to Chase, who was still on the phone. "Give me the phone."

He raised his brows, but silently handed her the phone. She immediately hung up on Dane, and called Maddox's phone back.

As she expected, Rick answered the phone. She didn't wait for the threat from him. "Let me talk to Brody."

"You're wasting time, bitch."

A chill ran down her spine at the threat in his words. "You said you wanted me, right? You're going to get me, but I need to make sure that everyone I care about is still alive when I get there. You know that I want to see you hang, and if I think you've already killed everybody, then I'm not coming. Let me talk to Brody." She was taking a chance, but she would never forget the pure venom in Rick's eyes as he glared at her across the courtroom. He would not want to let her go.

After a moment, the voice of the man she'd always considered her brother, even though she hadn't let him take that claim came on the phone. "Hey, Shorty. Long time no talk."

Tears filled her eyes at the sound of the voice she

hadn't acknowledged in so long. "What's the color?" It was the same question that the gang of teenage runaways had set up so long ago as part of their escape plans if things went bad. Red meant walk away. Red meant it didn't matter how great the loss was, it didn't matter how many things were at stake, because all that was left was survival. Red meant the only choice was to leave everything behind.

Green meant, obviously, all clear. Dance in the streets. Sing songs.

Yellow was the one she was hoping for. Yellow meant that shit had hit the fan, but there was still a chance. Maddox would tell her to walk away. Maddox would want to protect her completely, which was why he had shut her out from his own life.

The Harts had a different code. The Harts believed that every single one of them was worth saving. The Harts believed that there was always a chance as long as there was at least one of them still on the outside, still breathing the air of freedom, still available to figure out a way. No one was sacrificed, not on the inside, not on the outside. Everyone protected everyone, which meant that Brody saw her as an ally, not a weak female who couldn't fend for herself. If Brody thought it would be suicide for her to walk in there, he would give her the red light. But if there was an opening, he would take it, and he would tell her to take it, too.

He answered easily. "It's sunshine all the way, baby."

She closed her eyes, gripping the phone. *Yellow.* "What do I do?" she whispered.

"It's a full house—"

Before he could finish, Rick was back on the phone. "Get your ass over here, Hannah. I start shooting off body parts in nineteen minutes."

Her hands were shaking now, but she kept her voice

calm. "I'm leaving now, but I can't drive fast because of the snow. I need thirty minutes."

"Where are you? I'll send my brother to come get you."

Hannah looked around the room full of people she didn't want to endanger. "No. Thirty minutes or it's over." He didn't know where she was. He had to wait for her to tell him. She knew she had the upper hand, and she was going to use it...just like little Alfred had done to save Fluffy. He'd found his strength, and suddenly, for the first time in her life, she felt strong, too.

Rick snarled, but she knew she would win. His need for revenge was too unrelenting. "Fine, thirty minutes, but if you call again, or if you're late, I start shooting."

He hung up, and she took a deep breath. She handed the phone to Chase. "I got Dane thirty minutes. Tell him to save the men I love. I'm going to the bathroom." She turned away and walked down the hall toward the room she'd been in with Maddox.

She shut the door, walked over to the window, and hoisted the sash. The snow was deep, too freaking deep. For a moment, she hesitated. Then she thought of Katie, of Maddox, of the Harts, of Ava, and she knew that she was done hiding, done running away, done being afraid.

Maybe Maddox's story about Alfred and Fluffy had been for her, not Ava.

She climbed up onto the windowsill, scooched out on her bum, then dropped down into the snow. The snow came almost to her waist, an icy cold landing that sucked the air from her lungs. It took several precious minutes to flounder out of the snow into the plowed driveway, but once she was free, she raced across the driveway to Maddox's truck and opened the door.

The keys were still in the ignition, exactly as he'd left them. Her heart pounding, she swung up into the truck, slammed the door shut, and started the engine. She waited for a split second, expecting the Stocktons to come rushing out the front door, but nothing happened.

She realized the movie was playing too loudly, drowning out the noise from the truck's engine. Whispering a prayer of thanks, she shifted into drive and swung the truck around in a circle, and then headed down the driveway.

She left the headlights off until she had rounded the bend, and then she turned on the headlights, and hit the accelerator.

Chapter 24

MADDOX WANTED BLOOD.

Rick's blood.

The blood of the man who had murdered the sister of the woman he loved.

The blood of the man who wanted to kill the woman he loved.

He lowered his head, watching Rick pace restlessly, his heavy boots treading the same floor that Ava and Hannah had slept on that first night, when he had pulled the mattress out for them.

Maddox was barely aware of the blood trickling down his temple. He didn't care that his right arm was barely working. Every single part of his body and mind was focused on the man pacing back and forth.

Rick had to die. From the conversations between Rick and his brother, it was clear that Katie wasn't the first woman to fall victim to his temper. Their family's money had saved his name three times, but Hannah's testimony had damaged Rick's reputation.

He wanted revenge, and his brother was there to help

him get it.

Well, fuck that. Maddox wanted revenge, too, and he wasn't the one who had been born into silver spoons, silk sheets, and luxury vehicles. He was dirt, scum, violence, and death. All the things that were born to make revenge happen.

"Shit, Maddox," Brody muttered, under his breath. "The expression on your face makes you look like one scary bastard right now."

"I am one scary bastard," Maddox responded. "I never thought it would come in handy. Glad to know I was wrong." He hoped Chase had understood his message not to send help, when he had said not to let Hannah near the place. Yeah, he might have a concussion, and he might be handcuffed to Brody, but there was no chance that Rick was going to walk out of there alive.

Maddox didn't need help. He didn't want help.

He was going to take Rick down. If it had to be in cold blood, then fine. He was built for that, wasn't he?

Brody grunted as he tried to sit up, but he, too, had been hit in the head with a shovel and knocked unconscious long enough to be dragged in the house and handcuffed. His other three brothers hadn't woken up yet.

Maddox and the Harts had been prepared for an asshole who beat up women. They hadn't been prepared for two former military who had laid a well-planned assault on the house, which is why Rick and his brother had gotten the jump on them.

But they knew now, which meant the element of surprise was no longer on the table. What was on the table were five badasses who had survived hell when they were teenagers, who knew only how to fight dirty, hit hard, and fight until there was only one left standing.

Maddox had recognized kin in the Harts from the first moment he'd seen them. He'd already known they were intensely loyal based on how Hannah had described them. He'd figured they were scrappy survivors, willing to get their knuckles bloody in defense of those they loved. What he hadn't expected was that every single one of them carried the same shadow of darkness that he lived under. He didn't know what story each of them had, but he knew it was ugly, the kind of ugly that either broke a man, or turned him into a damned gladiator.

The Harts had all turned into gladiators, and Maddox planned to use that to his advantage.

"I don't like Rick," Brody said conversationally. "I don't really want to sit down and have a beer with him. You?"

Maddox looked over at the man. "I don't really have a sense of humor in situations like this."

"That's okay. I don't mind laughing at my own jokes. Sort of empowering." He was watching Rick pace just as carefully as Maddox was. "Where's the brother? Roger, right? Got any ideas?"

"He set up outside again. He'll be looking for anyone to show up, which is why I told my brother not to send anyone."

"He'll see Hannah when she gets here," Brody said.

A chill went through Maddox at the thought of Hannah facing Rick. "No way in hell is my brother going to let Hannah come here."

Brody looked over at him, and cocked an eyebrow. "You really think your brother could stop Hannah from coming? The man she loves is in danger. And not to toot my own horn, but we used to be pretty tight, too. I think she'd come just for me, but I know for an absolute fact she's coming for you."

Maddox stared at him, suddenly unable to breathe. "You told her to come here? Are you shitting me?"

Brody gave him a steady stare. "Do you really think

I'd endanger her?"

"But you told her to come!"

"Because we'll be all done by the time she gets here. It was the only way I could think of to make her come over here." Brody gave Maddox a steady gaze. "Hannah has been through hell. She doesn't trust anyone. She never even trusted us. I've never met anyone as skittish as she is, but I can tell from what you've told me, that she trusts you. Your plan to walk away from her after this is over is complete bullshit. You don't break the heart of a woman like Hannah when she's given it to you. She's coming over here, and you're going to stop that martyrdom shit. She's coming here because she loves you, and you sent her away because you love her. That's about the crappiest love story I've ever heard. So, when she gets here, change the story. Got it?"

Maddox stared at Brody. "Love story? Are you kidding me?"

"Hell, no. I'm a total romantic. Love is good, my friend. Plus, Hannah's my sister, and if you are what her heart needs to heal, then I'm going to interfere." He looked across the room at Rick, who was now by the window, watching the driveway. "So, I'm guessing we have about four minutes until Hannah gets here. Should we act now, or wait until the last second?"

Maddox stared at him. "What's your problem? This isn't a joke."

"Nope. It's not." Brody was still watching Rick. "My mom was killed by a man like him." His voice was low, suddenly ice cold. "I told you I don't like him."

Maddox looked sharply at Brody, his gaze narrowing when he saw the hardness on the other man's face. Son of a bitch. Brody was as dangerous as he was. He grinned. "Let's do this," he said.

"Hell, yeah. Now."

The two men lurched to their feet simultaneously, moving as one out of necessity, due to the fact their hands were handcuffed behind their backs together. They charged across the room, moving with lightning speed, reaching Rick before he could turn around. They slammed their shoulders into his back, crushing him against the wall.

Rick shouted a warning to his brother, but it took only two more quick hits before he was down and unconscious. Maddox dropped to his knees, searching for the key to the handcuffs. He could hear footsteps thudding outside, and he knew Roger was on his way.

He found the keys, jerked them out of Rick's pocket, and jammed them into the handcuffs. He unlocked the ones binding him to Brody, but the door swung open before he could get out of the second set that was locking his wrists behind his back. Brody hit first, using his full body weight to shove Roger out the door. Both Brody and Roger disappeared from sight, and Maddox lunged to his feet, making it to the door just as they rolled down the steps and landed in the driveway.

Maddox charged after them as Roger lunged to his feet and pointed a gun at Brody, who was still on the ground. "No!" Maddox launched himself off the steps and tackled Roger, knocking him to the ground just as the gun went off.

Sharp pain slashed Maddox's calf, and he knew he'd been grazed by the bullet. He stumbled, trying to keep his balance, but his momentum was too strong, and his balance was off due to his injuries and the fact that his arms were still handcuffed behind his back. He hit the ground hard, and rolled sideways fast, as another bullet exploded in the snow, right where he had been.

Brody lashed out with his feet, slamming his boots into Roger's ankle, knocking him off balance. Roger staggered, just enough for Maddox to leap up and shoulder slam him again. Roger was fast and wiry, but Maddox had the bulk and the range, and sent him flying.

As Roger sailed through the air, he pulled out his gun, and aimed it at Brody. Maddox shouted a warning, and Brody rolled to the side, but his body jerked at the same moment the gun fired.

Brody was hit.

Fury exploded through Maddox, and he lunged to his feet. He sprinted across the driveway to where Roger was scrambling to his feet. He slammed his knee into the other man's gut, launching him sideways. He was just rearing back for another hit when headlights flashed over him. He froze as his truck came to a skidding halt and Hannah leapt out of it.

Dear God. *Hannah had come.*

He froze, aware of the blood dripping down his forehead and his leg. He was aware of his right arm hanging uselessly in the handcuffs. Brody was on the ground, bleeding from his side, and Roger was also down, groaning.

It was just like the scene Beth had encountered, only worse, because there was so much blood.

Hannah stood there in the glow from the headlights, her mouth open as she stared at Maddox, her gaze going to Brody, and then to Roger. He knew what she was seeing. He knew the carnage that was sinking into her brain. He knew the damage and ugliness that was seeping into her, all because of him.

Maddox tensed, bracing himself for the inevitable, for that moment when it finally registered on Hannah exactly what he was...that moment when the look on her face shattered his heart.

Chapter 25

S UDDENLY, HANNAH SCREAMED, a scream that reverberated in Maddox's brain the way Beth's had for so many years after that night. The minute he heard Hannah scream, something inside him shut down, broke, fragmented into a thousand pieces. He couldn't move. He couldn't think. It was his worst nightmare—

"Maddox! Behind you!" Hannah pointed, a look of horror on her face.

Suddenly, it registered. The scream wasn't because of what he had done. The scream was because of something that was behind him... And there was only one thing behind him.

He whirled around as Rick staggered out of the cabin, a gun pointed right at Maddox.

"One move, and you die." But Rick wasn't looking at Maddox. The gun may have been pointed at him, but the bastard was staring at Hannah, a look of such depraved satisfaction on his face, that Maddox's blood went cold. He realized suddenly that he was wrong, that he had been wrong his whole life.

His dad hadn't been a monster. His dad had been a fucked-up loser who wouldn't hesitate to use his fists on his kids, and suck the life out of Maddox's mom. But he'd done it because he was too screwed up to do anything else.

But the man staring at Hannah right now was different, so different. The depraved greed in his eyes, the pure evil leaching from his smile, the smug satisfaction of knowing he was going to hurt the incredible woman standing in front of him, was so different than anything Maddox had ever seen on the face of his father.

His father had been a bastard.

Rick was pure evil.

Stunned, Maddox finally realized what Hannah had meant when she'd told him that she knew what real monsters were, and that he wasn't one of them. He knew, because for the first time in his life, he was staring into the eyes of a creature that was truly evil.

Rick limped down the steps, the gun still pointed at Maddox. "Get back in the truck, Hannah. We're going for a ride."

Hannah's gaze flicked to Maddox, and then to the side, where Brody and Roger both lay. Maddox knew that Rick would not take that gun off him until they had driven out of sight. He also knew there was no way for him to get to Rick before he could get a shot off.

He risked a glance to his side, and he saw Brody was still down. His chest was moving, and Maddox knew he was still alive, but he would be of no help. Roger was groaning, and he knew Roger would be up in a moment.

It was up to him. Only him. And there was only one way he could do it.

He had to go all out. One strike was all he would have. He would have to harness all his strength. He'd have to show Hannah what he was truly capable of.

He met her gaze, and she smiled at him. *Smiled.* His heart froze, and then suddenly, it began to beat. She loved him. She saw the blood. She saw the carnage, and she still loved him.

Suddenly, the weight of a thousand nightmares lifted from his shoulders. With a crow of victory, he launched himself at Rick. The monster swung fast, and pulled the trigger, but before the sound had even finished echoing, Maddox hit him. They landed hard, and Maddox slammed his knee into the bastard's throat, leaving him gasping as he rolled off him and leapt to his feet, spinning around to check on Rick's brother.

Roger was reaching for his gun. He rolled onto his back, taking aim as Maddox reached him.

He kicked the gun out of Roger's hands and then incapacitated him with a swift kick that left a satisfying crunch. Blood spewed out on the snow, just as it had so many years ago. He looked at the brothers, both of them unconscious, disarmed, and helpless...and he stopped. He didn't kick them. He didn't keep going. They were taken out, unable to hurt his woman, and he didn't want to hurt them anymore. He blinked, stunned by the revelation, but before he could process it, Hannah was racing across the driveway toward him, shouting his name, her arms outstretched. The woman he loved was running *toward* him, instead of away.

Toward.

Maddox braced himself as she threw her arms around his neck and flung herself at him, burying her face against his chest. Maddox bent his head, pressing his face against hers, breathing her scent, her warmth, her love. With his hands still behind his back, he couldn't hold her. All he could do was stand there as she held onto him.

"God, Maddox, don't ever get shot again, okay?" She

pulled back, tears streaming down her face. "Don't you dare tell me you don't love me, okay? I can't take it. I really can't." She gripped his shirt, staring up at him, tears staining her cheeks. "We need you. Don't you understand? We all need you. Me, Ava, your brothers. Everyone."

Maddox stared down at her, at the love burning in her eyes. There was blood on her shirt, and she was trembling from the cold, or the shock, or some combination, but there was no mistaking the expression on her face.

She'd seen his truth. She'd watched it. And yet, she was still standing there, loving him.

In that moment, the shackles that had trapped him his entire life suddenly dissolved. Just like that. One moment there. The next moment, gone. He took a deep breath, a breath deeper than any he'd ever taken in his life. "You see me," he said softly. "I can tell you do."

"Of course I do." She gripped his shirt. "I've seen you the whole time. You're the one who hasn't seen you." She searched his face. "What do you see now when you look at yourself, Maddox?"

He smiled. "I see a man who loves the most amazing woman, and her daughter."

The smile that lit up her face made him want to get down on his knees in surrender. "You love me?" she whispered.

"Of course I do. How could I not?" He bent his head and kissed her, the most tender, most gentle kiss he could deliver, needing to kiss her, needing that physical connection of beauty.

It was a long moment before he broke the kiss, but he barely pulled back, searching her face. "You're really not freaked by what you saw me do?"

She laughed softly. "Maddox, you saved my life, and Brody's. How could I be scared of you?" She tugged on

240

his shirt. "Ava and I need strength in our lives, Maddox. We need your strength, as well as your gentleness. Come home to us, Maddox. Please?"

He grinned. "Are you going to make me live on the ranch with my brothers?"

"Fuck that." Brody's voice drifted through the night. "She has to come live on my ranch. Mine's bigger. Nicer."

Hannah's heart tightened at the sound of her brother's voice. Slowly, she turned around, to see Brody lying on the ground, a stain spreading on his side. "Brody," she whispered. There were so many things to say. To apologize for not calling him back. To thank him for coming. To tell him about Katie. But only three words came out. "I love you," she whispered.

He grinned, his jaw tight against the pain. "Of course you do. Just because you blew us off for a decade doesn't change anything." He grimaced. "I love you, too, Shorty. We all do."

Maddox gave her a gentle nudge. "Make sure he's not dying. I'm going to get the keys to the handcuffs, and call Dane."

Hannah was afraid to move, so uncertain how to act with Brody. Maddox bent over and brushed a kiss over the side of her neck. "It's okay, sweetheart. Just follow your heart. Go say hi."

She stood there for another moment, waiting while Maddox dragged Roger and Rick further away, dumping them by the house after ensuring they were truly incapacitated, then he jogged inside to get the keys to the handcuffs, until it was only her and Brody in the driveway.

She swallowed hard, then made herself walk over to him. He was on his back, his eyes closed, breathing heavily. Silently, she knelt beside him, her knees cold in the snowy driveway. "Brody?"

Maddox came back outside, his handcuffs dangling from his hand. He snapped a pair on Roger, and then did the same for Rick. "The others are waking up," he told her. "I took off their handcuffs. Everyone's okay."

Relief rushed through her, but before she could respond, Brody's eyes opened, and flickered toward her. They were the same beautiful green as they had once been, so familiar that her heart turned over. "Brody," she whispered, unable to keep her voice from breaking.

"Hey, Shorty," he said, smiling at her. "I missed you. We all did."

Tears filled her eyes as Maddox crouched behind Brody and unfastened his handcuffs. The moment her brother was free, he held up his arms to her, the same way he had when she had said goodbye ten years ago, to head to Boston with Katie.

Unlike a decade ago, this time she didn't hesitate. She leaned forward into his embrace, hugging him tightly. His body was hard and muscular, padded with strength, unlike the scrawny, undernourished teenage boy she had left behind. Tears filled her eyes as his warmth poured into her, a reassuring strength that she had rejected for so long.

She felt Maddox's hand rubbing her lower back, and she smiled, her heart expanding. She pulled back, grinning at Brody as she leaned against Maddox, needing the contact with the man she loved. "Thank you for coming, Brody," she said. "I can't believe you came."

Brody raised his eyebrows at her. "Really? You can't believe we came? You lived with us for a year. How could it possibly surprise you that we would fly out here on a moment's notice when some asshole was on his way to kill you?"

She laughed softly, and inclined her head in acknowledgment. "Okay, I guess I knew you would come."

Her amusement faded, replaced by embarrassment and discomfort. "I didn't know how to reach out to you, Brody. I'm so sorry." As she spoke, Maddox wrapped his arms around her, anchoring her against his chest. She took a deep breath, allowing herself to melt into his strength.

Brody smiled. "Shorty, we accept you exactly as you are, and you don't have to do anything to earn it. Even if it took you fifty years to come back to the family, that would still be okay. Once a Hart, always a Hart."

She smiled. "I was never a Hart. I kept my own name."

"Just because your last name wasn't Hart doesn't mean you weren't one of us." Jacob spoke from the porch, and she looked up, her heart leaping as she looked into the face of one of the brothers she had tried to reject for so long.

"Jacob," she whispered, her heart aching as she said it.

He came down the steps, holding out his arms. She rose to her feet, and suddenly she was running toward him, her arms outstretched. She threw herself into his arms, and laughed as he swung her around, just as he had done so long ago. The next thing she knew, Keegan and Lucas walked out of the cabin, both limping, but grinning widely. They swept her up in a group hug, embracing her so tightly she felt like she would never be able to breathe again...which was okay with her.

She couldn't stop from crying, and when she pulled back, she saw that they were all crying too. "God, you guys are so emotional," she teased.

"Family matters," Keegan said. "You know it does." He ruffled her hair, and then looked over at Brody, who was stretched out on the driveway. He had crossed his ankles, clasped his hands behind his head, and was studying the sky, as if he were camping out for an evening of star-gazing, instead of lying on a snowy driveway, bleeding from a gunshot wound. "You good, Brody?"

"I could use an ambulance, if anyone cares to call one, but other than that, yep, I'm good." He looked at Hannah. "Actually, I'm great."

Maddox walked up behind Hannah and slipped his arms around her waist, resting his chin on her shoulder. With a sigh, she leaned back against him, a deep sense of peace settling in her as she listened to Maddox tease her brothers about how long they'd been unconscious. Brody chimed in from his spot in the driveway, but even as everyone was laughing and teasing, Lucas and Keegan were already at work wrapping Brody's wound and wrapping him in blankets, treating him with the same vigilant care that they always treated each other.

Humor, teasing, and absolute loyalty to each other.

How could she not have felt their love before? How could she have been so unable to feel their support?

Maddox pressed a kiss to her cheek. "Sweetheart," he whispered. "I love you, but if you ever race into a fight scene involving a gun and a murderer again, I'm going to be incredibly pissed. Please don't do it again."

"I promise, as long as you promise not to get handcuffed by a murderer."

He grinned. "Deal. Seal it with a kiss?"

"Of course." She smiled, and she realized she knew exactly why she was finally able to feel the love from her family. It was because of Maddox. He had taught her to trust, to love, and to be strong. She turned in his arms and slid her arms around his neck, beaming up at him. "I'm so sorry that I got mad at you for calling them."

He shrugged. "You should have gotten mad at me. I knew you would. I did it anyway."

She cocked her head. "Is that going to happen a lot?

You doing something that you know I won't like, and doing it anyway?"

"If it keeps you safe, yeah." He sighed, and ran his fingers through her hair. "It's who I am, Hannah. I—"

She put her finger over his lips, silencing him. "I know who you are, Maddox, and I love you. Unconditionally. Forever. Without reservation."

He searched her face, and then smiled, a breathtaking smile of such joy and such love that it filled her with the most beautiful sense of rightness. There was beauty shining out of Maddox's face, the beauty that she'd always known was inside him, that he had finally allowed to surface.

He framed her face with his hands. "I love you, Hannah. I love you and that amazing daughter of yours. If you'll have me, I'll stand by you both forever. I'll make sure you're safe every second of every day, so that you both can learn to laugh, to play, and to feel free again."

Her smiled widened. "If I'll have you? What are you asking?"

"I'm asking for forever, sweetheart. I can't go less than all in. I'm not capable of it." He searched her face. "I need you, Hannah. I can't go back to who I was before I met you. All my shields are gone. All my defenses have vanished. I need you in order to breathe. Say you'll be mine, forever."

She smiled. "I'll—"

"Don't answer him," Brody interrupted.

Maddox groaned. "Shut the hell up, Brody."

"No." Brody limped over to her, one arm over each of Lucas and Keegan's shoulders. "Hannah, if the man wants forever, he's got to put a ring on your finger. No promises of forever unless he promises to marry you."

Hannah's heart stuttered. "Marry me? I'm not going to get married. I'm terrified of marriage."

Maddox groaned. "Here we go again..."

She glanced at him. "What does that mean?"

He hooked his arm around her and pulled her close, nuzzling her gently. "It means that I'm willing to do whatever it takes to earn your trust, until you are willing for forever to include two circles of gold. You were afraid of men, and now you trust me. Whatever it takes, however long it takes until you're ready to marry me, I'm in this for the long haul, sweetheart."

Tears filled her eyes. "I don't think I'll ever be ready for that—"

He wiped his thumb over her cheek, smiling gently. "I think you might be wrong about that." Then he bent his head and gave her such a tender, sweet kiss that she thought maybe, just maybe, he might be right.

Chapter 26

THE ENDLESS OREGON sky was breathtaking, the kind of breathtaking Hannah hadn't been able to feel or see before she'd met Maddox. Today? It filled her entire soul with pure beauty and joy, echoing through the deepest parts of her heart.

Hannah hugged her knees to her chest, riveted by the incredible array of pink, orange, and purple illuminating the evening sky across the Oregon high desert. She was sitting on top of a wide, flat rock that was almost twenty feet wide and ten feet high. She, Ava, and Maddox were in the final evening of two glorious months on the Hart ranch, becoming a part of the family she'd rejected for so long. All the rebellious, damaged teenagers who had once saved her had become the amazing, loving family she'd never known how to have.

She'd fallen in love with them all over again, a love that had filled her heart with joy and a sense of belonging and roots that she'd never had before. It had also, however, brought with it new tears, because she could see the shadows in the eyes of every Hart, and she knew that they were all still healing from their assorted pasts. They all needed the same kind of healing she had found with Maddox. She hoped they each would get their chance at the life they deserved, especially Brody, who had more weight in his eyes than all of them put together. She had a feeling he was almost irretrievably broken, and getting closer to the precipice with each day.

Despite the burdens they carried, each one of her seven brothers and two sisters had the most enormous hearts, an unbending sense of loyalty, and a shared sense of camaraderie that shone light into even the darkest of moments. She'd even gotten to see Wyatt Parker, who, like her, had lived with the Harts for a while, but never taken their last name. Wyatt owned a ranch in town with his new wife, Noelle, who Hannah had adored immediately.

The Harts had taken to Ava the same way they'd taken care of Hannah and Katie when they were young, and Ava had flourished under their attention. Even Maddox had been drawn into their family, tempted back into his cowboy roots by her brothers.

Tonight was their last night on the ranch before heading back to Wyoming. Hannah and Maddox had wanted to do something special for Ava, and Brody had directed them to Sunset Rock as the place to go. He'd told them it was the perfect spot on the Hart ranch for an evening picnic, followed by a gorgeous sunset, and capped off by a few hours of watching shooting stars.

They'd arrived in late afternoon, enjoyed an amazing feast, and some Frisbee. After dinner, Maddox and Ava had ridden off to a nearby stream to play in the water, while Hannah had relaxed, relishing every moment of her amazing life. She looked up at the sky, and smiled, somehow knowing that Katie was looking down on them, smiling. "I love you, sis. I wish you could be here with us." But even as she said it, she knew in her heart that Katie was there, filling them with love. There was still sadness that would never leave, but at the same time, Hannah felt a sense of peace and acceptance.

Life was beautiful. She was so grateful that she and Ava had been given a second chance to find a meaningful life, and find it they had. Life was beautiful. Love was beautiful. Family was beautiful.

A shriek of laughter echoed across the plains, and Hannah turned her head toward the sound. Ava and Maddox were racing toward her on their mounts, both of them laughing and waving their cowboy hats like they were chasing down bandits in the Old West.

The most amazing sense of rightness filled Hannah as she watched her daughter, and the man she loved gallivanting in the rays of the setting sun. Maddox moved with the horse as if he were one with the animal, a truly gifted rider. Ava was a little less graceful, but she was fearless and bold, waving her hot pink cowboy hat as if she were taking on the world.

Keegan had presented Marble to Ava as soon as they had stepped out of Maddox's truck onto the ranch. Ava had been thunderstruck when Keegan had handed her the lead line and told her that the adorable brown and white pony was hers forever. Then she'd walked up to Marble, put her nose against his, looked into his eyes, and started whispering to him.

The bond had been instant, and Marble was coming back home to Wyoming with them. Hannah was pretty certain that she was going to walk into Ava's bedroom one morning and find Marble curled up on the bed with her, both of them sound asleep.

She waved at her daughter. "Looking great, sweetheart!"

Ava waved back, holding both arms above her head,

giggling with laughter as they neared.

Hannah rested her chin on her knees as she watched Maddox and Ava rein in, and dismount. Ava handled her pony with confident ease, whispering to him, the same whispers she used to use with Alfred.

There was so much light and excitement in Ava's eyes nowadays, but still, no words. But Hannah knew they were coming soon. She had a feeling Ava was almost ready.

Maddox patted the rock. "Climb on up, pumpkin. It's time for dessert."

Ava scrambled up the side of the rock with ease, her cheeks flushed with excitement. She plopped down next to Hannah, and helped herself to one of the chocolate chip cookies that Keegan had made for her. Surprisingly, Keegan was a baker, and owned a bakery in town. He'd loved meeting Lissa when he'd been in Wyoming, and the two of them were already plotting an online gourmet bakery.

In a few moments, Maddox finished taking care of the horses, and then climbed up. He looked incredibly sexy in his cowboy hat and boots. He'd traded in his bounty hunting gig for the moment, helping the Harts with the horses. She'd seen light in his eyes that she hadn't seen before when he was working with the horses, and she knew he'd found his way back to what he loved as well. He had already told Chase he'd help out on the ranch when they were back in Wyoming, and she had a feeling that they'd be settling down on the Stockton property before too long.

He sat down next to her and put his arm around her. "Gorgeous evening, isn't it?"

Hannah nodded. "It's so beautiful. I've had the best time here. I can't believe we're going back to Wyoming tomorrow."

Maddox was quiet for a moment. "Do you want to stay here?"

"Stay here?" She looked at him, startled by his comment. "But your family is in Wyoming."

He shrugged. "I like it here, too. Besides, the Stocktons are your family, too. The Harts have made it pretty clear that I'm in with them, so we both have family in both places." He winked at her. "Seems like getting you to love me is the secret ticket to being one of them, which is awesome, because I love your family."

Her heart tightened at his words. "I love them, too," she admitted, words she had never been able to acknowledge, let alone articulate, until Maddox had taught her about love.

"They love Ava, too." He looked over his shoulder. "Ava, sweetheart? What do you think? Do you want to live in Wyoming with the Stocktons, or in Oregon with the Harts?"

She held up two fingers, and both Hannah and Maddox laughed. "You want both?" he asked.

Ava nodded, chocolate chip cookie crumbs decorating her cheeks.

Hannah smiled, and rested her head against Maddox's shoulder. "I want both, too," she said. "Can we do both?"

"Yeah. Both works for me, too. I'd like that." he laughed softly. "Who'd have thought I'd be on board with all this family stuff? But I love it, and I will always love you for bringing all of them into my life, among other reasons, of course." Maddox pressed a kiss to her head. "How are you feeling, sweetie? Happy?"

She nodded. "My heart feels like dancing all the time." She pulled back to look at him. "These last six months with you have been incredible, Maddox. I didn't know what happiness was, until I met you, until you brought us into your family and brought the Harts back to me. I couldn't love them until you taught me how to love." She rested her hand against his whiskered cheek. "I love you so much, Maddox, to the end of time."

He smiled, a tender, wonderful smile that made her heart fill with sunshine. "I love you, too, sweetheart." He looked over at Ava. "And I love you, pumpkin."

Ava tapped her heart with her finger and smiled at him.

Maddox held out his hand to her. "Come here, Ava."

She grabbed another cookie, and then crawled across the rock and snuggled against his side, tucking herself in the crook between Hannah and Maddox. Hannah smiled, and kissed Ava's head, so grateful for how Maddox had also taught Ava to trust and to feel safe again. "It feels so right, the three of us together," she said.

"I agree." Maddox paused for a moment. "Hang on a sec. I'll be right back." He disentangled himself from them, then climbed down the rock to his saddlebags. He fished around in them for a moment, then climbed back up.

This time, however, he didn't sit with them. He knelt in front of them. "Ava, I want you to know that I never thought of having kids until I met you. You changed me. I love you, and I want to be a part of your life every moment, and be there as you grow up, to hold you when you fall, to cheer you when you leap, and to love you every moment."

Hannah's heart tightened, and she felt Ava nestle more tightly against her, the little girl's gaze riveted to Maddox.

He reached into his pocket and pulled out a small jewelry box. "This is for you, pumpkin."

Ava took the box and opened it. Inside was a heart locket. Ava opened it, and Hannah saw it contained a photograph of Maddox and Ava grinning at the camera, both of them covered in brownie batter from a kitchen food fight they'd had just before leaving Wyoming. They were both laughing so hard, their joy so vibrant that it was almost tangible. The love and joy in the picture was electric, and it perfectly summed up the bond between the two of them.

"Ava, hon." Maddox cleared his throat, his warm gaze steady on the little girl. "That locket is my promise to you that I will always be there for you. I want to be your dad. Will you be my daughter?"

Hannah's throat tightened, and tears burned.

Ava stared at him solemnly for a long time, then she nodded. "Yes."

Yes? Hannah gasped, and Maddox's eyes widened. He looked at Hannah, and she saw her own tears reflected in his eyes. *Ava had spoken.* After a year of silence, Ava was finally back, and she'd come back for Maddox.

He recovered more quickly than Hannah did, and he held out his arms. Ava jumped into his arms, clinging to him. "I love you, Maddox," she whispered.

Maddox hugged her back. "I love you, too, Ava."

Ava pulled back. "Can I call you Dad?"

He nodded, his face so alive with joy that Hannah knew she'd never stop crying. "You bet." He kissed her forehead. "There's one thing, though. I think we need your mom's okay."

Ava grinned at Hannah. "Mom, is it okay if Maddox is my dad?"

Mom. Ava had called her *Mom.* Oh, *God.* The tears wouldn't stop now.

"Wait. I want to ask her." Maddox tucked Ava on his hip and faced Hannah. "Hannah, these last six months with you have made me happier than I knew was possible. I love you more every minute. My entire soul settles whenever you are near, whenever I hear your voice, or brush against you. My life was darkness before I met you, and it has all changed. Every day, the sun shines brighter. I know I've got flaws, but if there's any way that you can put up with them..." He paused, reached into his pocket, and pulled out another jewelry box.

A ring box.

He flipped it open, revealing a gorgeous, sparkling diamond set in a platinum band. It was breathtaking. *Breathtaking.* "Will you marry me, Hannah? Will you be my wife, and let me be your husband?"

Elation flooded her. This time, she felt no fear. Just joy, more joy than she had ever felt in her life. Love. Happiness. Hope for a future that was more than she could ever have imagined, even six short months ago. There was no doubt in her heart, not even the tiniest whisper. Her soul knew the answer, and so did her heart. "Yes," she whispered. "Yes, Maddox, of course, I'll marry you."

He let out a loud whoop, then leaned over and kissed her, a deep, beautiful, passionate kiss that she knew was the first of many, many to come. Ava shrieked with laughter and wrapped her arms around Hannah's neck, almost knocking Hannah off balance. But before either of them could fall, Maddox wrapped his arms around both of them, anchoring them together, being their strength, their comfort, and their joy.

About The Author

Hailed by J.R. Ward as a "paranormal star, "*New York Times* and *USA Today* bestselling author Stephanie Rowe is the author of more than forty-five novels, and she's a four-time nominee for the RITA® award, the highest award in romance fiction.

For a complete booklist, visit:
www.stephanierowe.com

Keep up with the latest Stephanie Rowe news on Facebook at
www.facebook.com/StephanieRoweBooks

On Twitter at StephanieRowe2

Or by signing up for her private newsletter at:
http://stephanierowe.com/connect.php

Also by Stephanie Rowe